WITH THE MUSIC

WITH THE MUSIC

NICHOLA SCURRY

Fluffy Dog

Melbourne, Australia

Published in Australia by Fluffy Dog
5/230 Lygon Street, East Brunswick 3057, Australia

First published in Australia 2017
Copyright © Nichola Scurry 2017

A CiP catalogue record for this book is available from the
National Library of Australia

Scurry, Nichola
WITH THE MUSIC

ISBN 978-0-9954227-0-4 (paperback)
ISBN 978-0-9954227-1-1 (eBook)

Cover layout and design by Fiona Byrne
Typeset by Fiona Byrne
Edited by Lu Sexton
Proofread by Jessica Hoadley
Author photo by Linda Ly

*For Ivan Zabuga Rodley, good job you rode that horse across
Europe during the War. Otherwise none of us would be here today.*

*Also for Dorothy Scurry, thanks to your generous gift I was able to do
something halfway between frivolous and practical, writing this book.*

CONTENTS

Music may not save your soul, but it will cause your soul to be worth saving.

Korla Pandit

I Got You, Turning Japanese, Crazy Little Thing Called Love, Another Brick In The Wall (Part 2), Brass In Pocket, Can't Stop The Music, Space Invaders, More Than I Can Say, Funkytown, Please Don't Go, Tired Of Toein' The Line, Don't Stop Til You Get Enough, What I Like About You, Dreaming My Dreams With You, Upside Down, Moscow, You've Lost That Lovin' Feelin', Kiss Kiss Kiss, He's My Number One, Call Me, Babooshka, Woman In Love, Coming Up, Shandi, Blame It On The Boogie, Ashes To Ashes, (Just Like) Starting Over, It's Still Rock And Roll To Me, Emotional Rescue, Love Will Tear Us Apart, Whip It, I'm Coming Out, Dirty Mind, Geno, Girl U Want, Master Blaster, Everybody's Got To Learn Sometime, Could You Be Loved, Let Me Leave Open The Door, Holiday In Cambodia, Games Without Frontiers, Enola Gay, The Tide Is High, You Shook Me All Night Long, Take Your Time (Do It Right), Little Jeanie, Another One Bites The Dust, Once In A Lifetime, Steal Away, Echo Beach, Biggest Part Of Me, Ant Music, Never Knew Love Like This Before, Down Under, Embarrassment, Hungry Heart, Don't Stand So Close To Me, While You See A Chance, Don't Say Goodnight (It's Time For Love), Special Brew, Lady, Back In Black, Fire Lake, Love Stinks, Shining Star, Two Pints Of Lager And A Packet Of Crisps, Mirror In The Bathroom, Magic, Rock With You, Do That To Me One More Time, Cars, Cruisin', High Fidelity, Lost In Love, Ladies Night, Pop Muzik, On The Radio, All Out Of Love, Don't Do Me Like That, Fame, Misunderstanding, Off The Wall, Heartbreaker, Take The Long Way Home, Atmosphere, I Wanna Be Your Lover, In America, Refugee, Super Trouper, Feels Like I'm In Love, Disco, Xanadu, No Doubt About It, The Winner Takes It All, Going Underground, Morning Train (9 To 5), Atomic, Too Much Too Young, Bankrobber, Baggy Trousers, Do You Remember Rock 'n' Roll Radio, M, Icehouse, Over You, Fashion, Banana Republic, Tom Hark, Modern Girl, Dog Eat Dog, To Cut A Long Story Short, My Way Of Thinking, Poison Ivy, Rat Race, Celebration, Boys Don't Cry, Christine, I Can't Stand Up For Falling Down, I Know What Boys Like, I Am The Beat, A Forest, Will You, Private Idaho, Rapture, Ivan Meets G.I. Joe, Me Myself I, Breathing

Vinyl

TRACK 1 – MY PERFECT COUSIN

Here I am at the police station. I sit in a chair, swinging my feet and wondering if they'll ever be able to reach the ground.

'Hi!' I say when Mum arrives. She gives me a hug so tight, it makes me pant when I talk. 'A lady with a Chihuahua found me. He's a little dog from Mexico that yaps and nips and shivers. Can we get one? Pleeease?'

Mum ignores my question. 'Dot Kelly! Your father and I have been frantic! Frantic! Do not wander off, ever again!'

The police are looking at me and laughing, even though I didn't do anything funny.

'You should've kept a better eye on me!' I tell Mum.

'What did you think you were doing?'

'I was bored, so I went to look for records. Can I have a record?'

I already have one record. The cover is yellow with a picture of teenagers listening to music. The man at the party gave it to me. He said it came all the way from England. The song tells funny Beatle maniacs to go away because an ice age is coming. The man told me to look after the record because it's the future. The future's bright, he said. I keep the record hidden between my mattress and bed. It's my treasure.

Mum grabs my hand and pulls me out of the police station and down Malvern Road. We're both stomping.

'You should be happy to see me!' I say. 'Next time, I'll stay with that lady and her Chihuahua forever. I'll name him Jason, teach him tricks and we can join the Young Talent Team.'

We march home. Mum's not listening to me. I mutter to myself anyway. I'm mad at her and I'm imagining how nice it would be to join the Young Talent Team.

'You can sit at home and drink your dumb tea and you'll see me on telly, in my sparkly costume, singing with Tina Arena. I'll be famous and everyone will want to talk to me. But I won't talk to you. And then I'll stop having that annoying dream about Major Tom's capsule.'

I stop talking. I remember that my dream is a secret, my first secret. In the dream, I'm floating through space in a capsule. No people, no music, just me by myself, forever and ever. My stomach is a rock on mornings after I have that dream. I pretend this secret dream is a piece of paper with a rude drawing on it, fold it up tight and put it away.

Mum is walking fast, so I trot to catch up.

♫ ♫ ♫

I stand outside, looking at our house. The paint is peely and the roof isn't straight. Dad has planted some flowers, but weeds are growing too. When I stare long enough, the shapes of the window, porch and roof make a face that's smiling at me. All the houses in Prahran look the same. I like them.

I liked the place where that party was, too. It was far, far away; somewhere called the Dandelion Mountains. There are lots of little green frogs there, red mushrooms and fat gumnut babies, who live under the ferns and dance and eat cake on the moss.

'You, go straight to your room,' Mum says, as she unlocks the front door. 'Have a good, long think about being more careful in the future.'

'The future's bright!' I shout, but Mum has already disappeared down the hallway.

I stomp into my room and half-shut, half-slam the door. Obviously Mum's forgotten it's the Year of the Child, so I sing the 'Care for Kids' song as loud as I can.

When I'm tired of singing, I lie on my bed and have a think. Maybe this isn't my real family. I could be a kidnapped princess. Maybe there was another girl at the hospital, a girl with brown hair and mud eyes, like the rest of the Kellys.

Grandma says they're the emerald green eyes of Ireland, but they look like mud to me. Maybe a prince and princess were hiding from KAOS agents, so they had no choice but to swap their pale baby with that other girl. This could explain why I have that dream no one else does.

Mum comes into my room, and gives me a hug and a kiss, and tells me she was only angry because she was really, really worried about me. She loves me so much that if anything ever happened to me, she wouldn't know what to do. Then she sings me a song about a dusty lady who doesn't know what to do with herself. Mum isn't very good at singing.

♫ ♫ ♫

The first thing in my life I remember is when Mum left me and went to hospital. Eventually, she came home with Jack, who cried a lot, which made my teeth stick together. I sat in his cot, looking at the pictures in my *Muddle-Headed Wombat* book, and told Mum to send him back to heaven.

Jack is here to stay though, and sometimes I love him, but only when he's a good boy.

His real name is Colin, but one day he said, 'My name is called Jack.'

'No silly-billy, it's Colin,' I replied.

'Nope. Jack.'

♫ ♫ ♫

We're getting ready for the roulette party. My mouth waters, because soon the hidden Milo tin will appear. I've been thinking about that tin and the one- and two-dollar notes inside. If it was mine, I'd buy records, Crunchies and a trip to England for Mum. She misses England and the Beatles, but she's decided to stay here with us.

Mum likes chocolates, tea, jumpers that people have knitted, Barbara Taylor Bradford, hula hoops, *Dallas*, roulette and vacuuming. She's vacuuming right now, and I'm not allowed to help.

Dad is watching the news, but he's also tapping his foot. That's because he's an accordion player and always thinking about music. His band is called Now and Then.

'Got any gigs, Dad?' I ask.

'Next week.' Dad isn't talking much; he's concentrating on the news.

'Can I come?'

'No, little one, it's at a pub.'

The news ends, so Dad turns off the telly and gets out his accordion.

Dad likes Irish music, healthy food, the news, long walks and clean teeth. He inspects mine and Jack's teeth every night after we've brushed them. If we haven't done a good job, he'll brush them himself, which is terrible because he's rough and his hands smell like washing up. Besides teeth cleaning, Dad is teaching me and Jack to contribute, which means we need to do jobs or tell interesting stories.

Dad has five sisters and one brother. They're all coming to the party tonight.

I say their names. 'Mary-Margaret Rose, Ann-Maree, Theresa-May, Kathleen-Claire, Christine-Paul, Dad, Ted.'

Tappa, tappa, tappa, says Dad's foot.

'Dad?'

Squeak, squeak, squeak, says Dad's accordion.

'Dad!'

'What?'

'How come Aunty Christine-Paul has a boy's name?'

'She was named after a nun your grandma loved very much. Nuns can have boys' names, as long as they're saints' names.'

Grandma told me about saints, who can perform miracles like walking on water and looking after smelly people no one else likes.

Grandma is Dad's mum. Grandpa died of a heart attack before I was born. Beer, whiskey and cigarettes gave him the heart attack. That's why me and Jack are banned from Coke, McDonald's and tomato sauce on our chips. We don't want our teeth and guts and brains to rot.

Mum comes back into the lounge room and looks at Dad, then walks off. I think they must be talking to each other with their minds again because straight away Dad puts his accordion down and starts sticking streamers onto the ceiling.

I follow Mum into the laundry, where she's filling the sink with ice, beer, a box of wine and a bottle of lemonade for the kids, but not Coke. At another party, they forgot the kids drinks, and we were so annoyed that me and Jack drank all the milk. Then Mum and Dad couldn't have any tea the next morning, which served them right.

'Mum? How come we have so many parties?' I ask.

'Because we want to enjoy ourselves. People don't need to sit at home eating meat and three veg all day long just because they have kids.'

♬ ♬ ♬

This party is meant to start at seven thirty, but everyone arrives at seven. My aunts and uncles bring chips, chopped-up pineapple and mint, plus a sponge cake.

All Dad's party songs are about some boring lady called Mollie, with a black velvet band and smiling Irish eyes. I don't understand why everyone likes old, old music, and not the music that drills into my head with the beat of a drum and the jingle jangle of a guitar.

I like Blondie because she has blonde hair like me. I saw her singing on telly on *Countdown* and loved how she sang in a high, pretty voice surrounded by guitars and drums. The song about glass hearts is my favourite because it's soft like hearts and sharp like glass, all at the same time.

All of a sudden I remember the record hidden under my mattress. I haven't listened to it yet, so I go get it.

'Dad, can you play this one?'

Dad is bobbing his head in time with the fiddles. 'We're listening to The Chieftains, honey. Aren't they grand?'

'Please, Dad! It's just one song.'

Dad looks at my record. '"London Calling". Where did you get this?'

I picture that other party in my head. It must have been a long time ago because everything is misty. It was a cicada-noisy night and there were no other kids. Someone gave me a lolly in the shape of teeth, which I put in front of my real teeth, so I had a film-star smile. I showed my lolly teeth to the adults, who gave me their most twinkling party smiles.

I felt safe, like I was wrapped in a warm blanket. We sat outside in the dark. People were talking or listening to a black and silver ghetto blaster splashed with paint. After every few songs, a whispery voice on the radio said, 'EON FM!' and then played some more songs by Split Ends and Fleetwood Max.

The garden was a gypsy camp, with plants in pots, candles and big cushions everywhere. There was a fire burning inside a metal tube thing; flames jumped around on top and I could see a red glow through little holes on the sides. On the other side of the garden were vegie patches, with sweet corn, carrots and yucky pumpkin growing, and a flippy-floppy scarecrow protecting them.

I was sitting on some cushions talking to a man. He's a music man. He gave me the record.

'Oh, I just found it,' I tell Dad. 'Please, can we have a listen?'

'OK, just one listen. Attention, everyone! We're now going to play a song called "London Calling" as requested by Miss Dot Kelly.'

People are staring at me and I feel silly, but as soon as the music starts, everything else stops; the party disappears. Guitars and drums march along. I stomp my feet up and down. A man starts singing. He's calling me, warning me. An ice age is coming, but thanks to the man I'm ready. The river won't get me. I shut my eyes tight and let my body do whatever it wants. It wants to jump, so I jump and jump and howl like a wolf.

When the song ends, Dad looks at me for a long time before giving me my record back. 'That music isn't for me, but if it's for you, Dot, treasure it always.'

'Yes, Dad.'

He puts the smiling Irish eyes back on and goes into the kitchen.

Uncle Ted has just arrived with his new girlfriend Jocelyn, and they're looking at me. Uncle Ted is smiling, but Jocelyn isn't. She has short black hair and wears a stripy tee-shirt, red lipstick and dangly earrings. She doesn't talk or smile, but she looks like she could be in the telly audience listening to bands on *Countdown*. I run into the kitchen, where Mum and Dad are putting food on paper plates.

'Jocelyn is so pretty,' I whisper.

'Hmmm,' says Mum.

Dad says to Mum, 'Jocelyn's turned out to be a bit of a dud, hasn't she? She's got no good stories and never offers to wash the dishes.'

'She's a sour-faced cow,' says Mum.

I feel strange that Mum and Dad don't like Jocelyn and I do. I like how she stands there looking like a rock star and not talking. I want to be just like her when I grow up. I'll wash the dishes though, so Mum and Dad still like me.

The doorbell rings and the party goes quiet. I can hear little trumpets in my head. Even before the door's opened, I know it's my cousin Julie Ann and her parents. They walk down the hallway in a procession. Julie Ann's wearing a mustard-coloured velvet dress sewn by her mum, Aunty Mary-Margaret Rose. It has a little round collar, pearly buttons down the front and pleats.

'Oh, my word!' cries Aunty Ann-Maree, 'Jules is simply the most divine creature that ever existed!'

Julie Ann smiles and doesn't wriggle around like I do.

'What a glorious child and frock. Just glorious!' Aunty Kathleen-Claire says.

I stand in front of Julie Ann, but now squawking baby Dibble Dobble has arrived.

'He's an angel! An angel!' My aunties' voices are getting louder and louder; they sound like they're crying.

'What a darling, serene little prince!' says Aunty Ann-Maree. 'He's just perfect!'

'Like Buddha,' Aunty Christine-Paul agrees. 'So peaceful!'

'Buddha doesn't squawk like that. He sits on a cloud and teaches Monkey Magic lessons,' I say, but no one listens as my aunties are so frantic and rowdy.

Jocelyn doesn't talk about how wonderful my cousins Julie Ann and Dibble Dobble are. She rolls a cigarette and looks at herself in the reflection of the window. I look at my own reflection. My hair is wispy and messy, not a perfect bowl like Jocelyn's.

Dad's records are turned up louder, the men drink beer, the ladies drink wine and the roulette game starts. When they finish the wine, we'll be able to blow up the empty silver bag and use it as a football. I keep checking how much is left, to make sure I get it before Julie Ann or Jack.

The adults' faces are red and their eyes are glassy. Some of them play roulette and cheer whenever anyone has a win. Others stand around in the kitchen, talking in loud, serious voices about boring things from the news. They sound like they're arguing, but it's just what Dad calls bombastics, so I ignore them.

Jocelyn smokes cigarettes and eats all the green olives. I stand next to her, staring at her as I slurp red bits out of the olives, but she doesn't talk to me.

The next person to arrive doesn't ring the doorbell. Crash, bang, they thunder on the door. I hear bellowing and bottles tinkling.

'Ay yi yi!' someone shouts.

I open the door, but run back down the hallway before he can kiss me. It's Dr Ivanskiy, Grandpa Kelly's old friend who we kept even after Grandpa died.

Stomp, stomp, stomp. Dr Ivanskiy comes down the hallway, his arms full of bottles and chips. Everyone crowds around Dr Ivanskiy and he gives each person a big hug. I stand back; I don't want to get squashed or my ears blasted off by his shouting.

He spots me anyway, and puts a Cheezel on my finger, saying, 'Will you marry me, little Dot?'

'No way, Jose!'

Grandma wants Julie Ann to sing, so Dad gets out his accordion to play along. Julie Ann stands there, with her feet together and her hands neat and tidy by her sides. Then she opens her mouth wide.

Oh, Danny boy, the pipes, the pipes are calling,

From glen to glen, and down the mountain side,

The summer's gone, and all the roses falling,

'Tis you, 'tis you must go and I must bide.

Julie Ann's voice isn't wobbly like mine; it sounds like a cross between an opera singer and the kids on Young Talent Time. Aunty Christine-Paul has a tear in her eye.

'Encore, encore!' the adults shout.

Julie Ann sings the same song all over again. Dad plays along with the accordion, his foot tapping so loud I can hear the good dishes in the cupboard rattling. Everyone except me and Jocelyn sways and sings along with Julie Ann.

I stomp off to Mum and Dad's room, and jump up and down on their bed. I do it on purpose because it's something I'm not allowed to do. Out the window I see Jocelyn standing on the porch, fiddling with her dangly earrings and looking at the stars.

I wonder if that man who talked to me about music snuck in when I wasn't looking. I want to find him, so we can talk some more. I'll ask him how come adults love dumb songs like 'Danny Boy'. I walk through the party, looking everywhere.

At that other party, it was too dark to see his face, but I could make out his shape beside the orange fire. He was tall and thin, but not thin like a stick, and his hair was spiky on top. The thing I liked about that man was the sound of his voice. It wasn't a kid's voice, or a teenager's voice, or an old dad voice. He had a kind voice, and spoke slow, not like he was dumb, but like he was thinking about things. He didn't talk to me in that annoying, *Play School* voice lots of adults use with kids. I don't know what, but there was something about that man.

He told me about music. He listens to music and then he writes about what he hears. I knew by his voice he was smiling. We talked and talked and talked.

I don't think the man is at this party though. I can't hear his calm voice amongst all the chitter-chatter. Instead, I find Jack in the kitchen finishing off the Cheezels. His face and hands are covered in spit and orange powder.

'Julie Ann sing like dumb lady,' Jack says.

I hug him tight and we go back into the lounge room.

'Ay yi yi!' Dr Ivanskiy bellows, stomping around and clapping his hands in the air, loud like thunder. 'Tonight I feel right drunk!'

Mum steers Dr Ivanskiy into the hallway. 'Mind the table, Dr Ivanskiy.'

'I had a girlfriend like you, Margaret, back in Ukrainia,' he says. 'Right dowdy, she was. Really unusual character, but my, my, what a woman!'

Everyone is so sozzled they don't mind that I'm playing roulette. I take a two-dollar note from my piggy bank and put it on red. It's all the money I have.

'If you lose, you're not getting it back,' warns Mum.

The ball lands on red and I win two dollars, so now I have four dollars. I put it back in my piggy bank. I'm saving to buy a hundred litres of milk, which I'm going to freeze, then pour on the ground, so we can have snow in our street. The snow will remind Mum of England, and she'll like that.

I stare out the window, fiddling with my imaginary earrings, and pick out the biggest star.

Star light, star bright, I wish my wish comes true tonight,
I wish to have another party soon.

I liked talking about music to that man at the other party. I try hard to remember more things about him, but I can't. I miss him.

TRACK 2 – ANOTHER BRICK IN THE WALL

I'm dreaming about puppies. They look like black jelly beans and they're my best friends.

'Dot, time to get up for school.'

The puppies vanish.

'Don' like school,' I say in my asleep voice.

'Don't like was made to like,' Mum says.

She scoops up Jack from his bed and I roll out of my bed onto the floor. I lie there waiting for the puppies to come back, but they don't, so I get dressed and go into the kitchen.

'When I finish Saint Aloysius, I'll go to high school, won't I, Mum?'

'Yes, and university after that.'

University is a place where you sew patches onto the elbows of your jumper and read so many books you have to get glasses. Then you become a doctor or a lawyer or a businessman. Uncle Ted is a businessman, so I know what they get up to. Every morning they have a cup of tea and some muesli, then they take the morning train and work from nine till five. They sit at a desk and smoke a cigarette and their boss yells at them. They go home and have some chops for dinner and then they just sit there. I don't want to be a businessman. Dad says I don't have to, as long as I contribute.

I'll be in school a long, long time, as long as the universe. I think of the cartoon hammers and the kids singing.

'I don't need no education or thought control,' I say to Mum.

♫ ♫ ♫

At school we have to pray to God, Jesus, Mary and the Friendly Spirit. We touch our spectacles, tentacles, wallet and watch, and pray for nice things, like the end of the Cold War and healthy parents. In the chapel, the older kids eat a dry biscuit and take a sip of red cordial. I want to find out what those biscuits taste like, but Mrs O'Hoolihan says that first we need to have a special birthday and wear our wedding dresses.

Out the front of the chapel is a white statue of Mary holding baby Jesus. If you watch closely, you can see Mary's eyes moving. She's keeping an eye on us to make sure we're not naughty. If we're naughty, she'll tell Santa Claus and then we won't get a Christmas present. When I tell Dad about this he looks so surprised he has to put down his cup of tea.

He looks at me for a long time, then finally says, 'Dot, sometimes people have to go to certain schools to get a good education, but they don't need to believe all of the things they're told.'

'I don't get it.'

'Learn all you can, but also have a think about everything and make up your own mind.'

'OK.'

I have a think, and decide to play nicely, just in case Mary is watching. I wouldn't like it if I didn't get a Christmas present.

♫ ♫ ♫

Caitali has a black bowl haircut, brown eyes and tiny freckles on her nose. Me and Caitali are the exact same height, which means we could be perfect best friends. She's in the sandpit, playing with Georgina. I somersault across the sand, but I can't think of anything to say, so I just sit there.

Georgina sees me first. 'Whaddya want?'

Caitali looks at me and grins. Her smile is like the summer holidays.

'I like your hair,' I tell her. I ignore Georgina.

'Thanks!' Caitali replies. 'D'you know what "rootable" means?'

'No…'

'It's a girl that all the boys love,' she explains. 'My brother teaches me slang. He's thirteen and has hairy armpits.'

'Yuk!' I say. 'My brother is three and he has poo in his undies.'

Georgina stares at me with her hands on her hips; but Caitali laughs, and her laugh is like the flute in the 'Land Down Under' song. It makes me brave, so I ask her, 'Wanna be friends?'

'OK!'

♫ ♫ ♫

School is a way of getting used to real life. There are some strange kids at my school, and even though I don't have to be their friends, I have to get used to them. One of them is Zack, who cries every single day until his mum comes to collect him. Zack is really good at drawing, but he can't do anything else, not even write his name.

There's a boy in Grade Three called Milo, who's always in trouble. He's a bully and throws rocks at kids. His dad works all the time and his mum had to have a rest at the clinic. Milo's teacher sent him to sit with us because he was being a baby. I tell Mum about it on the way home from school.

'He didn't cry, but his face was bright red. And guess what, Mum, he's only eight and I can see a little moustache growing on his lip. Everyone laughs at him, even his friends.'

'I want you to be kind to that boy, Dot.'

'Why?'

'Because he has a sad life and will probably end up being thrown in Turana.'

♫ ♫ ♫

Caitali comes to my house to play. Jack is annoying, so we put him in the toy box, then sit on top so he can't get out. It's really funny, but Mum comes into the room.

'What's all this cackling about?'

We can't answer because we're laughing so much.

Mum asks, 'Where's Jack?'

'I in here!' a voice from the toy box calls out.

We get up and Jack pops out of the toy box.

'Da-daaah!' he shouts. 'Jack-in-a-box!'

'Dot, if I catch you doing that again, I'm sending Caitali home.'

'Sorry, Mrs Kelly,' Caitali says. 'We promise we won't do it again.'

Mum smiles and pats Caitali on the head. 'OK girls, but play nicely with Jack.'

'Yes, Mrs Kelly.'

'Baby bum-bum head,' I whisper to Jack when Mum leaves the room.

♫ ♫ ♫

The first time I go to Caitali's house a big boy answers the door, but blocks it so I can't come in.

'You have to take your shoes off.'

His voice is funny; some words are squeaky and some are growly. I unbuckle my sandals as Caitali's mum comes to the door to talk to Mum.

'Wheee!'

Caitali's sliding down the banister. I've never been in a two-storey house before. I can't wait to look upstairs, but as I run towards Caitali, I notice something golden through a door. It's a beautiful couch, all covered in plastic, with a high, swirly back.

'What's that room?'

'It's the good room. We're not allowed to play in there.'

Caitali looks around. The coast is clear; she grabs my hand and we run and hide behind the couch.

'Let's be princesses!'

I wiggle my toes in the deep red carpet, which is so soft I feel like I'm sitting on a cloud.

'Why does your brother talk funny, Princess Caitali?'

'The Queen told me his voice is breaking, Princess Dot.'

That's a good description. His voice really is like broken glass.

I peep out from behind the couch and notice a picture of a handsome prince playing a flute. There's also a statue of a blue elephant and the biggest television I've ever seen.

'Is that a colour telly?'

'Of course! Don't you have a colour telly?'

I think about Mum and Dad saving all year to buy our black and white portable.

'We're getting one soon,' I say.

TRACK 3 – MAD WORLD

Mum's always telling me about other children who have terrible lives. When I'm forced to eat disgusting eggplant, she reminds me that some children don't have enough food to eat and starve to death.

'They'd love to have some delicious eggplant,' she says.

Not if they're already dead, I think.

When I don't want to go to dumb school, I'm told to spare a thought for the children in Charles Dickens' time, who had to work all day in factories and coal mines. When I complain about having a brattish baby brother, Mum asks how I would feel if Jack was taken away by dingoes, like Azaria Chamberlain was. *As long as they look after him, I wouldn't mind.*

I ask Mum why we have an old bomb Valiant for a car. 'I want a yellow Volvo like Caitali's family has.'

Mum says, 'Dot, you should be grateful you can sit in that Valiant and not worry about a car bomb exploding, like the children in Northern Ireland do.'

Children are in danger everywhere, so I need to be very, very happy I've got such a nice, safe life. Then a bad thing happens to a boy from my class, so bad it's on the news.

Jimmy is playing in the park with his brother. They're throwing a red ball to each other, but it rolls away, so Jimmy runs into the bushes to find it. A man is waiting in there and asks Jimmy if he wants to see a puppy. Jimmy says yes, so then the man kidnaps him. The brother runs home and tells his parents, who tell the police. I know all this because it's on the news. Geoff Raymond looks at me through the television camera and describes the man, the red ball and everything that happened in the park. At school we say extra prayers to ask God, Jesus, Mary and the Friendly Spirit to return Jimmy to his family. No one cries, not even Jimmy's mum when she goes on the telly, asking the kidnapper to please send Jimmy home. But everyone looks very, very worried. The adults look just as worried as the kids, so there is no one to say magic words to make us feel better.

This gives me a cranky, scary feeling. Bad things could happen to me and not even my parents can save me. As I get older, I'll have to learn about more and more bad things, like one day I might break my leg, or someone I love will die, or *I* might die. If Mum and Dad can't save me from these things, who will?

'I suppose I'll just have to do it myself,' I sigh in the voice Mum uses when no one helps her wash the dishes.

If I can find Jimmy, maybe that will make everything bad stop. I look for clues everywhere: at school, in the park, down Chapel Street. I spot a man at the tram stop.

'Don't talk to that man, Jack. He could be a kidnapper.'

'OK!'

I see a soccer ball lying on the grass near the trees.

'I'm not gunna touch that ball in case someone jumps out and snatches me.'

'Well, it's not yours anyway,' Mum says.

♫ ♫ ♫

Jimmy comes home and a few days later he's back at school. He brings newspaper articles about himself for Show and Tell.

Jimmy's kidnapper wasn't an ordinary kidnapper like you see in movies; there was something unusual about him because he made Jimmy put lipstick on. Something weird had happened, but Jimmy can't explain it and the adults won't tell us. It's hidden behind a thick curtain, in a secret world I don't want to know about.

♫ ♫ ♫

I wake up crying. I'm having my nightmare again, the one where I'm stuck all alone in Major Tom's capsule. Mum and Dad say I can sleep in their bed, even though I'm not sick. I hum a little song to myself about how sometimes I don't know why I get frightened, but if you see my eyes you can tell I'm not lying. The song is familiar and comforting, like a hug from Grandma.

My humming turns into singing.

'Shush Dot, or you can get back in your own bed,' says Mum.

I keep humming, just quieter.

♪ ♪ ♪

Another of my baby teeth falls out. I hold it in my hand and poke my gums with my tongue. They're mushy and taste like metal.

'From now on, take extra care of your teeth,' says Dad. 'If your adult teeth fall out, you'll have to get false ones like Grandma.'

'Or have none like the man who lives in the box?'

'Who?'

'Doesn't matter.' Mum and Dad are always too busy carrying shopping from the supermarket to notice the old man who lives in a cardboard box in the carpark.

♪ ♪ ♪

Dr Ivanskiy is our dentist. He's tall and chubby with a brown and grey beard and a very loud voice. He has a nurse called Sharon who's a punk. Sharon has spiky pink hair and four earrings in each ear. She wears a nurse's uniform with bright green tights.

'Really unusual character, is Sharon,' says Dr Ivanskiy. 'She listens to right angry music, but she's a steady nurse and patients like her. Solid, like Ukrainian peasant.'

I can't decide if I'd rather be Sharon or Jocelyn when I grow up.

Dr Ivanskiy says, 'No problem with your teeth, little Dot. They're strong like a skyscraper.'

This is Jack's first time seeing Dr Ivanskiy, but he won't open his mouth.

'No!' he shouts. 'Your hands stink!'

Dr Ivanskiy roars with laughter. 'Ay yi yi! You're a comical one, little man.'

He gives Jack a pat on the head and a *Hooray, No Decay* sticker, even though he didn't get a look at Jack's teeth. I give Jack a little pinch.

♫ ♫ ♫

It's Christmas and Aunty Mary-Margaret Rose says we should stop giving everyone presents because the family is getting too big. I think this is the worst idea in the world and so does Dr Ivanskiy, who turns up at Grandma's with a giant Christmas ham and presents for everyone. He gives me a beautiful Japanese lady ornament, which Jack smashes the next day because he's a bone-headed little pest.

♫ ♫ ♫

Aunty Christine-Paul takes me and Jack to visit Dr Ivanskiy to thank him for our Christmas presents. He lives in a flat, with beautiful pink roses in the garden. I don't touch them though, because of the thorns.

'Wow, this flat is bigger than our whole house!' I say. 'What's that little button on the wall for?'

Jack's standing on his tippy toes, pressing the button, but no sound comes out.

Dr Ivanskiy says, 'In right old times, you'd press the button and maid came running to bring you a cup of tea. Doesn't work now, no maids round here.'

Dr Ivanskiy has no toys and no Tim Tams, just plain old Marie Biscuits. He gives us a pack of cards to play with, so I try teaching Jack how to play Snap, but he isn't good at concentrating. Aunty Christine-Paul and Dr Ivanskiy talk about dumb things from the newspaper. Just as I'm getting so bored I almost fall asleep, Aunty Christine-Paul says it's time to leave.

'Say goodbye to Dr Ivanskiy, kids,' she says.

'Bye-bye!' said Jack.

'Bye-bye! Ay yi yi! Right happy to go, I am,' I say.

When we're outside, Aunty Christine-Paul gives me a swift little slap. 'Dot! I'm so mortified. I never want to hear you being that disrespectful again!'

'Huh? What did I do?' I ask.

'Making fun of his accent like that! Don't you know how much Dr Ivanskiy does for this family? He helps us all so much! Don't you know he speaks four languages and came to this country all by himself with nothing? Don't you know what he went through when he escaped from the communists? Do you know how bad the communists were? They used to rape nuns!'

Aunty Christine-Paul's voice rises higher and higher, and her face grows redder and redder. Nuns are ladies who wear black gowns and are married to God and Jesus. They do good works and you have to respect them. There aren't any nuns at my school, but there were at my aunties' school. If you think about rude things, like how nuns have big bottoms and big bosoms, you have to tell a priest at Confession and he'll give you some roses.

'What's rape?' I ask.

'Something so terrible I can't even tell you.'

'I promise never to copy Dr Ivanskiy's accent ever again.'

When adults are listening, I add inside my head.

I think Dr Ivanskiy came to Australia on the Wishing Chair. First he was in Ukraine, then he was in Europe, and then he went to Yorkshire where he learned his funny English and worked at a place called The Pits. Finally he arrived here to become a dentist and our friend.

When we get home I grab Jack and we hide in Mum's wardrobe. I close the door and we sit in the dark. I can smell perfume, sweat, mothballs and wood.

'What we doing?' Jack asks.

'Hiding from communists,' I say. 'They're chasing after us and we have to hide.'

When it's night, I'll sneak out and find a safe place for us to live, a house with lots of music, where no communists or other bad stuff can happen, ever.

'They got a gun?' Jack asks.

'Yep, but if we stay real quiet they won't find us.'

'OK, but I not scared.'

I wonder if Dr Ivanskiy was scared. Just then, Mum whips open the wardrobe door and jumps a little.

'Gerrout, the pair of you! You'll squash my shoes,' she says.

I run down the hallway towards Dad's accordion-playing in the lounge room; the squeezy sounds make me feel relieved. With a bit of music in the house, we can be safe.

TRACK 4 – ECHO BEACH

We pass the Train Tracks Hotel. Dad's been going there with Uncle Ted and his friends since they were teenagers. They drink beer, talk about things in life they think are bullshit and listen to bands. One time I asked Dad what 'bullshit' means, but he just told me to stop swearing. We stop to look at the train. It's a giant blue and yellow one that's crashing out of the Train Tracks Hotel wall.

'When I grow up, I'm gunna be a punk like Sharon and have a train like that crashing into my bedroom!' I say.

A nice feeling wraps around me when I think about being a punk. My house will have parties all the time and I won't have to clean it or take a bath. I'll paint on the walls and dye my hair pink. Mum looks at me with her thinking face.

The real train tracks are right next to the Train Tracks Hotel, and we hear a ding ding ding.

'I think it's gunna be a red one,' I say.

'Blue!' says Jack.

'I think it'll be silver,' Mum says.

Mum's right. I like the red ones best, but they hardly ever come now.

♪ ♪ ♪

Our park is nice, but the one near my cousin Julie Ann's place is nicer. Caulfield Park is the biggest park I've ever been to and has the longest slide in the world. Mum tries to slide down, but her legs stick to the metal and she can't budge. We laugh so much my stomach hurts.

On the corner of Caulfield Park are statues of people. My favourite one is the boy with long hair and flared trousers, holding his schoolbooks. Sometimes on the radio, they play a song about that boy. He's a little boy waiting on the corner in front of a shop. He's been waiting all day and then he asks, 'What about me? It isn't fair.'

♫ ♫ ♫

There's a slide at the Prahran pools too. Dad makes me slide down all by myself.

'I'm a bit scared,' I say.

'Stop grizzling and slide down. It'll be fun!'

'Will I go under the water?'

'No, you'll just land on your feet, like on the slide at the park.'

I slide down, but when I hit the water I do go all the way under. Being stuck under water feels like being lost in space. Dad scoops me out, but water has gone in my eyes and up my nose. I sneeze out the snot and cling to the ledge of the pool, thinking about that lost feeling and wondering why it's followed me out of my dream.

♫ ♫ ♫

Grandma buys a holiday house by the sea. The entire Kelly family drive down for a holiday. Me and Jack jump out of the car as soon as we arrive and run to the front door of the yellow house, hopping up and down, waiting for someone to open the door.

There's a sign above the door which I try to read. 'Grey Sea Land.'

Dad stands behind me. 'Graceland. Grandma's named the house Graceland.'

Me and Jack run through the house and out the sliding door onto a balcony. The garden goes on forever, and there's a bungalow and a treehouse in an apple tree.

'This place is paradise!' I shout.

The adults unpack things. Me and Jack run from room to room. Grandma hangs pictures of Elvis Presley, Buddy Holly and the Pope on the walls. Aunty Mary-Margaret Rose puts plates and pans in the kitchen cupboards. Aunty Christine-Paul puts blankets in the bedroom cupboards. Dr Ivanskiy has to work, but he's sent furniture for the whole house.

Dad bought himself a brand new hi-fi with humongous speakers, and gave his old record player to Graceland. Uncle Ted found a box of records in the op shop. I don't like the look of these records – the covers show people with scruffy-looking clothes and long beards. I wish I brought my 'London Calling' record, but it's at home, hidden in its secret place. Finally, at the bottom of Uncle Ted's pile, I find a kids record called *The Jungle Book*. Me, Julie Ann and Jack sing and dance to the songs. My favourite song from *The Jungle Book* is 'The Bear Necessities', Jack's is 'Winnie the Pooh' and Julie Ann's is 'Feed the Birds', which is my worst song because it's so soppy.

Feeeeed the birds, Jack sings in an opera lady's voice and Julie Ann pouts.

'I'm not sure why you'd want to pay tuppence a bag to feed stinky old pigeons,' I say to her. 'Mum calls them winged rats and says they build their nests in poo.'

Graceland is small, but we all manage to fit. I wander around the house, checking where everyone is sleeping. Every room is set up with mattresses and beds. There are even tents in the garden, and sleeping bags in the tree house for Uncle Ted and Jocelyn.

'Where are me and Julie Ann sleeping?' I ask.

'We've set up some banana lounges on the balcony,' Mum says. 'Won't that be fun?'

I lie on my banana lounge that night, and listen to the adults drink tea and beer and talk about boring things, like what's happening in Ireland. Their bombastics are keeping me and Julie Ann awake.

'Shush!' I call out grumpily and Julie Ann whimpers.

They shush and after a thousand years they go to bed. Julie Ann is allowed to go sleep with Grandma, but I stay on the balcony.

In the morning, we all go to the beach for a compulsory swim. We have to slip slop slap sun-cream and then the kids take turns on the boogie board. We stay between the flags.

Lunch is salad sandwiches and water. After lunch, the adults lie around reading the dumb newspaper, but the kids are taken for a compulsory walk.

I hate compulsory walks. Me and Julie Ann say we won't go, but Dad says there'll be a treat at the end. We march up and down hills, and all we see are gum trees and ferns. Twigs scratch my legs as I stomp along the track. I'm puffed out and getting blisters on my feet, but the thought of the treat keeps me going. Finally, the walk ends when we reach a lookout where we can see the mountains and the sea.

'Can we have the treat now, pleeeease?' I ask.

'OK, but first let's appreciate the grouse view,' Dad says.

I stare at the bright blue sea and imagine I'm sailing across it in a yacht. The sun and wind on my face feel like a kiss. It's the opposite of being lost in space.

Eventually Dad pulls a packet of mints from his pocket; we're allowed one each.

♬ ♬ ♬

For Uncle Ted's birthday, we go to the beach pub for a counter meal.

While we're waiting for our chicken in pyjamas, Aunty Christine-Paul says, 'Look kids, there's a disco over there!'

'A real-life disco?' I ask.

'You bet, kiddo!'

In the middle of the pub I see a floor made of flashing, colourful squares.

Call me, call me, call me! sings Blondie.

I dance around, jumping from square to square. The music and flashing lights are hypnotising me. This is like a treasure, but not a treasure that's a thing.

I feel like I'm somewhere I always wanted to be, only I don't know where it is. I dance on the disco floor until someone calls out, 'Dot, your parma's here.'

I skip back to our table, and pass by a man with spiky hair playing Space Invaders. Something tells me that man is part of the disco too, but I'm too hungry to think much about it.

TRACK 5 – I AM THE BEAT

Discombobulation – Richmond Squat – 20th January 1979

If you don't already know, Discombobulation is a noise band formed by three Elwood High students two weeks ago. They're the best sound to come out of Melbourne's south-east since The Boys Next Door. But the thing about Discombobulation is that you can't go see them straight. My mate Stevo insists there's a special quality to these kids, only appreciated if you listen to them under some sort of influence.

With this in mind, two hours before the gig, we paid a call to a mate of Stevo's, a hippie from uni, who lives way out in Ferntree Gully. There was a party going on, full of uni students, and let me tell you, intellectuals are a pain in the arse with their fifty-cent words, perpetual grief over the ancient-history Dismissal and complete denial that men don't have long hair anymore! The best conversationalist there was this little kid who was a Blondie fan and didn't give a shit about Foucault's panopticon. Would you believe I gave her one of my precious Clash singles that Stevo brought back from England? We need to look after our future generations, don't we?

But I digress. The grotty mayhem of Richmond called. Discombobulation played in a junkie squat, their angelic, hairless faces nicely juxtaposed with the bashing together of various pieces of stolen metal, while the singer screamed one off-key note nonstop for a good thirty minutes. The combined forces of a few hundred of Melbourne's finest dole recipients pogoing with gusto, the Ferntree Gully weed, two bottles of Benadryl and half a cask of red wine resulted in a fine evening for Stevo and me.

It doesn't matter if the Discombobulation boys are great or if they're shit. What matters is they're doing something new. Do yourself a favour and go to the next Discombobulation gig before they're thrown in Turana. Rumour has it that they're playing at Harry's joint in Fitzroy next Thursday. The future's bright.

Personal Jesus, Here Comes Your Man, Love Shack, Pictures Of You, Fools Gold, Buffalo Stance, Janie's Got A Gun, Express Yourself, Dressed For Success, Sowing The Seeds Of Love, You Got It, Back To Life, Baby Don't Forget My Number, Like A Prayer, About A Girl, Especially For You, Love In An Elevator, Ride On Time, 38 Years Young, I Don't Want A Lover, Toy Soldiers, American Horse, I Won't Back Down, Batdance, Everlasting Love, My Prerogative, Black Velvet, Epic, Fight The Power, Paradise City, Loud Love, Bust A Move, Good Thing, Between A Man And A Woman, Love Buzz, Monkey Gone To Heaven, Pump Up The Jam, Beds Are Burning, If You Don't Know Me By Now, Deeper Understanding, She Bangs The Drums, A Girl Like You, Eternal Flame, Something's Gotten Hold Of My Heart, Down All The Days, Been A Son, The Living Years, Poison, I'll Be Your Shelter, Baby I Don't Care, Right Back Where We Started From, Leave Me Alone, Advice For The Young At Heart, She Drives Me Crazy, A Little Bit Of Soap, Big Cheese, Partyman, Hey Ladies, **Cassette** Hallelujah, Fascination Street, Hey DJ I Can't Dance To That Music You're Playing, I Want It All, We Didn't Start The Fire, Let Love Rule, Made Of Stone, Love Song, Lullaby, Magic Johnson, Belfast Child, Egg Man, Heads We're Dancing, Don't Let Me Down Gently, Punk Rock Classic, Tame, Baby I Don't Care, Runnin' Down A Dream, Fear, Get On The Snake, Free, Fallin', Get On Your Feet, Sun King, Hangin' Tough, Sweet Child O' Mine, Monkey On My Back, 18 And Life, Birdhouse In Your Soul, Lambada, Jennifer Lost the War, The Look, Debaser, So What, Mr Cab Driver, The Sensual World, Hands All Over, Sacrifice, Black Steel In The Hour Of Chaos, The Best, Can U Dig It, Pet Sematary, Closedown, Royal Station 4/16, Don't Ask Me Why, Electric Youth, Head Like A Hole, Knock Me Down, Let Him Dangle, Talent Show, Love And Anger, Wicked Game, Rhythm Nation, Shouting Street, The Last Of The Famous International Playboys, I'm Gonna Be (500 Miles), Bedroom Eyes, Tucker's Daughter

TRACK 6 – ANOTHER BRICK IN THE WALL (PART 2)

'Mum, do we have vinegar?' I ask as I do push-ups against the pantry door.

'In the cupboard. What do you want it for?'

'I need to drink a shot glass with dinner to digest all the chop fat.'

I read in *Dolly* magazine that drinking vinegar with a meal helps you lose weight. We were weighed and measured at school today, and I'm 159 cm, which makes me officially taller than Kylie Minogue! On a tragic note, I weigh 48 kg, which is way too heavy, so I'll have to go on a diet, even though dieting isn't exactly my forte. Right now, I'm thinking about dim sims and Chocolate Big Ms.

'I won't be fussing around with you if you turn out anorexic,' Mum says.

'Well, I won't!' I snap, my mouth watering as I watch Jack spread Nutella onto a slice of bread.

Jack sock-skates past, running the open Nutella jar under my nose. I snatch the jar from him and dip in my finger. I'll try the vinegar tomorrow.

'For chrissakes, Dot, use a spoon!' Mum says, but she looks relieved.

'I hope that's not your nose-picking finger,' Jack says, and I embrace him in a headlock.

Mum needn't worry about me being ana, seeing as I'm hungry like all the time. I must confess, though, that I think there's something glamorous about anorexics. Karen Carpenter may have sung dorky songs, but I'm fascinated by her. Sometimes I fantasise about lying in a hospital bed, hooked up to a drip, with my bones sticking out all over the shop. Hordes of people visit me, bringing presents and crying about my condition.

Caitali, or Cat, as she now prefers to be called, says half the girls at her school have an eating disorder; but I've met some of them and they just look like normal kids to me. I can't tell whether they're fat or wasting away, hidden behind the giant Country Road bags they're always carting around.

I check myself out in the full-length mirror in Mum and Dad's room. I miss the straight-line body I had when I was a kid. My hair is darker too, which I'm spewing about. As soon as I finish school, I'm peroxiding it the same shade as Deborah Harry's. I'd do it now, if I didn't go to such a fascist school. I saunter into the bathroom to backcomb and blow dry my hair. I add hairspray and study the results in the mirror. Not bad, but I wish I had a spiral perm.

'Mum! Can I get a perm?'

'Don't be daft!'

'Tight-arse,' I mutter.

'I heard that!' Mum calls back. 'Your father and I have enough expenses, what with your school fees. We don't have money to throw away on fancy hair-dos for a teenage girl.'

I sigh and continue gazing at myself in the mirror. I know it's trendy to have a tan, but I think Joe Strummer would be impressed by my pale complexion, protected at all times from the hole in the ozone layer, courtesy of 15 plus sun-cream and my extensive collection of hats.

I wander back into the kitchen and announce to anyone who's listening, 'Sometimes I stare at the people tanning on the beach, and think about how they'll all end up looking like old boots, riddled with melanomas by the time they're forty. And I'll still have my ravishingly youthful looks.'

'Nah, you'll just be a prune with a baby face,' Jack says. 'And what's going on with your hair? Did you stick your finger in an electric socket?'

'Get stuffed!' I tell him.

'Why don't you, moon-girl?' Jack answers back. Mum laughs.

'I've had enough of you people!' I cry, and retire to my bedroom.

My room is my sanctuary where I can listen to music, read and think about life, uninterrupted by fools. When we first moved to Glen Huntly, I did my own interior designing. The look I went for was a Norsca deodorant ad, white walls and dark green trimmings. The effect is excellent, so cool and fresh!

I seriously miss Prahran, because the closer you live to the city, the cooler you are. A bigger house was in order though, as it would have been child abuse for me to still share a room with that smelly little skinner, Jack. In this house, Dad has his own music room, so we can close the door and not hear his toe-tapping accordion-playing day and night. Another good thing is that Glen Huntly is a ten-minute bus ride to Chadstone, where I can meet my friends to go shopping or whatever.

Sometimes I go for walks around the neighbourhood. The streets are wider and the houses are bigger than in Prahran, but less interesting. There are no trains crashing through walls and no old men sleeping in boxes in the supermarket carpark. The ding of the trams is a comforting noise, but Glen Huntly's just not that punk. At least there aren't too many bogans or families with bratty little kids here. That'd suck.

One day I'll return to the inner city, but Glen Huntly will do for now.

'Change out of your uniform, Dot,' Mum says. 'I don't want you falling asleep and getting it all creased again. I've got better things to be doing than ironing your scruffy clothes all the time.'

'Der! I'm not falling asleep. I'm doing my damn homework!'

'No swearing!'

Geez, she's lucky I don't crack out the f and c words! I can't be bothered with the grief though, so I change out of my uniform. Mum and Dad are so strict about school stuff. I've got to take extra special care of my precious uniform, get good marks, be mindful of the massive fees they're forking out to send me to St Lutgarde's College, and feel happy to miss out on stuff like getting a spiral perm or a trip to Queensland to see Expo 88. Apparently Jack and I are going to become amazingly excellent people, just because we go to fancy schools. Dad monitors our marks like a maniac, using the threat of the local state school to keep us on our toes.

'First term reports are coming out soon, aren't they?' he asks at dinner.

Jack shrugs and I mumble, 'Dunno.'

'If you kids mess up, it's straight to Carnegie Secondary with you.'

Dad's been making that threat since the day I started at St Lutgarde's, or Sluts, as it's affectionately known.

I don't push it, because I really don't want to go to Carnegie Secondary. State school girls are sooo unfashionable with their extra short dresses, when they should know that longer dresses are in. At Sluts, if your dress doesn't touch the ground when you're kneeling, you have to buy a new one. Madonna's 'Like a Prayer' sums up my life at school, because I'm always down on my knees and I'd get crucified if I pashed a black Jesus, or any guy for that matter.

'Life is so unfair,' I grumble, while the family's still laughing. 'Jack gets to go to a co-ed school, while I'm stuck at a dumb old girls school.'

'Oh, Dot, it will do you good to concentrate on your education without any distractions,' Mum says.

'There's plenty of better places where I can concentrate on my education,' I reply. 'I could go to Caitali's school.'

Mum starts laughing again. 'If you think we can afford those fees, you've got another think coming.'

'It sucks being a pauper!' I snarl.

'Well, get a good education, then you won't be one.'

There's no point arguing with these people.

♫ ♫ ♫

Cat's school is a private school, but it's modelled on English public schools like Eton and is even posher than normal private schools. Most Proddie schools have the word 'Grammar' in their names, but Cat's school is the only one that's just called Grammar. It's so well known, it doesn't need further clarification.

'Oooh err, Gwammar!' says Jack with a faux-aristocratic accent, when Cat shows up in her thousand-dollar uniform.

'Rack off, skinner!' says Cat, as she pulls up her white knee-high socks and smooths out the pleats in her skirt.

'Can't get a girl, get a Gwammar boy,' Jack sings with glee, as he practically skips out of the room.

The kids who go to Grammar are way wilder than the kids at Carnegie Secondary. They do what they want, like smoking, shoplifting and throwing crazy parties with alcohol and drugs. They're so rich, their dads buy them cars when they turn eighteen, and they have heaps of designer clothes like Levi 501s, Doc Martens and Country Road.

Cat and I shut the door to my bedroom, so we can discuss our favourite topic in privacy.

'So, have you got with any boys yet?' she asks me.

'Nope, not yet.' I'm mortified, and burst out with, 'This is strictly my parents' fault for sending me to a girls school! I don't know any boys my age.'

Cat has already got with three boys, even though only one was a French kiss. Besides, her school is co-ed.

'Next holidays I'm gunna introduce you to some spunks,' she comforts me.

'You better!' I say. 'I'm going mental at Sluts!'

♫ ♫ ♫

As well as the tragic lack of boys at my school, the teachers are obsessed with periods. It's all they talk about, and they pronounce the word 'period' in such a gross, creepy way; like they're discussing some feral secret, which they are.

'What's wrong, does she have her peeer-iod?' they ask every time one of us is upset. *Der, you can get upset about other stuff, you know!*

'Some boys will tell you they can smell when you have your peeer-iod. But it's not true, girls. As long as you have good hygieeene, they'll never know.' *This is the single most terrifying thing I've ever heard in my life!*

'Three girls got their peeer-iods at school this week. Ask your mothers to buy sanitary pads to keep in your lockers at all times.'

Lucky for me, I didn't get my period at school, but during the holidays. Lucky for me, Cat tells me pads are just for old, old ladies and that I should use tampons.

Mum also has helpful advice. 'Wash your face properly from now on, Dot, or you'll be covered in pimples.'

♫ ♫ ♫

More important than getting good marks at school is not to be classified a hanger – someone who hangs off other people but doesn't contribute to the conversation and is really boring.

Besides not wanting to be a hanger, I want to be a High Court judge. That means I need to improve my marks, since you need straight As to get into law. My first term report arrives and it's mostly Bs, plus an E for recorder. Recorder is not a proper subject, but Dad is still annoyed.

'There was a bit of a surprise in your report, Dot,' he says. 'Every subject is important, so pick up your game, or I'll send you to Carnegie Secondary.'

I leave the room as fast as I can to find Mum, so I can complain.

'Dad probably wants me to play the recorder in his daggy Irish band or something, but that would be over my dead body. None of the other girls' dads play accordion in a band. They're all doctors, lawyers and businessmen.'

'Stop being ignorant,' Mum tells me. 'There are kids from all walks of life at your school. Their parents are just normal, hard-working people like us.'

'Ha ha! I doubt there's anything normal about this family!'

When people ask me what my dad does, I tell them he's a manager. He is a manager, a manager of a dorky Irish band called Now and Then. Lucky we're not as destitute as when I was a little kid, since Mum got a job and Now and Then have more gigs these days.

Mum and Dad finally joined the twentieth century and bought some items every other normal person got years ago: a colour TV, a video player and a car that isn't an old bomb Valiant. Our new car is less than five years old and doesn't have beaded car-seat covers, so now I don't have to ask Mum to park around the corner when she's picking me up from school. A lot of the other girls' parents drive Mercedes and Volvos, but at least our car isn't so embarrassing it makes me want to cry like that old Valiant did.

A few days later, Jack's report arrives and it's worse than mine, all Cs and Ds. Dad is livid.

'This is the worst report I've seen since Christine-Paul was at school! I don't want anything lower than a C, Jack, or it's straight to Carnegie Secondary with you!'

'I don't care,' Jack replies. 'Some pretty cool skateboarders go there. I wouldn't mind being friends with them.'

'How does a skateboarder earn a decent living?'

'Gets sponsored by Coke and goes to America to be filmed in rap videos.'

'Ah, bullshit,' mutters Dad. 'Coke and rap music will rot your brain.'

He stomps off to the music room to play his accordion, and I go to my room to listen to The Clash and mark off the days until the next holidays in my Dinky Diary. I'm excited because Amanda is coming to Graceland with me.

♫ ♫ ♫

A day before we leave, she rings me. 'I'm really sorry, Dot, but Mum says I'm not allowed to go away with you after all.'

'Why the hell not?'

'We had a family meeting and decided I'm too young to stay the night at other people's houses...'

'Jesus Christ!' I shout.

I hope her mum heard that. Amanda's parents are strict because they're religious maniacs. She has to go to Mass all the time and have really shiny shoes. Plus, she's not allowed to catch the bus by herself, so she never comes to Chadstone with me.

I'm disappointed, so I call Cat to rant, 'Her parents are total squares who need to wake up and smell the coffee. This is the eighties, and teenage girls shouldn't be kept locked in an attic like Mr Rochester's mad wife!'

Making friends with people who aren't Cat is near-on impossible. In the end, Cat comes to Graceland with me and it's a rage. We hit the beach every day, and walk up and down the sand looking for boys.

'The coolest thing about this beach is that there are loads of spunky boys here,' Cat says. 'And they're mostly from private schools, so we don't have to worry about accidentally meeting a derro!'

'Yeah. That would suck,' I reply.

We don't talk to any of the boys, but we look at them…a lot.

At night we sleep in the tree house and laugh about sex stories.

'Has anyone in your year had it off yet?' Cat asks me.

'Not that I'm aware of.'

'There's a girl in my class who knows how to give a hand job. She gave us a demo with a carrot.'

My body feels tired after endless giggling and I sleep well.

In the morning, *Video Hits* is on TV. Jack is hovering, wanting to watch the cricket, but we shoo him away. We choreograph a deliciously daggy ribbon dance to go with 'Eternal Flame' and then we jump around and cut sick when something by Transvision Vamp comes on. I'm not really into Top 40 stuff, but mucking around with Cat is fun.

While she's having a shower, I sit on the balcony railing, looking at the gum trees and wondering where the people with the cool music are. I want to sit by a fire at a party with a cute guy and talk about songs that changed the world. I want to hear jangly guitars and cicadas and the sound of a nice voice. I'll find him one day, I know, but it gets boring as bat shit waiting.

TRACK 7 – PRETTY VACANT

I sit opposite Jack and scratch my face with my middle finger so I'm giving him the bird without Mum or Dad knowing. He opens his mouth wide, to show me his vomity, chewed-up cereal.

'Ooh, you could win a prize for having the world's grumpiest face, Dot,' Mum says.

'Who *would* have a happy face, if they had to look at this family every morning?' I reply.

'Some people would give their right nut to hang with a family as cool as ours,' chirps Jack.

'Geez, Jack,' I say. 'When's your voice gunna break? If I hear that soprano one more time, my ear drums will burst!'

'When're you gunna stop being so flat? You're making the ironing board jealous!' he comes back at me.

That comment pisses me off, so I stalk off to my room. I keep my unimpressed face plastered on, but really I feel like crying, which is annoying as it's not how I want the world to see me. I want to be this glamorous girl who stands around at parties, not saying much, but because I look so cool, people flock to me. I don't want to be some sook who tears up every two seconds.

'You needn't be sulking in there if you're expecting me to take you shopping this afternoon,' Mum calls out.

'I'm not, I'm doing homework!'

'Yeah, right,' I hear Mum say in a fake teenager's voice, which is mega embarrassing.

Mum is taking me to Chadstone to buy new clothes. About time too, because at the moment I have zero clothes, which is seriously endangering my reputation. I told Mum it's breaching the *United Nations Declaration on the*

Rights of the Child if she doesn't buy me something decent to wear. I've got a hundred dollars in birthday money but I'm not sure it's enough, so I call Cat.

'Is a hundred dollars OK for an annual clothes budget?' I ask.

'Prolly not, but if you don't have enough of your own clothes, just klepto someone else's,' she advises. 'All the kids at my school are kleptomaniacs. How do you think my wardrobe got so excellent?'

'So if I see someone's clothes I like, I just take them?'

'Sure, but part of the thrill is to be real brazen and wear their clothes in front of the person.'

'Well, I think I'd rather just stick with my own clothes, or at least ask someone if I can borrow theirs.'

'There is no private property at my school. You just take what you can get — clothes, food, boys. It's the ultimate socialist state.'

I'm not sure that's the definition of socialism, but I don't say anything. I hang up and think about whose clothes I can borrow. There are Julie Ann's hand-me-downs, but she's so incredibly unfashionable. She wears tracksuits all the time and her bedroom is covered in posters of Richard Marx. Cat is busy klepto-ing other kids' clothes and Amanda probably isn't allowed to lend hers, so I'll have to make do with what I buy at Chadstone.

'I'm not waiting all day for that bus,' Mum says when we're ready to go. 'We can walk.'

'What?!'

'You heard me, miss. Now, gerroff your arse!'

The walk is so incredibly tedious. I trudge along, sighing and imagining we're on the Kokoda Trail. Every time a car passes, I walk on the other side of Mum, so people can't see me being forced to walk all the way to Chadstone. If someone from school saw me, I'd die.

We eventually arrive at Chadstone and I tell Mum, 'I wanna buy some baggy shirts from Cherry Lane, a denim jacket and some Converse high-tops.'

'You can get shoes exactly like those Converse in Kmart for half the price.'

'Um, don't you realise how tacky it is to buy knock-offs from Kmart? I have to get the *actual* brand!'

'Sometimes I don't know which planet you're on, Dot. A shoe is a shoe. Here, take your money and meet me at the food court in an hour.'

'OK, cool.'

'And don't be buying any suggestive clothes.'

'Whatever.'

I don't know what Mum's on about telling me not to buy anything suggestive. Baggy clothes are what's fashionable, and she should know better than to assume I'm some sort of scrubber who wears low-cut tops. I buy black Connies, a bandana and two baggy shirts – one is a flannie – but I don't have enough money for a denim jacket.

I still have time before I need to meet Mum, so I decide to check out the Angus & Robertson bookshop, which is right by the food court. I walk past the new releases to the music section and look for books about the punk scene. I find one full of photos of something called Melbourne's Little Band Scene. Teenagers not much older than me sit around looking coolly bored in messy houses and dingy pubs, surrounded by guitars, drums and home-made synthesisers. I hear echoes of the music they would have listened to as I stare at their faces that look both familiar and far away. I could be their friend. My thoughts are interrupted by a bossy-voiced woman talking to the man who's working here.

'Excuuuse me, do you stock *The Power of One?*'

She sounds intimidating, so I stare down at my book, but I'm eavesdropping for sure.

The man pauses, then says, 'Nah…it's sold out. Sorry 'bout that.'

He talks a little slowly, like he's considering things, and he has a kind voice, even though I have a feeling he doesn't like this woman.

'Oh my, that's terribly unfortunate. I shan't be shopping here again!' exclaims the woman as though she's Marie Antoinette, and flounces off.

I'm grinning because I've worked out this man decided not to help the woman because she isn't a nice person. Besides, there are a million copies of *The Power of One* right where she was standing at the front of the shop. I flick through a few more pages of the book.

'Great book,' the man says. I'm the only one in the shop, so he must be talking to me. 'That was a fantastic music scene. Seminal.'

'Yeah…' I say, lost for words as usual. I'll have to look up 'seminal' in the dictionary when I get home.

I can't bring myself to meet the man's eyes. Instead, I check the book's price, which is over my budget, and furtively leave the shop to find Mum. On my way out, I sneak a peek at the man, but he's tidying some books behind a shelf, so I can't see his face. I'm annoyed at myself for missing out on a conversation about music. I wish I could just talk to people like a normal human being, but I can't. I must have a disability. Some people are blind or deaf, but my disability is that I'm too shy to have conversations with people I don't know.

At the food court, Mum practically kills me with embarrassment. She's scoffing down all the free food samples like a greedy pig and she's carrying around a massive Target bag – the daggiest clothes store ever! She's talking to one of her friends, who sports a massive country-town poodle perm and skin-tight leggings. I catch snippets of their conversation, which is about nothing.

I roll my eyes and hope my conversations are never that boring. I prefer to discuss cutting-edge issues with my friends, like the hole in the ozone layer and nuclear testing. Things get worse when two of the popular girls from my year walk past, just as I'm standing with Mum, her Target bag and her bogany friend.

'Hi, Dot!' they say.

'Hi…' I feel myself blush.

I make sure my Cherry Lane bag is visible.

'Been shopping?'

'Um…yeah.'

'Cool! Well, see ya at school.'

'Bye…'

That was the longest conversation I've had with those girls. I wish I could join in with them more at school, but I'm so tongue-tied I'd most likely spend the entire lunch break trying to think of one decent thing to say.

Mum and I begin the arduous journey home, and I'm lost in thought, dreaming up ways I can become cooler. If I had a more extensive wardrobe, I could simply stand around looking fabulous and it wouldn't matter what kind of personality I had.

'Mum, I really need more money for clothes,' I tell her.

'When I was your age, we had three outfits. One for school, one for after school and one for special occasions.'

'Well, now I'm my age and I need more clothes. Pleeease, it's important I fit in.'

'Why don't you just be yourself, Dot? Everyone will love you for who you are, just like your father and I do.'

'Huh?'

'Well, if you want more clothes, get yourself a job to pay for them.'

We finish the walk home in stony silence.

Luckily our annual roulette party rolls round, and with it the opportunity to make some money. I set up a catering business, employing Jack, Dibble Dobble and my youngest cousin, Jade, to walk around the party carrying platters of corn chips, salsa and this new coriander dip all the adults think is bloody marvellous. Why would you eat coriander when it tastes exactly like mowed lawn and weed killer?

I'm mixing vodka tonics when Jack comes into the kitchen with an empty platter.

'Man, there's some boring conversation in there. Babies, Berlin Wall, Julie Ann's wondrous singing voice, Bob Hawke weeping, blah, blah, blah.'

I saddle Jack up with stubbies of beer, wine coolers and the vodka tonics.

'Give 'em these. Maybe they'll stop talking if they're drunker.'

We hear a whoop; someone must have had a big win. Later on, I'll see if I can double my catering money by sticking it all on red.

'What's that taste like?' Jack points to the vodka tonics I'm mixing.

We each take a sip, then spit it out.

'Gross! Petrol!' I grimace.

Jack leaves with the drinks and Jade arrives with another empty platter.

I load her platter with cheese cubes and kabana on toothpicks.

'How's it going out there?'

'Uncle Ted's talking about a sexy woman who gave him the eye on the tram. What's that mean?'

'It means he's a perve.'

Uncle Ted broke up with Jocelyn recently and now all he talks about is women. It's creepy and gross to hear people over thirty talking about the opposite sex in the same way people my age do.

We're getting paid five dollars an hour for our efforts, which is pretty excellent. The only things lacking at this party are cute boys and decent music. I take a break from preparing finger food to rifle through Dad's CD collection, but it's more dire than ever – The Chieftains, The Fureys and The Bushwackers. I've still got my 'London Calling' single, but we got rid of the record player. I'll buy some decent CDs as well as clothes with my pay.

In the next room, I hear Julie Ann strike up with 'Danny Boy'. I'm getting pretty over that song and the smug look she has when she sings it. I keep out of the roulette room until she finishes, but when I go in, everyone is still talking about how fantastic she is.

'Jules is going to Sydney to compete in an inter-school singing competition,' says Aunty Mary-Margaret Rose.

All the adults are highly impressed.

'What else will you do in Sydney, dearie?' Grandma asks her.

'Oh, I'll see all the touristy stuff like the Sydney Harbour Bridge and Opera House. Plus I'm playing in a Snap tournament with Helen.'

I say, 'If I was going to Sydney, I'd go to see gigs at the Annandale Hotel. I'd stand at the back of the band room, listening to the music, and one of the band members would notice I know a lot about music and come up and start talking to me.'

As usual, no one's listening.

TRACK 8 – HEROES

'Guess what, I've got a girlfriend,' Jack says.

We're in my room, about to watch *Neighbours* on the black-and-white TV, seeing Dad insists on watching the news on the colour one. Jack and I are supposed to alternate the TV every six months, but I do my best to make Jack forget when it's his turn.

'Bullshit,' I tell him.

'Yeah, I do. Here's a photo. Her name's Nancy.'

Jack produces his class photo and points out a girl who looks like the Scandinavian daughter of Deborah Harry. She makes me feel cranky.

'Oh, well done, Jack! And here's a picture of *my* boyfriend!' I point to a poster of Joe Strummer. 'As if that girl would go with a skinner like you,' I continue.

'Well, she does,' Jack replies.

It turns out he's not bullshitting, because later on Jack asks Mum to ring Nancy's mum to ask if she can go see *Batman* at the movies with him. Then on Sunday morning, the girl from Jack's school photo turns up on our doorstep.

'Are you Jack's girlfriend?' I ask.

'Yes,' she replies.

Jack sticks his tongue out. He and Nancy are still little kids, but they've already overtaken me. I'm mortified. While Mum is dropping them off at the cinema, I call Cat in distress.

'It's not fair! I've never had a boyfriend, never got with a boy, never been on a date. I can't even think of a boy I *know*, thanks to Mum and Dad sending me to a girls school.'

I can hear 'Blame it on the Rain' in the background at Cat's end, but I'm definitely blaming it on Mum and Dad.

'Cheer up, Dot. I don't have a boyfriend either,' Cat says.

'Yeah, but at least you can talk to boys. I'm quiet as it is, but around the opposite sex I'm *literally* mute.' I twirl the phone cord round and round my fingers.

'Don't worry, your time will come, girlfriend. Jack just has a kiddie romance. You'll have fireworks!'

Cat's saying all the right things, but I'm not in the mood to cheer up. I retire to my bedroom for a decadent sulk.

The only men in my life are Joey Ramone, Sid Vicious, Iggy Pop, Paul Weller, Joe Strummer and Ian Curtis – and some of them are dead. My bedroom walls are covered in posters of these musical men. I've even stuck pictures on my ceiling.

Mum's back from Chadstone; she sticks her head in my doorway.

'Clean your room for chrissakes, Dot,' she says. 'It looks like *Steptoe and Son* live in here.'

Whoever they are.

'Don't touch a thing, Mum! This room is a shrine to coolness.'

Mum bursts out laughing.

I close the door on her face and put on one of my mixed tapes. I had to scan every single radio station day and night to find these songs. In between the airwaves of commercial music, opera, news shows, horrible football and dad music, I found some treasures.

I wonder if I'm the only person in the world who feels cheered up when they listen to Joy Division. Ian Curtis sings in a voice as deep as the ocean and as I lie on my bed my worries float away like feathers. I close my eyes and try to remember when I was a tiny little kid, and I can see a chink of light in the corner; that's where the music is. That's why I love music like Joy Division, Blondie, The Clash and The Specials so much. It's the first music my brain knew, so now it's stuck in there and New Kids on the Block, Roxette or 1927 are never going to budge it out of there, ever.

The phone rings and Mum bangs on my door. 'Your mate's on the phone, but don't be tying up the line all day.'

It's Amanda. 'Hi!' she says. 'How's it going?'

'Not bad... Hey, who do you like best, Joy Division or New Order?'

'Who?'

'Don't you know? They were seminal to the Manchester music scene in the late seventies. Joy Division became New Order. "Blue Monday" is an anthem!'

'Oh, I'm not really into that stuff. Have you heard Kylie and Jason's new duet? It's sooo excellent!'

No one's into my stuff. Cat loves New Kids on the Block, Julie Ann is a Bette Midler fan and Jack only listens to rap. I'm out of place, as usual.

Mum's hovering, so I don't talk to Amanda for long.

'It's Sunday afternoon, Dot. Have you thought about your homework?' she asks as soon as I hang up.

Instead of doing homework, I sit on my bed reading *Gone with the Wind* and taping songs off the radio. I've found this community radio station, One Eleven FM, which plays heaps of post-punk and alternative. Right now they're playing some Birthday Party.

I shove my book aside, draw my curtains so no one can see in, and dance. I let myself go wherever the music takes me. Where it takes me is to dance in the style of Ian Curtis. I have the impression girls aren't meant to dance like that; I'm probably meant to be prancing about in bike pants doing synchronised aerobics moves, à la Collette. I sway and jerk with my eyes closed, imagining I'm at The Crystal Ballroom, losing myself in a haze of cigarette smoke and red lipstick. If only I wasn't underage, but I have enough trouble looking fourteen without trying to pass for eighteen.

At least the people on this radio station get me. The next song they play is 'A Message to You, Rudy' by The Specials. The joyful, brassy music fills me up and I sing along at the top of my voice.

'*You* better stop your messing around and think of your future. Do your homework, Dot!' Mum shouts from the kitchen.

I turn the music up and keep dancing, keeping an eye on my closed door in case someone barges in. I dance and dance, a huge smile plastered on my face, all the way till dinnertime.

After dinner, I really do need to start some homework. We've got an English essay about role models due tomorrow. The happy feeling the music gave me crumbles as I open my notepad. I write about Lynda Day from *Press Gang*. I think she's unreal because she's feisty, argumentative and sometimes she stuffs up, but boys still have crushes on her. Also, Lynda is a journalist, which is my backup profession if I don't make it as a High Court judge. I wish I was more like Lynda, or maybe Scarlett O'Hara without the slaves.

Instead, I'm just me, Dot, the girl teachers think should speak up more in class, my peers think of as too quiet, and boys never notice. I'm not popular but I'm not a loser, I'm not a genius but I'm not dumb, and I'm not sporty but I'm not a couch potato. There's nothing bad about me, but I wonder if there's nothing amazing about me either.

To stop feeling sorry for myself, I think of someone from the real world who could be my role model, someone who's a bit like the me that I am now and a lot like the me that I'm going to be. I remember Jocelyn, who never had to say a word to give off an air of attractive coolness.

Like Jocelyn, I know how to put together cool outfits and I'm already untalkative, so it'd be pretty easy for me to go to parties looking great and spending the entire night staring mysteriously out of the window. Boys will admire me from afar, and wish I was their girlfriend.

I don't get why no one in my family liked Jocelyn, not even Uncle Ted in the end. I guess it's because if you don't do the washing up or have some amusing anecdote or song about Ireland, you're nothing to the Kellys.

'Good kid, Dot,' Dad says when he spots me slaving away unloading the dishwasher. 'Contribution is the key to society.'

That night, I dream I'm floating in space in Major Tom's capsule, but this time there's a boy in there with me. He's got his back to me, but I can tell by his hairstyle that he's handsome. He's typing on a Macintosh II and quietly singing.

Dottie, a message to you,

Dottie, a message to you.

He disappears and I'm left all alone in that bloody capsule. Then my alarm goes off, which puts me in a bad mood.

♫ ♫ ♫

When I'm finally released from school, I catch the train to Prahran and wander through the side streets, looking at all the little houses. They're made of wood or stucco; some are scruffy and some are done up. I prefer the scruffy ones, with their ramshackle porches, dusty windows and overgrown plants. Each house has a door and one window on the side, so they look like a friendly, winking face. I'm not sure why, but I feel like the little houses are hypnotising me; my heartbeat slows down and I feel mega calm and relaxed. I feel like even if I am the only person like me in the universe, it doesn't matter. I breathe deep and slow, and smile to myself. It's the same feeling I had as when I was listening to The Specials last night.

I walk past the Train Tracks Hotel. The train crashing out of the building is still there, and I gaze at it for a while, wondering what ever happened to the red and blue trains. My reverie is interrupted by a man dashing out of the pub. There's something familiar about him, but he's covered his face, avoiding the wind so he can light a cigarette. I hurry off to catch the actual train home.

TRACK 9 – TEENAGE KICKS

It's a cold, rainy day and Amanda, Stephanie and I are huddled around the radiator, looking like war orphans in our grey and dull blue. St Lutgarde's has the ugliest uniform in the whole fascist history of making kids wear uniforms. We're damp from outside, and our jumpers smell like wet dogs.

'I wonder how many boys I can get with if I wear my uniform to the GW this weekend. Three? Four?' Roberta O'Brian says.

I feel my jaw drop.

'You should! I dare you!' Carmel Santamaria replies.

'Are you guys going to the GW?' I ask Amanda and Stephanie.

'I'm not allowed,' says Amanda, and Stephanie screws up her face in disgust.

I wouldn't mind going, but I wouldn't go without my friends, in case no one talks to me. After school I call Cat, to see if she wants to come.

'What is it?'

'It's this blue-light disco in Glen Waverley that runs once a month. The main objective is to see how many boys you can get with in one night.'

Now that I describe it, the GW doesn't sound that great. I remember long-ago discos that twirled their sounds around me, creating magic in the air. Do they still exist?

'Don't worry about that *suburban* disco,' Cat says. 'Come with me to my friend Fleur's party in East Melbourne. It's going to be excellent! East Melbourne, on the other side of Wellington Parade, is one of the most elegant parts of the city.'

'Geez, have you been reading *Home Beautiful* or something?'

It's true though, the Victorian terraces of East Melbourne are so fancy that Mr Darcy would probably live there if he was Australian. Instead, I think about the other side of Punt Road, with its small, scruffy cottages.

'I reckon Richmond is cooler,' I say.

'What? Too many derros and students. *Puh-lease*!' Cat replies in a mock-American accent.

The party is going to be a movie marathon, but with boys, alcohol and cigarettes. Amanda, Stephanie and I normally just go bowling for kicks, so I'm excited and nervous to be going to my first proper teenage party.

I meet Cat under the clocks at Flinders Street Station and we catch the tram to Fleur's house, which is actually more mansion than house. Some kid lets us in, then runs off to find Fleur.

'Wow!' says Cat, standing in the hall, which is a proper hall, not just a skinny passage. 'The whole place looks like it's been decorated by Laura Ashley. It's so pretty!'

'Is it?' I whisper. 'Don't you reckon it looks too busy with all those little flowers everywhere?'

'Um, that's like the *fashion*!' Cat replies in her American accent.

Fleur comes running down the hall. She's wearing Doc Martens and a dress covered in tiny blue flowers, perfectly matching her wallpaper. Cat told me that Fleur is bulimic, but you can't tell by looking, as her dress is baggy and practically ankle length.

'Cat!' gushes Fleur, and pecks her on the cheek, just like an adult.

I've noticed the girls in my school have started doing that too, pecking each other when they arrive each morning. I like the sophistication; it reminds me of Audrey Hepburn parties, but I'm uncomfortable initiating bodily contact. Besides, Amanda and Stephanie think it's gross.

'Fleur, this is Dot. Dot, this is Fleur.'

Fleur gives me a peck too. 'Nice to meet you, Dot. What school do you go to? Merton Hall, Timbertop, St Cath's, St Mick's, Sac, Star, MLC, PLC, Camberwell Girls, Shelford, St Leo's, MacRob, Fintona, Lauriston, Loreto or the Purple People Eaters?'

'St Lutgarde's College.'

I wait for her to make a joke about Sluts, but instead she says, 'Oh. Never heard of it…'

Then I'm introduced to Fleur's parents and her dad asks me the exact same question, and also stares at me blankly when I tell him the name of my school. I wish I could sail away, and I want to tell Cat that these people are such splendos, but she seems so happy to be here.

Fleur's parents are relegated upstairs.

'Remember Fleur, no hanky-panky,' warns her mum as she walks up the stairs.

'Ooh, hanky-panky!' We all giggle.

The movie marathon is held in a huge room at the back of the house, featuring the biggest television I've ever seen. It must be at least forty inches. Unlike the floral hall, this room is ultra-modern. When I get my own place, I'm definitely having a room like this, with black leather corner couches, soft maroon carpet, smoked glass coffee tables, a compact disc player and blackout curtains. It'll go nicely with the train crashing through the wall.

Fleur may be a snob, but she has excellent taste in movies. All my favourite videos are spread out on the coffee table – *Ferris Bueller*, *The Breakfast Club*, *Pretty in Pink*, *Heathers*, *Stand by Me* and *The Lost Boys*.

The television is still turned off and people are standing around in small groups, talking. Cat disappears to chat with some girls, so I retire to the corner. It's the perfect opportunity to try out acting like Jocelyn, so I stand there in my stripy tee-shirt and black A-line skirt, gazing pensively into the distance. No boys approach me, so I check out my reflection in the window. Instead of glamorous, my posture is slumped and apologetic. I'm mortified.

Cat looks over. 'Dot, what are you doing? Nobody puts Dot in a corner! Get over here!'

Cat and I sit side by side on one of the corner couches and at last the television is turned on. Everyone gathers to watch *Heathers*. All the girls sit on one of the corner couches and all the boys sit on the other. We watch

Heathers in a pretty civilised manner, but as Fleur's sister's putting on *The Lost Boys* this boy, Alec Brown, perks up.

'How about we get this party started?'

He produces a packet of aspirin and some cans of Coke.

'Don't be a tard, Brownie,' another boy, Joshua Hawkins, laughs, 'Everyone knows Coke and aspirin's only an urban myth.'

'Well, I'm gunna give it a try anyway, just to confirm,' Alec says. 'Anyone else up for it?'

In the end, we all try some. Combined with aspirin, the Coke is fizzier and tastes bitter, but I don't feel any effect. Maybe it's just the caffeine, but some of the boys hoon up and begin throwing cushions around and standing on the couch playing air guitar to the Doors song from *The Lost Boys* soundtrack. I spot Alec eyeing off Fleur's dad's liquor cabinet.

'Well, well, well. What do we have here?'

'No way, Alec!' Fleur sounds worried. 'My dad will crucify me!'

'Relax, Fleur. We'll just mark off how much we drink and top it up with water or something. He'll never know!'

'Then we'll eat all these party pies and sausage rolls, so no one can smell grog on our breath,' Joshua suggests.

Joshua is clearly the alpha boy, so with his sanction, Fleur says it's OK for us to try some of the alcohol.

'But just take a little bit out of each bottle, rather than finishing one entire drink, OK?'

'No problemo!'

'And don't get too wasted! My dad's an alcoholic and he can sniff out drunks,' Fleur continues.

Joshua and Alec mix some drinks with the Coke and pass them round. We all take a tiny sip of whiskey and Coke, vodka and Coke, Midori and Coke, and red wine and Coke. Every drink is feral.

'This is cool fun, isn't it?' Cat remarks.

'Yeah…'

I'd actually rather just watch *The Lost Boys*. The other kids don't really drink that much either, as they're all scared of getting caught, with the exception of Alec who sculls the leftovers, burps, jumps around a bit, then falls asleep on the couch. Another boy, William Lee, gets out a pen and draws little tears falling down Alec's cheek. He's frowning in his sleep and the tears make him look like the crying clown from all the posters, which is pretty hilarious.

Joshua rubs his hands together. 'Now, who's up for Spin the Bottle?'

My heart races. I really don't want to play Spin the Bottle. Some of these boys are cute, but I don't want to have my first kiss in front of everyone. What if I'm really bad at it and the boy is grossed out? What if my breath smells? What if he gropes me? I'm wearing a feral beige bra Mum got me from Target, and I don't want anyone finding out about that!

I almost pass out with relief when some other kids say they don't want to play either. I sit down to watch the rest of *The Lost Boys* with Fleur's little sister, a couple of other girls, this boy, Martin Jones, and Alec, who's still asleep. I hadn't previously noticed Martin Jones because he doesn't say much, but now that I do, I realise that I've never met anyone as good looking as him in real life before. I wonder why he's not playing Spin the Bottle, as I'm sure all the girls would go for him.

I work up the courage to speak. 'Don't you wanna play?'

'Nah…that game's immature. Anyway, I really wanna watch *The Lost Boys*.'

I stop talking, in case Martin Jones doesn't want to be interrupted while he's watching the movie. He looks like River Phoenix in *Stand by Me*, with green eyes and a light-brown flat-top. He's starting to develop muscles, but his arms are still hairless and smooth. Martin Jones reminds me of an expensive racehorse, bred to win at life. I wonder what I'd have to do to end up with a boy like that, and I wish I had the guts to do it.

I force my attention back to the movie and Kiefer Sutherland's perplexing mullet, but we're interrupted by a loud gasp. We turn to see Cat and Joshua full-on pashing! I've never seen people kissing in real life before and it looks way different from movie scenes, definitely not as romantic. They're both fairly unco at it, they move their heads around too much and I can see spit, even from where I'm sitting. So now, instead of worrying about the logistics of kissing, I just think it's gross. Everyone cheers when Cat and Joshua finish and wipe their faces, blushing but also looking pretty proud of themselves.

'Come out for a smoke, Dot,' Cat says, as she extricates herself from the group.

'So…how was it with Joshua? Do you have the hots for him?' I ask as soon as we're alone outside.

'Totally! I hope he asks me to go with him!'

'He seems really…nice.' And by nice, I mean popular. 'What's it like, kissing?'

'Excellent! It feels like the whole room is spinning and there's no one else alive but me and him! You should try it, Dot. You *gotta* lose your lip virginity before Year Ten!'

I suppose I do, if I'm going to join the rest of the human race. I wish I could be all romantic about it like Cat is, but I'm just not. Instead, I'm jealous that she likes it and I don't.

'I saw you talking to Martin Jones. Do you like him?' she asks.

'He's *sooo* good looking! But I doubt he'd like me since I can never think of anything to say.'

Cat rolls her eyes because I'm being a downer. Martin Jones is beyond cute and I like that he doesn't get all loudmouth like the other boys. He'd make a great boyfriend, but for some reason I can't imagine kissing him. If Martin Jones, or even Joe Strummer, wanted to pash me, I'm not sure I'd want to.

I'd rather just hang out with a guy and talk about music. If we talked about music, I'd be able to see his soul; not his God soul like the one we have to pray for at Mass, but a soul that people have hidden behind their eyes that only switches on every now and then. This is something I'd never tell Cat, in case she thinks I'm a weirdo, but although I like the idea of boys, I don't want to pash them as much as other girls do. Thinking about this stuff makes me feel empty and alone.

Cat breaks the silence. 'Come on, let's have a ciggie.'

We position ourselves out of line of vision from the upstairs windows where Fleur's parents can look out. Cat takes out her beloved soft pack of Peter Stuyvesants – all other brands are for bogans, she tells me – and lights up. I happen to know it's the same pack of cigarettes she acquired at the start of the year. She only smokes one or two cigarettes at parties, but she lets people think it's a different pack each time.

'Want one?'

'Nah…it's OK.'

More and more kids my age are starting to think smoking is cool and light up whenever they get a chance – school camps, at the park, behind the library. Fuzzy Peach perfume from The Body Shop and a packet of Juicy Fruit chewing gum are the ultimate masking agents.

Even Amanda smoked at the last school camp. 'I just wanna do something that would make my mum mad,' she told me. 'But without her finding out…'

I'm pretty much the only person who's never had a puff. I think cigarettes are feral and I don't want to end up dead like Yul Brynner, or worse, with yellow fingernails and teeth. The only problem is that I'm starting to feel left out. I'm not really interested in stuff like smoking, drinking and pashing, but I don't want to be different from my friends, especially Cat.

'Actually, can I have a puff?'

Cat grins. I present her with two fingers in the up-yours gesture, and she places the cigarette between them. I take a little puff and quickly blow the smoke out before I swallow. *Gross!* It tastes like stale ash and reminds me of that off smell in the house the morning after a Kelly family party.

Cat laughs. 'Oh, you doofus, Dot. Don't bum-puff, you gotta inhale!'

Bum-puff? Inhale?

'How d'you do that?' I ask.

Cat wrinkles her brow, thinking. 'You know what? I don't actually know!'

'Cat…?'

'Hmm?'

'D'you reckon in some parallel universe a guy like Martin Jones would go out with me?'

'Anything's possible, Dot,' Cat replies, stubbing out the cigarette. 'As long as he doesn't find out you're secretly an axe-murderer!'

We both crack up laughing, and for the first time in ages it feels like we're on the same wavelength.

TRACK 10 – THAT'S ENTERTAINMENT

The world is changing. I know this because I've started watching the news with Dad. I watch a teenage boy with a mullet shoving rubble out of the way and jumping over the Berlin Wall.

'Watch and learn, Dot!' Dad says, almost spilling his tea with excitement. 'This is history!'

'I wonder what that boy will do now,' I say, but Dad's attention is back on the news, so I talk to myself. 'I reckon he'll go to McDonald's, then get a decent haircut.'

'Quiet, please!' Dad says.

I imagine the boy moving out of his drab flat and becoming a rock star instead of a factory worker. He's probably quite good looking without that mullet.

Mum comes in with a fresh pot of tea, and I rifle round in my pocket.

'Can you sign this, Mum?'

'What is it?'

'Permission slip. We have to do Community Service giving food to poor people.'

'You needn't roll your eyes, Dot. It'll do you good to see how other people live,' Mum says.

♫ ♫ ♫

Amanda, Stephanie and I stand in the corridor of the boarding house, clutching paper cups and a flask of vegetable soup. Mrs Boukavalis waves us on with a nod of encouragement. I knock on the first door. It's opened by a friendly looking old man with hair as white and fluffy as a cloud.

'Well, hello!' His voice is deep and wise, like that old guy on TV, Charles 'Bud' Tingwell.

I don't know what to say to the boarding house man, so I say nothing until Amanda pokes me. 'Hi… D'you want some soup?'

'Why, that would be meritorious.'

I don't know what that means, so I just stand there until the old man continues, 'Yes please, I'd love some soup.'

Stephanie pours soup into a cup and I try to look past the old man into his room. There's no whiff of stale beer, wee or other signs of debauchery. I wonder how he ended up here. His whole house is smaller than my bedroom.

'I thought all these old dudes would be derros,' I say, once we've visited a few more men. 'But they're nice and they seem smart. How come they don't live in a house with their families?'

'They've had hard, sad lives, Dot,' says Mrs Boukavalis. I jump at the sound of her voice as I didn't realise she'd followed us up the corridor. 'And you can show some respect.'

'I do. But how come they ended up all alone in a boarding house?'

'Never you mind. Just love your fellow man, girls. And pray for him.'

Like Soft Cell, I don't pray that way. Instead of loving the men, I'm afraid of ending up like them, all alone in a tiny little room with no one to talk to at night and no one to stop the feeling of being lost forever in space. My heart races at the thought of it.

If only I could find a boy who liked music as much as me; we could protect each other from getting lost. Maybe, if I married someone like Martin Jones, I wouldn't have to go and live in a boarding house. We could live together in a yacht, and sail around the world going to music festivals.

Someone is leaving one of the rooms.

'Bye Bob, see ya next time,' the someone says in a slow, kind voice.

Before I can turn around to see who it is, Mrs Boukavalis says, 'Come on girls, it's time to leave.'

♫ ♫ ♫

Next school holidays, I head to Graceland with the family. It's spring now, so we're keen to enjoy the slightly warmer weather, 'slightly' being the operative word.

We've barely finished unpacking the car when Dad says, 'Right, you kids get down to the beach for a swim. I need a cup of tea and to relax without being bothered by your nonsense.'

'Is Julie Ann coming?' I ask.

'Never mind about her. *You're* going for a swim, and that's all *you* need to worry about,' Mum says. 'And you needn't look at me with that thunder face.'

I glare at Mum a little longer, so she knows I'm not obeying her, then follow Jack and Dibble Dobble down the hill.

The wind spits bullets of sand onto our legs, so we run into the water. We stand around for a bit, surveying the incoming waves.

'Man, this water is like melted bits of Antarctica,' Jack says, through chattering teeth.

'Yeah, how come none of the adults are down here swimming?' Dibble Dobble asks.

'How come Julie Ann isn't?' I growl.

'Hey, here comes a big wave,' Jack announces.

The boys swim out and begin body surfing, but I'm not in the mood. I look at my hands, which have turned purple.

'This is bullshit,' I announce in a dad voice and stomp out of the water and back up the hill to Graceland.

If Julie Ann can laze about with the adults, then so can I. I'm only a year younger!

The next day is no better. Jade and I are setting up Monopoly on the kitchen table when Dad marches in, takes one look at us and booms, 'Kids, out!'

We skulk off to the lounge room where the boys are watching *The Curiosity Show*, but Mum follows.

'I'm not having you kids lounging around on piss-stained mattresses all day,' she says.

This comment is directed at Jack and Dibble Dobble, who, when they were younger, indulged in more than their fair share of bed-wetting. The mattresses smell faintly of urine to this very day.

'Mum, you really need to learn to appreciate Eau de Jack cos I think Chanel wants to bottle it and make a million!' Jack says.

'Just gerrout of the house, you lazy little gits!' Mum snaps. 'I'm gagging for a cup of tea after dealing with you lot.'

So we head off to the beach – again – while Julie Ann weasels in with the adults by making tea and washing the dishes. *What a suck-up!*

The boys swim out deep, where the surfers are. I feel grumpy that they're more fearless than me, so I swim out to join them. Before I catch up, a massive dumper wave curls over me. *So this is what it feels like to be in a washing machine.* The wave roars in my ears, and then everything is quiet and I have the same creepy feeling I get whenever I have that dream about being stuck in Major Tom's capsule. I can't tell if it's forever or just a couple of seconds before the wave slams me on the shore. I stand up shakily, forcing myself to laugh.

'That was excellent!' I say in a loud voice, for all to hear. *That's the last time I ever swim out to the big waves.*

While the other kids swim, I slow jog across the sand, trying to warm up. Ahead I see a group of boys. I stop still when I realise that one of them is Martin Jones. *Imagine if he caught me running towards him, like a loser!* He's looking out to sea, so I have a perfect opportunity to study his profile. The other boys are flicking each other with towels, but Martin Jones is just looking at the waves with a slight smile on his lips. He's so handsome, I can hardly breathe!

Go up and say hi, a little voice in my head says.

But why would he want to see you? A louder voice pipes up. *He won't remember who you are and he doesn't want to be interrupted. Besides, you'll never think of anything to say.*

I turn away.

Coward! whispers the first voice.

Jade calls out from the water's edge, 'Hey Dot, come swim with me!'

I run out to join her, relieved I no longer have to debate with myself about talking to Martin Jones.

On the way back to Graceland, we pass the town's one and only café. People are sitting outside with cappuccinos and cake, a luxury that is denied us Kellys. Something draws my attention to a couple in their twenties. The woman facing me is cranky-looking, sipping coffee, wearing a stripy tee-shirt, red lipstick and dangly earrings. She reminds me of Jocelyn, sitting there looking beautiful in her stony silence. The man has his back to me, and he's reading the newspaper, scarcely acknowledging the woman's presence. The couple are the only people I see who are separate entities from each other; every other couple at the café is a unit. I never knew you could be alone even when you have someone.

♪ ♪ ♪

In the afternoon, we sit in the tree house, digesting salad sandwiches. Julie Ann refuses to join us, preferring instead to listen to jazz records in the front room. *Jazz!?!* Jack, Dibble Dobble, Jade and I loll about, torn between boredom and relaxation.

I'm jolted out of the silence by Jade saying in a posh voice, 'Oh helllooo, Dr Ivanskiy! I'm here to get my teeth seen to.'

'Ay yi yi!' Jack joins in. 'What are you wearing, Mrs Jade? Your fashions are right dowdy, like peasant from my neighbouring willage.'

'No problem with your teeth though, Mrs Jade,' says Dibble Dobble. 'They are strong, like a skyscraper.'

'Your husband is right ugly, Mrs Jade,' I say. 'He looks really untrustworthy, like Stalin.'

We collapse into laughter and can't continue. I don't hear anything, but I'm overcome by a disapproving vibe. I look out of the tree house and see Julie Ann frowning at the bottom of the tree.

'Guess not everyone's cool enough to have a sense of humour,' I mutter.

'Don't you guys think it's time you stopped making fun of Dr Ivanskiy?' she asks prissily, 'Don't you realise…'

'Yeah, yeah. We realise all he's done for the family!' I snap. 'But lighten up, Julie Ann. Without comedy, the world is nothing!'

'Yeah, but not comedy at someone else's expense.'

'So crucify us for being hilarious! I appreciate good dental care and all… but geez!'

'Don't you know Dr Ivanskiy saved Grandpa Kelly's life?'

'No…' This is actually a story I haven't heard. How is Julie Ann obtaining family information I don't have?

'Well, he did and that's why he's a hero to the family! When Grandma and Grandpa first got married, Grandpa would hit the pubs after work and drink as much as he could before six o'clock, because he was an alcoholic and that's what men did in those days. One time Grandpa stumbled out of the Menzies Hotel, pissed as a fart, and stepped in front of a tram. Luckily, Dr Ivanskiy was there at the same time and managed to push Grandpa out of the way, saving his life.'

'Wow!' says Jack, his eyes shining. 'Dr Ivanskiy saved our whole family, cos if Grandpa had've died that day, none of us would've been born!'

'And I'd never get to play soccer with the council flat kids when I grow up…' Dibble Dobble adds, always one to bring up his lifelong dream.

'Uh, yeah…' Julie Ann continues, 'So that's the kind of man Dr Ivanskiy is.'

I don't reply, but I wonder if maybe this serious side to Dr Ivanskiy is more interesting than the comedy.

♫ ♫ ♫

The holiday finishes and I head back to school. The feeling the world is changing continues. I remember hiding from communists in cupboards when I was little, but now that seems silly. I see my first ever dead body when photos of an executed Ceauşescu are plastered all over the papers. For English I write an essay about the boy with the mullet who tears down the Berlin Wall so he can go to McDonald's. I get an A.

Another development is that for the first time since the War, Dr Ivanskiy receives a letter from Ukraine. It's from his nephew Kolia and contains over forty years of news. Dr Ivanskiy's brother was sent to Siberia in the fifties for owning too many ponies for Stalin's liking, never to be seen again. His son Kolia is the only surviving relative. As well as pages of beautiful Cyrillic writing, there's a photo of a man, woman and little girl around Jade's age. It's a photograph with a sky blue background like they use for school pictures, but the colour is washed out like Mum's old photos from the seventies. The man has dark hair but the females are fair; they stare at the camera in outfits fifteen years out of date and don't smile or touch each other.

I can't imagine not having my family in my life for one minute, let alone forty years. I hear the clink of china in the kitchen and find Mum taking cups and saucers out of the cupboard. I give her a hug from behind and don't let go even when she walks over to the kettle.

TRACK 11 – THE MODEL

Dear Dot,

You won't believe what's happened! Because of my woeful marks in maths, I'm grounded! No going out and no phone calls until they improve. I'm even having to sneak this letter to you. Write back care of my cousin – she's cool and will pass it on without lagging to the parental units.

Mum and Dad are such fascists! They've got one of my brother's nerd friends to be my maths tutor. He's covered in pimples and smells like wet clothes that have been put away in the cupboard for a few weeks. Quelle grossness! Mum loves him and probably wants us to get married. Vomit!

Anyway, here's some excellent news for you! Remember Martin Jones, the boy you spoke to at Fleur's party? I asked him if he wanted to go on a date with you and he said YES!!! I've given him your number, so look out for his call. He's a really nice guy, so just stay cool and you're in!

Miss you!

Love,

Cat

Cat's handwriting is big and friendly, with circles instead of dots above each 'i'. As soon as I open the letter, my eyes pounce on the words 'Martin Jones' so I read that bit first. I feel like I'm having a really happy heart attack. Martin Jones is the best-looking boy I've ever seen and he's actually going to ask me on a date! Me, Dot! The girl even the most average-looking boys overlook because I'm so quiet.

If this date goes well, Martin Jones might ask me on another and then we might start going with each other. Eventually we could get married and talk about music forever. Martin Jones could be the boy with the music, the one who stops my terrible dreams about being lost in space. I'd never feel lonely, or different or sad ever again. This is the most excited I've ever been! I can't think of anything but Martin Jones, and my stomach feels like I've done two hundred sit-ups in a row.

Cat's over at her cousin's place and sneaks in a phone call. I ask her to tell me more about Martin Jones.

'Well, Joshua is the most popular boy in our year, but Martin Jones comes a close second. He'll probably be dux in Year Twelve and he plays in the A-Teams for cricket and footy. Oh, best of all, he's in Myer catalogues!'

'Really? He's a model?'

'Yep. Take a look in the latest catalogue.'

A few days later, it arrives in our letterbox. I flick straight to the adolescent section and there's Martin Jones in a denim jacket, smiling off into the distance with teeth so big and white they could be fridges.

On Saturday morning, the phone rings. Jack and I race for it, but he beats me, the little grommet.

'Ooh Dot, it's a boy!' he chirps. 'I almost fainted with shock.'

'Shut up, jerk!' I snarl as I snatch the phone.

I wait until Jack leaves the room before saying, 'Hello?'

'Hi Dot, it's Martin Jones. How's it going?'

'Um, good…'

'I hope you don't mind me calling. Cat gave me your number.'

'Nah, it's OK…I mean, it's cool!'

My words range uncontrollably from a growl to a squeak, like a boy whose voice is breaking. Martin Jones' voice hasn't gotten too deep yet, but it's husky. Actually, it's sexy.

'Great!' he says. 'Anyway, I was wondering if you wanted to go see a film tomorrow.'

It's actually happening, my first ever date and it's with the future dux of Grammar! I bite my knuckle so I don't squeal out loud and I'm breathing real quick. *Say something interesting, say something interesting!* It doesn't work. My brain is frozen and I've got nothing.

Eventually Martin Jones asks, 'Dot? You still there?'

A hiss of air escapes my locked jaw, 'Yeeeeep.'

'Pardon?'

Calm blue ocean, calm blue ocean! 'Sure, that'd be excellent.'

'Cool! Any particular movie you want to see?'

'Oh… I don't mind. You choose.'

'Well, how about *Dead Poet's Society*? It's on at one o'clock at Russell Street.'

'OK.'

I feel like kicking myself for sounding like such a boring loser, but Martin Jones doesn't seem to notice.

'Let's meet at Flinders Street Station under the clocks,' Martin Jones says. 'See you tomorrow, Dot.'

When I hang up, I almost knock the phone to the floor, I'm in that much of a swoon.

'Was that a boy, Dot?' Mum asks. I'm not sure why she's hanging around, dusting ornaments that have no dust.

'Yeah…we're going to see a movie in the city tomorrow.' I try to sound casual.

'OK,' says Mum, but as I'm leaving the room she adds, 'Jack can come too.'

'What?!?'

'Well, I'm not having him moping around all weekend. It'll do him good to have an outing too.'

'I can't bring an *uninvited* guest. It'd be rude.'

'I'm sure your friend won't mind.' And then Mum grins slyly. 'Or is this a date?'

'Nooo!'

I'm spewing I said no, but it's out now.

'Good, because I think you're a bit young to go on a date with a boy we don't know.'

So the next day, I meet Martin Jones under the clocks, with Jack in tow.

'Um, hi,' I say to him. 'This is my brother.'

Martin Jones doesn't bat an eyelid, 'Hey dude, how's it hanging?'

He gets better looking every time I see him; today he's sparkling. His voice is confident but not showy and his eyes are dreamy; dreamy handsome and dreamy like he's half asleep. My heart rate is up because I'm in the presence of such a good-looking boy, but I'm also perturbed because he addressed Jack first.

'Sweet,' Jack answers Martin Jones. Thank goodness he didn't say 'a little to the left' like he normally does; otherwise I would have died.

'What footy team do you go for?' Martin Jones asks him.

'Hawthorn.'

'Cool. I'm Carlton.'

'Shall we get going?' I ask. My voice comes out cranky-sounding.

As we walk to Russell Street, Martin Jones and Jack chat about footy, skateboarding and Game Boys. I just gaze at Martin Jones. I try to join in, but I know nothing about these topics.

We make our way to the back row of the cinema, so we can throw Jaffas at people, but it's already full of kids. With all the milling about and trying to find three empty seats, somehow Jack ends up in the middle.

I pinch him and he says, 'Oh, d'you wanna sit here?'

He speaks too loud and Martin Jones turns to look at me. I feel my cheeks heat up like they do when Mum puts too many chillies in the curry.

'No…it's cool.'

Jack raises an eyebrow and settles into his seat. I'm mad at Mum for inviting Jack on *my* date; I'm mad at Jack for taking my seat; I'm mad at Martin Jones for liking Jack more than me; but most of all I'm mad at myself for not being the kind of person I want to be. If I was Jocelyn, I'd sit down without saying a word and Martin Jones would rush to be by my side. Instead, I'm Dot, and the best thing I have going for me is an entertaining brother.

After the movie, we go to McDonald's for some fries. Dad's banned us from this establishment, but when he's not around… The conversation shifts from the movie to sport again, and I feel like a third wheel on my own date. Then again, at least I've been on a date, unlike Amanda and Stephanie.

'Who's your favourite band?' I ask Martin Jones when I can finally get in a word.

'Oh, probably Public Enemy.'

'Hey, me too!' Jack interjects. 'D'you like the Beastie Boys?'

'Do I!'

Great! Martin Jones looks like he could be the boy with the music, but I didn't think that the music would be rap. And I certainly didn't consider that the boy with the music would like Jack more than he liked me!

We're catching different trains, so we say goodbye at the platform entrance.

'Thanks for a great day,' I say.

'No worries. Bye, guys!' Martin Jones replies.

Guys?!? What the hell? I didn't think I'd get a goodbye kiss with Jack lurking about, but I also didn't think I'd be called a guy!

On the train, Jack says, 'Martin's cool. We might go skating together.'

'Good on ya!'

I feel my face turn red yet again, but this time it's from annoyance rather than embarrassment. I'm used to guys preferring other girls to me, but when they prefer my little brother it's an all-time low! I stare out the window at the blur of graffiti whizzing by.

After a while, Jack says, 'You know, you can see Martin without me. I can still tell Mum I'm coming with ya, for cover.'

'Thanks,' I smile, coming round. 'But you know what, you guys really hit it off, so you can hang with him too.'

I have a total crush on Martin Jones and I seriously want him. I'm not sure what I want him for though – to kiss, to marry, to talk about music with? If my life was a television, every channel would show up in bright, clear colours except one, which would be unviewable static. Maybe Martin Jones could tune in that station. Or maybe not. I also have an annoying little nugget of a vibe that nothing's ever going to happen. I turn back to Jack.

'That Martin Jones is right clean-cut,' I say in my best Dr Ivanskiy voice. 'Must be a bloody Nazi.'

'Ay yi yi!' Jack joins in. 'His Converse are red, so he must be a communist!'

'Really unusual character!'

We hoot with laughter and the adults on the train glare at us. I feel better, but I file away a sadness that Martin Jones isn't into me.

It turns out it's not all bad having an unreturned crush though. On Monday, I decorate my locker with cut-outs of Martin Jones from the Myer catalogue.

'Ooh, who's that?' asks Amanda.

'Martin Jones. He goes to Gwammar and yesterday he happened to take me to a movie,' I reply in my most nonchalant voice.

'That guy took *you* to a movie?' Roberta O'Brian, who's stuffing folders into the locker next to mine, asks.

'Yep,' I blush.

Roberta, who's never said a word to me since we started at Sluts, looks impressed. Of course, I don't mention that Jack was there too.

'Are you going with him?' Amanda asks.

'Oh, it's early days…' I say.

'Good for you, lady,' Roberta says, and I blush some more.

That night Cat calls to ask how my 'date' went. I can't bend the truth with her, seeing she knows Martin Jones, so I tell her everything.

'Don't worry about him,' she comforts me. 'The more I think about it, the more I think he's kinda weird. He's never mentioned anyone, real girl *or* supermodel, who he likes. And remember how he refused to play Spin the Bottle?'

'D'you reckon he's gay?'

This is the only reason I can think that Martin Jones wouldn't be interested in girls. There's silence on the other end of the line as Cat ponders.

'No…' she says eventually. 'It's like he's not really interested in anyone.'

'Yeah!' I agree. 'It's like his eyes lit up when Jack spoke about sport and rap music, but they didn't light up when he saw me, even though he was very nice and polite. I wonder why he even bothered to ask me to a movie.'

'Who knows, but screw him. It's not you, it's defo him!'

'Yeah…'

Martin Jones probably invited me out because Cat asked him and he was too polite to say no. He still is the best-looking boy to have come my way, so I continue with this one-sided crush. I don't hear from him again, but he does invite Jack to his next birthday.

'We're going skating in the City Square, then having lunch at McDonald's. You should come!' Jack says to me.

'There's no way I'd turn up somewhere *uninvited*,' I say. 'Besides, I can't skate, and the only people who sit around watching skaters are bimbos and pot dealers. I'm the kinda girl who *does stuff* rather than watches other people doing stuff!'

This isn't exactly true, as much as I want it to be, but I feel like I'm flying when Jack looks at me admiringly and says, 'Good for you, sis.'

TRACK 12 – SHEENA IS A PUNK ROCKER

I'm at Cat's house, practising dance moves in front of MTV in the good room. Womack & Womack come on, who I don't care for, so I flop onto the plastic-covered couch to take a break. Cat shimmies up to me, lip-synching 'Teardrops'.

'All the girls at Gwammar are planning to marry stockbrokers,' she says, during the musical interlude. 'I reckon I might too.'

'D'you even know what a stockbroker is?' I ask her.

'I think it's like from *Wall Street*. Well, they earn enough money to buy a yacht and a Porsche, as well as all the designer clothes you could ever want!'

'If it's so cool, why can't *you* be a stockbroker instead of marrying one?'

'Um, not sure…'

'We can be whoever we want, Cat. That's what you always tell me.'

'Yeah…yeah, we can. And right now, what I want is a packet of Twisties. Let's go to the milk bar!'

On the way Cat says, 'So…on Saturday I'm going to Melissa Cain's slumber party and my parents hate her. Also, there's going to be boys there… So can I tell them I'm staying the night at your place?'

'Sure. But how come they hate Melissa?'

'Oh, she takes taxis instead of being picked up by her parents, so my folks think she's too wild and bohemian. And that's just cos of the taxis. They don't know about the bottle of bourbon she has hidden in her undies drawer!'

'Ha ha!'

'So make sure you're the first to answer the phone on Saturday night, just in case my parents ring to check on me.'

'OK. I'll just tell them you're doing a massive poo if they call.'

'Perfect, and realistic too!'

We walk along in silence, and my brain goes off on a tangent. I've kind of assumed that Cat and I will both marry musicians and live next door to each other, throwing dinner parties every night. When our husbands die we'll move into an old folks home and laugh at all the other old ladies. We'll have a pact that if either of us develops a tragic illness, we'll go for a walk on a cold, bright-blue day and the well one will roll the sick one's wheelchair off a cliff. Being such sweet old ladies, the jury will feel sorry for us and let us off the hook. I used to think that's the kind of friends we were, but lately I'm wondering if it's possible we're on completely different paths.

Cat speaks. 'Actually, why don't you come to Melissa's slumber party? I'll think of a different alibi…and we've got that bottle of bourbon!'

I predict the party will involve everyone growing giggly and strange on petrol-tasting alcohol, then getting with the boys, while I sit alone on a couch hoping, yet not hoping, someone will talk to me.

'Nah…I should prolly do some homework.'

We pass a family walking a large, grey, shaggy dog with a pointy snout, yellow eyes and bits of oily food stuck to its wispy hair.

'Gross. That dog looks like a Skeksis from *The Dark Crystal*,' I laugh.

'Oh, don't be mean, Dot. That's someone's pet.'

Her tone is self-righteous and I'm embarrassed my humour isn't appreciated.

We reach the milk bar, but instead of buying Twisties, I eye off the tram stop. A tram is approaching.

'Actually, I just remembered I need to help Mum with something…so I might go home.'

'Really? No Twisties?'

'Next time. Bye.' I wave and sprint for the tram.

I sit on the tram, my stomach grumbling for Twisties, confused with myself. *Did I crack it just because Cat didn't appreciate my joke?*

A few days later, she calls and all she can talk about is parties, boys, alcohol and smoking.

'Cool, cool,' I say. 'Hey, d'you reckon Nick Cave made better music before or after he went to England?'

'Huh?'

'Nick Cave, the singer.'

'Oh, I don't know about your music, Dot. So, you sure you don't wanna come to Melissa's party tonight?'

'Yeah. I'm behind on my homework...'

I should be going to parties like every other normal teenager in the world, but that time at Fleur's party I had the same feeling I had when I was a little kid in the pool at Prahran Baths, out of my depth and not wanting anyone to see the water and snot streaming from my nose.

I don't even want to hear anything more about Melissa's party, but Cat rings first thing the next morning.

'Guess what, Dot! Last night I got with a seventeen-year-old!'

'Oh...cool.'

There's a boy who lives down the road who's seventeen and I'm terrified of him because he's six foot tall with a deep voice and hairy legs. I still feel like a kid, and I couldn't imagine kissing someone who looks like a grown man.

'By the way, I don't need you to sneak ciggies off your rellies for me anymore, cos now I know heaps of people over fifteen,' Cat continues.

♫ ♫ ♫

Her daringness escalates over the next few weeks. She sneaks out to parties once her parents are asleep, folding clothes in the shape of a body under her doona and placing a wig of long, black hair over a balloon on her pillow. I'm no longer required for alibis.

She rings to crow about yet another party. 'Someone had illegal fireworks from Canberra. It was so excellent!'

'Wow, but weren't you worried the cops would find out? Or your parents?'

'Nope! And if they do, I'll just tell them I have to fight for my right to par-tae!'

I um and ah as Cat keeps on babbling.

'Also, I got with Joshua for like the fourth time. He's so cute! Oh, and I almost forgot the best part, last night I got stoned! I chucked up and had to tell my parents that I had gastro, but it was sooo excellent!'

I don't say anything, so Cat continues, 'You should defo come with me one time, you'll have a rage!'

'Thanks…'

I'm too mortified to tell Cat I'm terrified to go to those sorts of parties. What if someone spiked my drink and raped me? Or worse, what if no one noticed me and I had to stand in a corner by myself, with eyes pleading like a puppy for someone, anyone, to come over and talk to me?

♫ ♫ ♫

I get a job babysitting Dibble Dobble and Jade, and spend my weekends scouring op shops for interesting clothes to buy with my earnings. The other kids wear bandanas, but I prefer old lady-style scarves decorated with pictures of anchors, wagon wheels and horses. I hunt down stripy tops, waistcoats and brightly coloured sixties-style shoes with little heels. I vow never to set foot in Chadstone again.

Between parties, Cat comes to my house and wrinkles her nose as she peruses my wardrobe.

'It's great you're trying something different, Dot, but there's *absolutely nothing* here I can wear.'

'Well, I like this stuff,' I reply. My voice comes out whiny.

Cat smooths out her floral dress and stares at my clothes, perplexed. She's taken to wearing more and more Country Road, and even some splendo Laura Ashley. Our clothes swapping days are at an end. Not that I mind, I like the op shop clothes better.

I'm withholding more and more stuff about my life from Cat. I don't tell her I read the dictionary, or play her the songs I've taped off One Eleven FM, and I certainly don't talk about the boy with the music I'm going to meet someday.

Cat closes my wardrobe door and oh-so-nonchalantly announces that she's officially going with Joshua. She has a boyfriend.

I feel instantly sick in the guts.

'Congratulations. I'm so happy for you,' I say in a monotone, and force myself to give her a hug, because that's what's expected.

I guess it's normal to be jealous when your best friend gets a boyfriend before you do, but why didn't someone warn me that when jealousy hits you, it feels like a train crash?

I turn to the pile of school books on my desk and poke holes in the bubbles of contact paper with my compass. Cat keeps talking about how cute Joshua is. I collect myself, but I don't really feel like being best friends with her anymore.

When she leaves, I put some music on, fling myself on my bed and cry for ages. I want the old Cat back; my cheeky childhood friend is gone.

Mum barges into my room with a pile of folded clothes. I wipe my face on my pillow. She puts the clothes on my desk.

'Have you been crying?' she asks.

'Nooo!'

Mum hesitates, but then says, 'Suit yourself.'

I follow her into the kitchen, where she's folding Jack's clothes. 'Mum, who's your best friend?'

'Your father.'

'No, not your husband. Who's your best female friend?'

'Oh…probably Rhonda.'

'Who's Rhonda?'

'We went to school together. I haven't seen her for years though, probably not since I left school.' Mum stops folding clothes. 'Did you fall out with Cat?'

My voice can't be relied upon, so I nod.

Mum gives me a hug. 'Don't worry, love. You'll have plenty of friends in your life, and you'll probably meet a wonderful man like your father.'

I've never felt so depressed.

♫ ♫ ♫

After that, I stop calling Cat. She's probably off pashing Joshua anyway. I'm angry at her for turning out differently from me. It's something I don't want to think about, so I listen to more Clash and try to concentrate on other stuff.

I take refuge in my friends from school, Amanda and Stephanie, who are more straight-laced and straightforward than Cat. We go to Pizza Hut for lunch, pitch a tent in Amanda's backyard and rent *The Boy Who Could Fly* on video. Occasionally, we have a puff of a cigarette, but that's as far as it goes. I feel at ease with my gang, but when I catch myself thinking too much, I feel hollow. It's like there's something else out there, something that's not Cat's wild parties, nor these comfortable gatherings. *I miss Cat*, an annoying little voice in my head squeaks, but I tell it to shush.

A song I recently taped starts playing in my head. It's by Roxy Music and they sing that *more than this, there's nothing*.

Jangle, jangle, go the guitars; squeak, squeak go the synthesizers. Maybe I should be sad because there's nothing more for me, but instead the music gives me hope that at the very least there are people out there who feel the same way I do. One of them is that boy I once dreamed was with me in Major Tom's capsule. I know I'll meet him in real life one day, and in the meantime I guess I'll just hang out and try to have some sort of fun along the way.

Sometimes something unexpected is fun, like how I'm reading the dictionary and discovering new words, such as 'problematic' and 'quintessential'. My English marks increase a little plus my Scrabble scores improve, which I find meritorious.

'Wow-wee Dot, if you keep this up you'll be able to beat me soon,' Dad says, even though he just tripled my score.

'Ooh Dot, you're sooo good at Scrabble! Can I get your autograph?' Jack says.

'Put a sock in it, you philistine, nihilistic jerk!'

'Good on ya, Dot. I can read the dictionary too, ya know!'

'You can't even read Enid Blyton books!'

'Whatever!'

'Stop squabbling, you two!' Mum interjects. 'And one of you go make us some tea.'

I stalk into the kitchen and put the kettle on. As I pass the phone, my hand twitches towards it, wanting to call Cat, but instead my brain makes my body march into my Norsca-green bedroom. I retire with my dictionary and my secret music.

I pore over my mixed tapes, soaking up music no one else my age has heard of – The Undertones, The Look, Bow Wow Wow, Public Image, Altered Images and X-Ray Spex. One day, all of this music is going to rescue me, and in the meantime I let the soundwaves settle into my brain.

♪ ♪ ♪

In science we're studying reproduction, which is the highlight of the academic year because what better amusement can you get at school than discussing penises? We watch a video about a lady squeezing a baby out of her fanny, which is enough to scare me off having kids forever. When we finish studying reproduction, we get to ask any questions we like.

'OK girls, questions?' Mrs O'Reilly asks nervously at the end of the class.

Hands shoot up faster than Carl Lewis.

'Yes, Elizabeth?'

'What's a sixty-nine?'

Mrs O'Reilly blushes red as a fire engine and says, 'Um…well…it's not really required for the exam…so we don't need to discuss it. Roberta, what's your question?'

'What's a brothel?'

Mrs O'Reilly stammers, but we keep going, firing her with the rudest questions we can think of.

'What's an orgy?'

'What's anal sex?'

'What's fisting?'

Finally, Stephanie asks a question Mrs O'Reilly can answer. 'So, you definitely need the man's sperm to fertilise the woman's egg to make the baby?'

Mrs O'Reilly sighs and says, 'Yes, Stephanie, it's what we've been studying for the past three weeks.'

'So you need a man and a woman?'

'Yes, of course.'

'Two people are definitely required?'

'Yes, yes!'

'What about Jesus, then? How was he born?'

'Well…' says Mrs O'Reilly. 'All normal babies are conceived by the sperm fertilising the egg, but Jesus was a miracle, praise the Lord. You know that from RE. Come on girls, these questions are silly!'

I don't think Mrs O'Reilly answered the question properly, so that night I ask Dad.

'Jesus had a mother and a father, just like every other person,' he tells me.

I haven't thought about this stuff before, but what Dad says makes sense. There was no miracle from the Holy Spirit, just like the Mary statue eyes don't really follow you around. In fact, I'm beginning to find the Bible stories tough to believe. The only part of the Bible I like is when Jesus is up on the cross calling out, 'Daddy, Daddy! Why have you forsaken me?' That bit has raw emotion in it, and would make a great movie scene.

'So, he was just an ordinary man?' I ask Dad.

'That's right, but he was a very good man.'

I decide to keep believing in God and Jesus, just in case I end up like the girl in *The Exorcist*, but I wonder how the teachers at my school can tell us stuff that's not true.

'How come you've sent me to a religious school if you don't even believe in this stuff?'

The *7.30 Report*'s come on, so Dad's getting distracted.

'Dad?'

'So you can get a good education and your brain doesn't rot. Now go and do your homework.'

Dad is gazing at Mary Delahunty, enrapt, so I know the conversation is over.

♫ ♫ ♫

A week later, I find an unexpected good side to religious activities.

Amanda invites me to a party her Antioch group is throwing in a church hall. I go along, comfortable that I won't be challenged by the sight of rowdy, drugged-out teenagers.

Top 40 music is pumping out of the loudspeaker. I decide to be open-minded and dance to the commercial music, along with everyone else. I feel mega embarrassed at first, and shuffle awkwardly from foot to foot, but after a few songs I warm up and I'm carried along by 'Baby I Don't Care', jumping around in a circle of kids. I dance with Amanda, some other girls and this boy with braces called Elliot. It's fun. I feel as though I'll never have anything to worry about ever again, as long as I keep dancing, and I feel a big smile form on my face.

All of a sudden, a slower song comes on, something by Simply Red. Elliot grabs me and starts slow dancing. He's not a spunk and he's definitely not the boy with the music, but he's not fugly either. Plus he's friendly, so I don't mind dancing with him. And then, without realising how it happened, all of a sudden he's kissing me! Elliot's tongue swirls round and round in my mouth, like a Kreepy Krauly pool cleaner, and he moves his head from left to right with increasing speed. My eyes are open, but they lose focus because he's so close and his two eyes merge, making him look like a dorky cyclops. I push Elliot away and he stands there grinning proudly, with one of my long hairs caught in his braces.

I hadn't noticed, but Elliot had danced me into a corner away from the supervising adults, so they don't see us. Some of the kids do though, and they cheer 'woo hoo!' and I feel myself turn redder than a chilli, but I smile at the attention.

Amanda waves me over and we bustle off to the toilets to talk.

'Wow, Dot!' she says. 'What was it like?'

A lovely, glowing feeling comes over me, and now I understand why Cat talks so much about her exploits. It's not the thrill of what you do, it's the thrill of talking about it with your friends, the feeling of admiration you get because you've done something they haven't.

'Excellent! It feels like the whole room is spinning and there's no one else alive but me and him! You should try it, Amanda. You *gotta* lose your lip virginity before Year Ten!'

'Elliot is great, isn't he?'

I'd actually forgotten about Elliot. The sight of my hair hanging from his mouth led me to the split-second decision that I'd never go out with him.

I didn't particularly enjoy kissing, but I didn't hate it either. Anyway, I'm so, so relieved that I've finally got it over and done with. The only issue is that Joy Division would have been better background music for my first pash, instead of daggy old Simply Red. And Cat, not Amanda, should have been the person who basked in my reflected glory.

TRACK 13 – I COULD BE HAPPY

Dick Smith Heads – the Corner – 15th September 1989

The Dick Smith Heads are the sort of band who will cheer you up, no matter how down you feel. Regular readers will know that I'm still recovering from that disastrous holiday down the coast with my erstwhile girlfriend. No matter, I feel a whole lot better after seeing the Dick Smith Heads at the Corner last night.

I was on the train to the concert, listening to The Birthday Party. Even with my Walkman on, I could hear these kids talking in a terrible imitation of an Eastern European accent and laughing as though their heads were about to fall off and I recognised something I'd been missing for ages – joy. Joy that fills you with sunshine; joy that makes you realise everything's always going to be all right. The train pulled into Richmond Station. 2-3-4, drum music with an exit theme played in my head, and I stepped onto the platform smiling.

The Dick Smith Heads are a Sydney band consisting of three guys and three girls, all with long, black wavy hair and bright red lipstick. Their music is brassy, mischievous and joyful. Each of their eleven songs is a beauty. Every member of the audience danced from start to finish of the gig, kicking up their legs as high as their Doc Marten 14-ups would allow.

I urge you to check out their debut album, We're All Dancing, *as soon as you can. I guarantee you won't be disappointed. If life's getting you down and you're wondering what you can possibly do next, listen to this music, feel the joy and let the dancing Docs stomp over your worries. Follow the trail of jangly guitars, tootling trombones and intense vocals. Don't worry that the sound is slightly flattened by the sticky carpet. Stand proud with your fellow music lovers, pot of beer in one hand, durrie in the other, and feel the joy.*

The future's bright.

Common People, Glory Box, Born Slippy, 1979, When I Come Around, Wonderwall, Car Song, All That I Need Is To Be Loved, Disco 2000, Girl From Mars, Lump, Ode To My Family, I Kissed A Girl, Karmacoma, I Don't Want To Grow Up, Everything Zen, My Friends, Hurt, Some Might Say, Army Of Me, I Got A Girl, Wake Up Boo, Waterfalls, All Over You, Caught By The Fuzz, Just A Girl, Tomorrow, Morning Glory, Walking Contradiction, Life Is Sweet, Don't Look Back In Anger, Black Steel, Aeroplane, Hold Me Thrill Me Kiss Me Kill Me, Alright, The Universal, Ironic, Sick Of Myself, Fake Plastic Trees, Bullet With Butterfly Wings, Country House, Glycerine, Mis-Shapes, Roll With It, Breakfast At Tiffany's, Free As A Bird, Brain Stew, Hand In My Pocket, It's Oh So Quiet, In The Summertime, Time Bomb, Gangsta's Paradise, I Spy, Creep, Another Night, Take A Bow, Here Comes The Hotstepper, The Rhythm Of The Night, The Diamond Sea, Boombastic, All I Wanna Do, Sorted for E's And Whizz, I'll Stand By You, Lightning Crashes, Baby Did A Bad Bad Thing, This Is A Call, Dear Mama, Vow, Champagne Supernova, Don't Speak, Queer, The Bends, I Got Id, The Reefer Song, Mouth, Apartment, Zombie, Paninaro, Where The Wild Roses Grow, Short Dick Man, Party, Put Yourself In My Place, You Are Not Alone, Sour Times, Kitty, Greg The Stop Sign, Evidence, Heroin Girl, I'll Be There For You, Hyperballad, Sparky's Dream, Warped, Rock 'n' Roll Is Where I Hide, She's Electric, Stupid Girl, Wynona's Big Brown Beaver, I'll Stick Around, Stayin' Alive, I'll Never Be An Old Man River, Blubber Boy, Miss Sarajevo, Purple Sneakers, My Island Home, Downtown, Apple Eyes, Brown Sugar, I Alone, Heart Of The Party, You Oughta Know, I Can Dream, Psychoactive Summer, (Let's Go) Smoke Some Pot, 21st Century Digital Boy, Sunday, All Homeboys Are Dickheads, Protection, This Is How We Do It, Ventolin, Freak Like Me, Feel Me Flow, Nights Introlude, Pencil Skirt, Ponderosa, In Dust We Trust, Charmless Man, Original, A Northern Soul, Liquid Swords, Geek Stink Breath, Israel's Son, King For A Day, The Memory of Trees, Do You Want More, She's Automatic, Misery, Root Down, Medication, Inner City Life, So Many Dreams, Reverend Black Grape, Serpentine Pad, To Bring You My Love, Just When You're Thinkin' Things Over

CD

TRACK 14 – HOT CHILD IN THE CITY

I tack my Ishka rug onto the wall, concealing the cracks and mildew, and stand back to admire the effect. I'm finally moved in!

Margaret picks her way through piles of books, CDs, candles and scatter cushions. She leans against the rickety old wardrobe that's bursting with clothes, and sighs. 'Ooh, all this clutter is giving me an asthma attack!'

Jack and I have started calling our parents by their first names. Mum and Dad are such childish titles.

'*You* don't have to live here, Margaret,' I say. 'I like anti-minimalism. Come on, I'll make us a cup of tea.'

'And don't think I didn't notice that watering can full of ciggie butts next to your stinking old couch on the porch,' Margaret says.

'My housemate smokes,' I lie.

We weave through the small rooms with their grimy windows and poky fireplaces, until we end up sitting in the concrete-paved garden, permanently shaded by a huge banana tree. We sip tea and eat Ferrero Rochers.

'Reminds me of Prahran when we first moved in,' Margaret says. 'Mmm, this tea's lovely! If your father and I taught you one thing, it's how to make a decent cup of tea.'

'Thanks…'

'But don't forget that Dr Ivanskiy has offered to pay for you to live in one of the colleges. I think they have cleaners there.'

'Nah, the colleges are full of rich kids from the country. Too daggy for me.'

Margaret raises an eyebrow. 'Well, this tea's hit the spot.'

As she's leaving, she unexpectedly leans in towards me, and I jump back. 'What're you doing?'

'Giving you a kiss goodbye, of course!'

'But we never kiss goodbye.'

'Don't we?'

I let her peck me on the cheek, but she still stands there. 'Are you coming round for dinner tomorrow night?' she asks.

'What're you cooking?'

'Think I'll do roast lamb.'

'Then I'll be round for sure!'

I watch as Margaret drives out of my street, back to the burbs. I'm pretty stoked to be living in Richmond. I love the yeasty aromas of Abbotsford Brewery on a summer's morning. I love the narrow streets, workmen's cottages, trams, proximity to anywhere that's anywhere, pubs, souvlaki and noodle shops. I love the migrants in the council flats, the smackies, the uni students and the old people who stand outside all day and tell off anyone who dares park in front of their houses. I do not love the footy crowds and the Bridge Road bargain shoppers, but at the end of the day, I'm so relieved to be back in the inner city.

♫ ♫ ♫

I go to a student union dance and who should be there but Cat. I haven't seen her since Year Nine. She's standing with her back to me, but right away I recognise the tilt of her head and the studied way she flicks her cigarette ash. She's cut her long hair to resemble Winona Ryder in *Reality Bites*, but she's the same old Cat. I'm struck by the lightning realisation of how much I've missed her all these years. Mortification with how I cut her off makes me consider sneaking past, but a glass of cheap champagne gives me Dutch courage, so instead I tap her on the shoulder.

'Excuse me, are you bum-puffing or inhaling that cigarette?'

Cat turns around and her smile is brighter than the sun. 'Dot!! Oh my godfather!'

At that moment, 'London Calling' comes on, and Cat grabs my hand and we walk together to the centre of the dance floor. Finally, I'm ready to join Cat in the glittered world of alcohol, nightclubs, parties and men!

Music has exploded. Blondie, The Clash, New Order, The Cure, Morrissey, The Happy Mondays, The Stone Roses, Blur, Supergrass, Pulp, Elastica, Suede and Oasis; they're all here! Suddenly the guy with the music is everywhere: in clubs, at parties and even in lecture theatres. It's as if I'm in a room full of mirrors though, and I can't tell who the actual guy with the music is and who is just his reflection. On a scrap of paper I write down the lyrics of a song that reminds me of him and Blu-Tack it to my wardrobe door. *I miss him, but I haven't met him yet; he's so special, but it hasn't happened yet.*

In between all this magic, I'm supposed to be studying law at Melbourne University. It was a choice between Melbourne and Monash; of course I opt for the university that isn't in the burbs.

When I tell people what I study, they give me a look as if to say, *Ooh, aren't you fancy.* They're clearly jealous. My girlhood dream of becoming a High Court judge is on the horizon, but I wonder if it still is my dream. I'd rather be going to the Blur concert than studying for my constitutional law exam. I'd rather be enjoying a latte in Greville Street than finishing my evidence assignment. I'd rather be hitting the bottle than learning about the snail in the bottle. Now that I have a life, I don't like all this studying imposing on my time. My grades go down and my happiness goes up.

It's almost light when I get home from the student union night. My housemate, the Vegetarian, has decreed that no meat may pass the threshold, so I eat my souvlaki on the porch, sobering up on the saggy, sun-faded couch, gazing at the fruit bats as they fly home to the Botanical Gardens.

I think about how I'd envisaged my first housemate. I was hoping for someone who'd turn out to be a new friend, someone I could exchange gossip with during the ad breaks of *Melrose Place*. I was hoping for a housemate who'd introduce me to new scenes and perhaps some cute guys. But I was so keen to move out of home that I forgot to have an in-depth housemate interview à la *Shallow Grave.*

The Vegetarian studiously pursues a quiet life, communicating with me via notes. I've only been here a month, and so far I've received about a dozen post-it notes, sinisterly decorated with smiley faces and accompanied by requests such as:

Hey Dot,
Would it be OK if you lock
all windows and switch all
appliances off at the mains
before you go out?

Dot...
Sorry to bring up something
awkward, but can you please not
flush tampons down the toilet?

Hi Dot,
I found your smoked salmon in
the fridge and threw it out.
Don't bring meat here as this
is a Vegetarian Household.
And yes, fish is meat.

Next morning I discover an infuriating note stuck to my bedroom door. I march down the hall to the lounge, where the Vegetarian is ironing sheets.

'So I got your note about keeping the noise down.'

'Oh. Sorry if I came across as harsh, but I had a migraine.'

I'm not interested in her migraine and my indignation rises. 'All I did was unlock the front door and tiptoe down the hall to the bathroom to clean my teeth. I'm not sure what else I can do to keep the noise down, but I guess I can always stop brushing my teeth and let them rot away. I hope you'll enjoy the rancid odour.'

The Vegetarian blushes and says, 'Well, I guess it was a one-off, with my migraine and all.'

'Indubitably.'

So the Vegetarian is not the person I dreamed of sharing this wonderful house with, but she was here first. Also, she spends most of the time locked in her room studying, so I have free range of the house. When it's her birthday I'll buy her a pair of ear plugs.

♫ ♫ ♫

I catch the train to Glen Huntly. Gerald's recently painted the front of the house, so the place seems slicker than it did when I lived there. Margaret lets me in and the roast lamb fumes smell so good my stomach somersaults. I can also smell clean washing, vacuumed carpet and my childhood.

At dinner, as we're eating the roast lamb, Jack and I eye the bone.

'Margaret, whose turn is it for the bone?' I ask.

'How the hell would I know? Aren't you two old enough to work it out for yourselves? You're like a pair of dogs.'

'I reckon it should be me. I'm a growing boy.'

'Come off it, Jack. Any taller and we'd think you have that giant's tumour thing. I need it more than you anyway, on account of my iron deficiency.'

'You kids stop squabbling,' Gerald growls and snatches up the bone.

The fact that some things will never change now seems exciting rather than depressing. Jack and I watch Gerald tuck into the bone with relish and grin at each other.

'How's the law, Dot?' Gerald asks when he's finished with the bone. He calls it *the* law, like I'm some sort of Oxford scholar from the eighteenth century.

'Well, having to study all the time is torturous, but I'm hanging in there.' This is the best I can tell him.

'That's why I'm not ruining my eyesight and posture swotting away,' Jack declares. He recently found a job at a sports store advising kids on which trucks, wheels and grip tape to get for their skateboards and ripping off any rollerbladers who come his way.

'Good kid, Dot,' Gerald says, ignoring Jack. 'Contribution is the key to society.'

I'm not sure whether I'm contributing anything, but I'm certainly not getting something for nothing. Cruelly denied any form of government grant, my uni fees will be taken out of my salary once I start working full-time, and now I have a part-time job that pays for my rent, textbooks and food. I'm proud that I'm self-sufficient, but it's irritating that my friends are less so.

'You know, Cat's parents bought her a car *and* pay for her uni expenses.'

'Well, that's her and this is you,' says Margaret, which is her answer for anything unfair in life.

'Don't worry, Dot,' Jack grins. 'Guys love an independent woman of the nineties.'

'Don't I know it!'

♫ ♫ ♫

I'm still adjusting to this, but all of a sudden…guys like me! When we're out they come up to Cat and me – the cool guys, the losers, the ravers, the indie boys, the ferals, the bogans, the suits, the guys still getting over the death of Kurt Cobain, the poets, the gangsta rappers, the gym junkies and the occasional old man over thirty. A night without being hit on is a night not worth going out, and it doesn't matter if we tell ninety per cent of them to piss off, the attention is fabulous!

I select a kind-looking but unmemorable guy to get the process of losing my virginity over and done with.

It's another student union night and after a two-hour conversation about nothing, I ask, 'Your place or mine?'

I can't quite believe I blurted that out, but it's done now and the boy, whose name I forget, looks stoked. He lives in a college, so we don't have to go far.

'This is my first time,' I warn him before he's even closed the door.

We get a towel in case of mess, but there isn't any, just like there's no music. Who would have thought all those romantic movies lied? Oh well, another box I can check off.

Student union nights are random like that, but my real life happens at The Tube – Melbourne's premier indie club night, which rotates between locations in the city, Carlton and North Melbourne. Cat and I are there every Saturday night between the hours of eleven pm and five am, and the rest of the time we're buying clothes to wear to the club, listening to CDs we heard at the club, stockpiling Cockatoo Ridge champagne to drink before heading to the club and stuffing our faces with vegies and water so we're healthy enough to recover from the club.

It's The Tube – OK The Tube and a joint – that inspires me to throw a fabulous house-warming party.

'How about we take a break from studying and throw a party?' I suggest to the Vegetarian.

'Um…'

'I'll take care of everything. I'll even do the cleaning the next day. Come on!'

Jesus, why is talking this girl into anything remotely fun so difficult? Margaret has more of a social life than she does!

Then a miracle happens.

'Oh sure, why not?' the Vegetarian says. 'I'll make mini vol-au-vents.'

Maybe I'd underestimated her. 'Cool! And we should totally have a theme!'

'A theme?'

'Yep. I'm thinking the theme should be utensils, as in everyone should dress up as a kitchen utensil!'

OK, that was the joint talking – but now I've said it, it's not such a bad idea. Everyone has seventies parties or colour themes, but I bet Melbourne's never seen a utensils party before.

'Um, OK…' the Vegetarian agrees, as though she has a choice.

I believe in this party like some people believe in God. I'm friendly with Jordan, the DJ from the chill-out room at The Tube, and he's agreed to come and play music. Cat always has an entourage of people to bring to any party, and I'm getting more comfortable with her friends these days, rather than being intimidated by them, like I was in high school. I invite a few of The Tube regulars, plus Amanda, Stephanie, Jack and whichever girl he's shagging at the moment, and my teenage cousins Dobbler and Jade. Even the Vegetarian manages to invite a few sweater-clad friends.

It's the afternoon before the party and I'm heading home from Safeway, armed with booze and nibbles. A guy lurches up to me. Not unfortunate looking, even if his nose is a little big.

'Hi, remember me?' he asks.

'Nope…'

'It's Zack. From primary school.'

Zack – the kid who used to cry every day and who was amazing at drawing but couldn't read properly, even in Grade Six.

'Zack…how's it going?'

'Good. I catch a train to Richmond for my dish-washing job and I also see my doctor here. Then I catch the train back to South Yarra where I live with my mum. Do you have any hobbies and interests?'

I had been considering Zack as a potential, possibly on the grounds that he's wearing a cool tee-shirt. At first I assumed he was acting weird because he was drunk, but now I realise he really is weird. Weirder even than when he was in primary school.

'Do you have any hobbies and interests?' Zack repeats.

'Oh, I dunno,' I say in my fading-away voice. 'I guess I like listening to music...'

'I also like music! I enjoy the Macarena. I also enjoy drawing. Do you want to keep in contact?'

Oh, boy! Luckily I'm well-practised at knocking guys back, not to sound arrogant. 'I'd love to, but it's just I'm really busy at the moment...cos I'm about to move to England.'

'That's OK. Bye-bye.' And off Zack goes.

I watch him walking stiffly down the street before I rush home to call Cat.

'Hey lady, guess who I ran into?'

'Who? Damon Albarn?'

'I wish! Nah...you remember Zack from Saint Aloysius?'

'The kid who used to cry the whole time? No kidding! Is he cute?'

'Kinda big nose, but decently dressed. Really weird though. He has a funny walk and speaks like a robot. He asked about my hobbies and interests!'

'Ha! Did you invite him to the party?'

'Certainly not! This is a party for cool people only.'

Still, I'm nervous that it'll be a shit party, so I open my bottle of Cockatoo Ridge early. By the time things get going, my evening has become a whirl of colours and music.

Most of the utensils costumes are pretty lame, just real utensils tied onto regular street clothes, but someone carts around an actual kitchen sink full of beers and Cat's friend Edie has sewn together a cute A-line dress made entirely from kitchen wipes.

Jordan arrives, sets up in the garden and starts cranking out some wicked tunes. Jack and Dobbler hover, pestering him for a go on the turntables, but he shoos them away, like the teenage flies they are. People dance or just sit around and chat.

The little house is heaving; more people than expected turned up. My parents, aunts and uncles are here too, even though I didn't tell them about the party. The hallway, laundry and even the bathroom are packed. The Vegetarian and her friends are relegated to her room, politely munching on chips and sipping Coke, but they don't complain about the noise. Amanda, Stephanie and my other school friends are in my room. I pop in from time to time to check they're having a decent night.

'Ladeeeez!' I say, slurring a little, as I'm onto my second bottle of champagne. 'Let's smoke some pot!'

Surprisingly, Amanda agrees and we sit on my bed, passing the joint between us, reminiscing about school days. After a while, I realise I'm doing all the talking and Amanda is just sitting there with a weird grin on her face.

'You OK?' I ask her.

Still grinning, Amanda lowers her head and spews all over my floorboards.

I'm starting to feel a little off myself, so I head to the kitchen and scull a litre of water while Stephanie cleans up Amanda's sick.

'Did somebody throw up?' asks the Vegetarian as she's scuttling back from the toilet.

'Relax, it's being cleaned up,' I say, and lollop off down the hallway.

I head to the porch for some fresh air. Dobbler and Jade are out there.

'Check this out, Dot!' Jade says.

She sprays Impulse deodorant all over her jeans, then lights them with a match. A gassy blue flame dances up and down her legs, and her eyes twinkle.

'Isn't it hot?' I ask.

'A little, but it doesn't burn.'

Two teenage boys open the front gate and wave at Dobbler.

'Who the hell are these kids?' I ask.

'From the council flats down the road. We're gunna arrange a game of soccer!'

I can't stand in the way of his lifelong dream, and two more guests can't hurt. I leave the kids to it and check on the scene in the back garden. Jordan is taking a break, so I join him.

'Thanks for DJ'ing.'

'No dramas.'

We talk about The Tube, uni and stuff. When Jordan starts up his next set, Cat sidles over.

'He likes you…'

I'm about to deny it, but I'm having such a good night, so instead I say, 'So he should!'

We dance to Jordan's tunes, but after a while I leave Cat and wander through the house again. Everyone is here and enjoying themselves and a guy likes me, a guy who's a DJ. Maybe he's the guy with the music!

For the rest of the party, I feel like I'm in a champagne bottle. I know I'll find that guy with the music soon because he's the second half of my heart. And while I'm waiting, I'll swim around in the golden, bubbly light.

At the end of the night, Cat says to me, 'You've arrived!'

It's the best thing I've heard in my life.

TRACK 15 – FASHION

My lifestyle as an indie clubbing aficionado won't pay for itself, so a few months ago, like Melanie Griffith in *Working Girl*, I got a job. Every Monday and Friday morning, I drag myself into the office for a day of filing, talking to moronic customers and comforting colleagues who are patiently awaiting their redundancy packages. The work doesn't fill me with joy, but I have somehow managed to find an office with the best view in Melbourne. My back is facing it, but when I swivel my chair, I can see the sparkling bay dotted with ships, the ferry on its way to Tasmania and the Westgate Bridge curving away to the mysterious western suburbs.

As well as admiring the view, the aspects of work I enjoy are gossiping with colleagues, earning more money than my friends, being the youngest person in the office, Friday night drinks and dressing up in cute outfits.

Fashion is my next great love after music and clubbing. Shiny shirts, Union Jacks, pixie haircuts, John Lennon sunglasses and even trendy tracksuits – like the ones Damon Albarn wears and in no way like the ones bogans wear. Cat's friend, Edie, is a fashion designer who sells us stuff with hardly any mark-up. She buys all this fabulous fabric from Italy and stays up all night, sewing and snorting speed.

Edie's studio is above a dingy shop in Smith Street. I'm meeting Cat there to hang out after work. Beggars gather in the street below, but they don't speak to me.

Up in the studio, we sip red wine from Vegemite jars and try on Edie's latest creations.

'What do you want to get, Dot?' Cat asks, as I'm trying on salmon three-quarter length pants.

'Defo these. And that metallic gold jacket. Oh, and I really love that cream corset top, but I better get that next time, cos the Vegetarian's at me about the phone bill.'

'And I have to get this,' says Cat, as she twirls around in a clingy black maxi dress with a plunging neckline.

Both Cat and I are pretty flat-chested, but that's nothing a Wonderbra can't fix.

'You both look fabulous,' Edie says.

♫ ♫ ♫

It's Friday morning and I'm not sure if I feel groggy from the crappy red wine last night or just from the thought of starting a day's work, so to delay the tedium, I ask my desk neighbour, Tony, to tell me about the gay clubs from the eighties again.

He perches on my desk, cup of tea in hand. 'Well, they were always hidden away in some nondescript building, they only let you in if they recognised you. Less people were out in those days and we wanted our nightclubs to be a hidden so people like you couldn't find us.'

I pout.

'Oh Dot, people need to have separate worlds sometimes, where they can be free.'

Tony sips his tea and continues, '"You Spin Me Round", "Blue Monday"…when songs like that were played, there wasn't a man standing still in the whole place!'

I picture hundreds of buff, moustached men dancing their hearts out to synth beats so exciting they sound like fireworks. Echoes of the men's pre-Grim Reaper joy reaches us fifteen years later.

My phone rings, breaking the moment. Tony walks back to his desk with a sigh and I pick up the headset.

When I hang up, I realise I feel hot. I'm wearing my new metallic gold jacket and salmon pants. Everyone else is wearing boring old suits. I also ended up buying the cream corset top – Dr Ivanskiy gave me money for the phone bill – and when I take off my gold jacket, I catch Tony raising his eyebrows.

'Well, it's Friday and I'm going out tonight!' I say. 'Besides…no one around here notices me or what I'm wearing.'

Why not fish for a compliment on a sunny Friday morning?

Tony takes off his glasses. 'Dot, do you know what every straight male, who's not related to you, is thinking whenever you, or any female, for that matter, walks in the room?'

'Prolly nothing. They're just going about their business.'

'They're deciding whether or not they want to sleep with you. And they'll make that decision within one second.'

'What, all men?'

'Yep.'

'Even old men or guys with girlfriends?'

'All men. Some of them may decide they don't want to have sex with you, or they do but they'll never act on it, for whatever reason. But that's what they're thinking about whenever you walk in the room.'

'Ew! Maybe they should be thinking about my fantastic work skills or that I could be a nice friend for them. Maybe they should mind their own business and not think about me at all.'

'Maybe. But they're thinking about sleeping with you.'

I feign scandalisation, but I'm actually delighted with this piece of news. I gloss over the part where Tony said men are thinking this about all women and assume it's just me who's special.

After work, I catch a tram to meet Cat. I sit demurely on my seat, looking at the businessmen, and I know what they're thinking. Maybe they say yes, maybe they say no. Who would have thought? Why did I waste my teenage years being a wallflower? Even though I'm alone, I burst out laughing, and all the suits glare at me.

I look around for a face that I've never seen before, yet is instantly familiar, but he's not here.

TRACK 16 – (WHITE MAN) IN HAMMERSMITH PALAIS

We step out of the taxi across a gutter overflowing with water and rubbish.

'Debris!' I announce. I like the sound of the word, and Cat giggles.

The hotdog man is still setting up and there are only a few people waiting out the front of the club, which is great, as places with long queues are strictly for losers. The streetlight is dim and The Tube façade is painted black; it's a nondescript entrance to heaven.

Leigh, the security guy, sees us and ushers Cat and I past the queue of three. We stand in the entrance where Cat's old school friend Fleur sits on her throne. She holds the most powerful position in Melbourne: The Tube door bitch and holder of drink cards. She also runs the cloakroom.

'Hiya, Cat. Hiya, Dot. All right?'

'Hey, Fleur. Yeah, good. How're you?'

'Yeah, all right. Come back and see me later, innit?'

'We sure will!'

Fleur stamps the insides of our wrists, slips a couple of drink cards into our hands and waves us through before we can pay. Fleur, or Miss London, as we now call her, recently returned from a twelve-month stint in the UK with a slumming-it attitude and a faux geeza accent. The snobby teenager with her Laura Ashley flowers has been replaced by a friendly chick with a pink fringe, eyebrow ring and tales of Cool Britannia.

We step past Miss London's booth and we're home. Uni's fine, but it's just a place to go to become a white-collar worker one day. Work's OK, but it's just a means of getting money. My house's nice, but the Vegetarian is a drag. I love my family, but I want to be with my friends. So I mean it when I say that

The Tube is my whole world. If I'm stressing about uni, tired from work or upset that some guy doesn't think I'm as wonderful as he should, the moment I step inside The Tube all those irritating feelings fly away on the wings of a synth beat. The happy-go-lucky guitars, polite drumming and English-accented vocals of the music make me feel like I'm floating, like I want to run around the room, like I'm never going to grow old.

I look at the smiling faces of my fellow clubbers and know that they feel the same. The Tube is where Melbourne's indie kids take refuge from the bogans, football fans, mainstream tools and R&B losers who frequent clubs at the casino.

Cat and I stand at the entrance for a moment, so everyone can take note that we've arrived. The club is dark and scruffy, the only light being the ultraviolet lamp and the glow-in-the-dark test tube drinks sold by girls walking around in bikini tops and tracksuit pants. Comfortable old couches, pool tables, bar stools and, off to the side, the chill-out room where videos of *Astro Boy* are played and Jordan DJs. Central to everything is the dance floor, which is a flurry of Converse, glitter and the latest trend, old school uniforms.

Cat heads to the bar to buy drinks, and I stand on the edge of the floor looking at its colourful, flashing squares, imagining it's a beautiful lagoon, waiting for the perfect moment to dive in and start dancing. My heart beats in time with Saint Etienne's 'He's on the Phone', but just as I'm about to launch, I feel a presence.

'Interesting music, but the time has come to admit I'm too old for this,' a man's voice says.

My heartbeat changes and a strange, relaxed feeling comes over me. There's something about his voice, but as I turn to reply, he's walking out of the club with his back to me.

Cat shoves a beer into my hand, but after one small sip I put it on a nearby table and jump into the dance floor. We dance about, checking out cute guys. We raise our left or right eyebrow, depending on the location of the guy, wink if he's cute and wrinkle our noses if he's not. Someone must be approaching now because Cat raises her right eyebrow, pauses, considering, and then winks.

We dance a little further apart so the someone can join us. He's cute, but he has an extraordinary hairstyle, à la John Travolta in *Pulp Fiction*. The three of us jump about to a couple of frenetic numbers by The Prodigy, pogoing like the punks used to at Sex Pistols gigs, only with more joie de vivre and less spitting.

Once the song ends, I head over to my beer, while Cat dances off with a girl wearing what is obviously a Sacré Cœur school uniform. The guy dances up to me.

'What's ya name?'

'Esmerelda.' Cat (Gertrude) and I prefer to go by pseudonyms when being picked up.

'Fantastic! I'm Greg.'

Greg rummages in his lunch box for a packet of cigarettes and offers me one, which I accept. 'Morning Glory' starts playing, with the volume turned up extra loud, so Greg has to lean in to talk. His designer mullet has grown sweaty; it's almost dripping onto my shoulder.

'So, what do you do, Esmerelda?'

'Live my life.'

Greg laughs and takes a long drag of his cigarette. Some of his mates appear, so I say hi, then excuse myself to look for Cat.

As well as random guys like Greg, there are The Tube regulars. I see them on the dance floor now. There's the Old Man, a guy in his thirties, balding, but still pogoing with the best of them; the Beatles, four mop-topped guys dressed in matching suits, so very cute; and the Fairy, a girl who's always by herself, dancing happily with her wings and wand.

I spot Cat alone in the middle of the dance floor. The Old Man is sidling up to her, so I drag her over to Greg and co.

'Thanks for the rescue!' she grins.

'Gertrude, this is Greg.'

'Nice to meet you,' Greg says, and shakes Cat's hand.

He's still sweaty, and I see Cat wipe her hand on her pants once Greg turns away to find his cigarettes again.

The pack on the nearby table is evidently empty because Greg turns back to us and says, 'I'm gunna buy some more. Back in a tick.'

As Greg walks off, Cat mimes spraying deodorant in his direction. I laugh so much I accidentally spit beer on the Old Man, who's somehow made it back to us. 'Beautiful Ones' comes on, and Cat and I run back to the dance floor, along with the rest of the club.

'Can I buy you a drink?' Greg asks a bit later, as Cat and I flail about, unsure whether to dance to something by The Divine Comedy or take a break.

'Sure! Can you get one for Gertrude too?'

'No worries.'

At another point, Cat and I are getting our photo taken by a character with eyebrow slits, and Greg materialises at my elbow.

'Where do you live?' he asks.

'Richmond.'

'Want to share a cab on the way home? My shout.'

'Brilliant! We need to drop Gertrude off first though.'

By then, things are blurry, and all I remember about what happens later with Greg is when a perfect drop of sweat falls from his forehead directly into my ear.

The next morning, when he's gone, I remember how cool the girl in her Sacré Cœur uniform looked.

I ring Margaret and ask, 'Have you still got my old uniform?'

'Have I 'eck? I flung it out when you finished school.'

'Oh. What about Jack's?'

'What do you want his uniform for?'

I don't reply because I realise she would have got rid of our old clutter as soon as she could, but I feel a bittersweet nostalgia for my old things that were associated with a time I'm fast leaving behind.

Margaret continues, 'I don't know sometimes, Dot. The fashions are right daft these days. Last time I saw your cousin Jade, she was wearing a petticoat and sucking on a dummy. She looked like something out of the cast of *Les Misérables*!'

'Ha!'

'By the way, your brother's on his way over to your place to show you his new car.'

'Cool.'

♫ ♫ ♫

While I've been spending my money on clothes and clubbing, Jack saved his for a car. I join him out the front of my house to admire the old bomb Valiant; the type of car that was embarrassing when we were kids is now cool.

'Let's go for a spin,' he says.

The car is full of junk food packaging, and some god-awful hip hop is emanating from the cassette player. I turn the music down and look out the window as we drive alongside the river, well over the speed limit.

Jack asks, 'So how's The Tube going?'

'Fabulous! Last night a photographer from *Beat* magazine took our picture, and I'm pretty sure we'll end up in print, because why wouldn't we? Jack, you should totally come one time.'

'Maybe for a special occasion, but they don't play enough hip hop.'

There aren't any hip hop clubs in Melbourne, but Jack's recently invested in a turntable that's currently sitting in the boot of his car. He already has a few house parties lined up. Jack reckons he's in demand because he orders records from America that no one else has. I think he loves the attention he receives from a never-ending supply of dingy-looking chicks in oversized baseball caps and overalls.

'Ugh Jack, hip hop is rough. You should try something new.'

'What, like the Spice Girls?'

'Ha! Actually Cat quite likes them, which is cause for concern... She always did have a soft spot for stuff that's way commercial. I thought we'd gotten through this, but the other night she was actually trying to get me to check out the clubs in the casino!'

'You're such a snob, Dot. You might enjoy yourself at the casino.'

'I might enjoy living in the outer suburbs and rotting away. And yet I don't.'

Jack laughs. Maybe I'm judgmental, but I can't help it if I have an innate sense of what's cool and what's tacky.

'How is Cat, anyway?' he asks.

'Why're you asking? She'd never consider *you* unless you take that manky lip piercing out.'

'And I'd never consider her until she *got* a manky lip piercing. Can't I ask about your friends without having any underhand intentions?'

'She's well. I wish she'd tell her parents to piss off, though. They want her to focus on her boring old commerce degree, which is seriously jeopardising *my* social life.'

Jack rolls his eyes, but I don't think he gets it because he has so many friends to hang out with. I have friends too, but I depend on Cat. I'm not quite up to going to The Tube by myself like the Fairy does, and having dinner in family-friendly restaurants in the burbs with Amanda and Stephanie has lost its appeal.

I'm surprised that Cat's parents have a say in her social life, considering she's an adult, and yet they do. She's allowed out, as long as she gets good marks at uni and doesn't set foot in what her dad calls a 'den of iniquity'. Her parents have the same non-existent idea of what she gets up to as what they had when she was fourteen. They think her Saturday nights are spent studying with nerdy students or watching a PG movie with me. It's only because I'm such an old friend that she's even allowed to crash at my place when we go to The Tube – or order takeaway pizza and watch *Pride and Prejudice*, if you believe the official version. And as for the guys she sometimes visits late at night, her parents don't know she's even been kissed! As long as she brings home First Class Honours, gets a decent job when she graduates next year and looks them in the eye and lies, then my nights at The Tube are safe. For now.

TRACK 17 – LAST NIGHT A DJ SAVED MY LIFE

Miss London lets us into The Tube for free and gives us drink cards, and in return Cat and I stick around till closing and accompany her home. She still lives with her parents in the Laura Ashley house in East Melbourne, so the three of us plan to head back to hers for breakfast to debrief on our night. It's near closing, and my stomach is calling out for jam toast and a cup of tea. Miss London and Cat are gossiping in the cloakroom, and I offer to help Jordan pack up his CDs.

'Cracking night tonight,' I say.

'Yeah,' he agrees.

We're both too tired to say much. I bend down to scoop up a pile of CDs from the floor and Jordan bends down to help me. Our faces are so close to each other that it's inevitable we end up snogging. We stand up together, still snogging, which would be really romantic, but I lose my balance and fall back, almost knocking over Jordan's deck. I hear cackling and cheering, and look up to see Cat and Miss London standing in the doorway.

'Yeah, yeah,' I mutter. 'C'mon, let's go home, girls.'

After breakfast with Miss London, Cat and I walk home down Wellington Parade, singing 'Champagne Supernova' at full volume and smirking at the early morning losers on their way to work. I'm still buzzing from the incident with Jordan.

He's the first non-random guy that I've ever snogged. Usually it's easier to kiss unknowns in case my interest wanes and I need to get rid of them. That happens with me a lot; I snog guys but soon after, I want them to go away. I'm starting to be concerned that I still haven't met a guy I actually genuinely fancy, apart from Martin Jones at school, but he, like a fool, wasn't into me. There's also the guy with the music, but I haven't even met him yet, or have I? Is it Jordan after all?

Although I didn't get butterflies when we kissed, I'm excited to see Jordan the following Saturday. At the end of the night, we snog again and do the same the week after. Soon it becomes a regular thing, and I invite him home with me.

Hallelujah, I've finally found someone, and he's a DJ! Tick, tick! I just wish he wasn't so skinny. When we kiss, I've noticed his shoulders are narrower than mine, which makes me feel like a heifer. Maybe when we've been going out longer, I'll ask him to take up rugby or something, so he can bulk up and I can feel more feminine.

On Sundays, Jordan sticks around at my place longer during the day and we start hanging out together during the week. We never have a conversation about it, but I start referring to him as 'my boyfriend' and it feels nice to say those words. Things aren't how I predicted though.

Prediction: Having a boyfriend should mean I'm so busy doing fun stuff, there's no time for TV.

Reality: Having a boyfriend means watching TV pretty much every night because we can't think of anything else to do.

Prediction: Having a boyfriend should mean receiving unexpected flowers.

Reality: Having a boyfriend means listening to constant sneezing, on account of his pollen allergy.

Prediction: Having a boyfriend should mean being with someone who always understands me.

Reality: Having a boyfriend means continually having to explain things, in case he gets offended by something I didn't even realise I said.

Having a boyfriend should be like landing on a planet of music; he's the guy with the music and I'm the girl with the music. We'll fill a house with music, and, when I'm thirty, we'll have little musical babies. When we want to visit our friends, we'll fly back to Earth in Major Tom's capsule, the musical babies playing guitar and singing to entertain us on our journey. This is not the case.

I'm happy to finally have a boyfriend, but I'm also disappointed.

'Do you even like Jordan?' Cat asks the next time we're in a taxi on the way to The Tube.

'Of course. He's too skinny, but he's not that bad looking. Well…I don't feel sickened when I look at him close up.'

'OK…'

'It's a relief to no longer feel upstaged by Jack, who's had girlfriends since he was twelve. Besides, if I ever get invited to a wedding, I now have a plus-one.'

I glimpse the taxi driver struggling to suppress a smile in the rearview mirror, so I keep talking to convince him and Cat, as well as myself. 'Jordan's a really nice guy and we have heaps in common.'

'OK…'

I know there's no romance or passion, and I know now that Jordan isn't the guy with the music, but I guess I'll worry about all that later.

As we step out of the taxi, we may as well be film stars arriving at the Oscars. I've gone from being the friend of a friend of the door bitch to being the girlfriend of one of The Tube DJs. The Tube really is my *Cheers* now, because everybody knows my name.

'Hi, Dot! Hi, Cat!' say the bouncers, Miss London, the bartenders, the club manager, the DJs, the regulars and the girls selling blue drinks in test tubes.

Cat says, 'Well, I reckon the most sweet-arse thing about you dating Jordan is that it's placed you directly in The Tube in-crowd. And, by default, me too!'

It's true. Jordan may not have set my heart on fire, but he's set my social life on fire! At least he has on The Tube nights, and no one knows about the television nights. Cat links arms with me as we head to the bar, loaded with drink cards.

No one knows that on the inside I'm still Dot, quiet and full of self-doubt. On the outside I'm Dot who dates a DJ, has a pixie haircut spiked with glitter gel and is capable of having a bubbly conversation with anyone I meet.

We rest our vodka tonics on the table nearest the dance floor and slide onto the flashing squares, à la John Travolta in *Saturday Night Fever*. The Fairy waves us over, so I peck her on the cheek and admire her new wings.

'Fabulous, sweetie,' I tell her.

I catch the Britpop DJ's eye, and he puts on 'London Calling'. I arrived at my utensils party, but dating Jordan means that I'm here to stay.

I like these developments a lot, but Jordan has become a cartoon character. The cartoon Jordan is my fabulous DJ boyfriend, who's turned my life into a glittery whirlwind of popularity; but then there's the real Jordan, who I sometimes have to think about during moments of sobriety.

One Sunday morning, we're enjoying a fry up in Bridge Road. I drain my latte, followed by a glass of water, waiting for the caffeine to take effect.

'So, what made you become a DJ? Did you always love music?' I ask Jordan.

We've been seeing each other for a couple months, but I only just realise we've never had a getting-to-know-you convo. We've been out to breakfast before, but we normally just read the paper, waiting for our fatigue to melt away. Today I want to talk.

'Not really,' Jordan says. 'I fell into this when one of my mates told me it's good money. DJ'ing's just a thing I do to support myself through uni.'

How can anything related to music be 'just a thing'? I guess the caffeine isn't working yet as I don't understand what he's saying, so I continue. 'Wouldn't you love to go to Ibiza when you finish uni?'

'Hardly. I've already started interviewing at the big four banks.'

So Jordan's future lies in suits and management, not touring with Paul Oakenfold, Underworld or Faithless, with me in tow. All around me people are chattering and enjoying their breakfast, but I'm no longer part of the crowd. Instead, I'm being sucked into a yawn of a black hole. My bacon and eggs taste funny as I imagine Jordan dreaming about money, rather than music.

I'm struggling, but persist with the conversation. 'What're you doing next Saturday before The Tube?'

'Probably studying.'

What kind of person spends Saturday night studying?

'Why don't you blow that off and come to Gerald and Margaret's roulette party?'

'Hmm, I dunno…'

'It'll be fun! Besides, I want you to meet my family. And wouldn't it be great to do something outside The Tube that's not just watching TV?'

Jordan seems more focused on his food than me. He dips a chip into runny egg yolk, and the sight of the yellow goo makes my stomach jump. A waiter materialises to take the plate I've shoved aside. He's cute.

'Come on, Jordan…you might win some money!'

Jordan takes his eyes off his eggs at the mention of money. I feel a little irritated, but at least he agrees to come.

'The only thing you need to do to impress my family is tell them a brilliant story or wash some dishes. After that, you're in for life!'

'Won't they be impressed by my interviews with the banks?'

I don't answer, and order a cup of Earl Grey. Jordan grabs a newspaper abandoned on a nearby table and I stare into my cup.

♬ ♬ ♬

Jordan and I stand on the doorstep at Glen Huntly, holding a six-pack of beer and a plate of California rolls.

'Don't forget, good stories and washing up,' I whisper to him.

Before Jordan can reply, the door flies open.

'Dottie!' Gerald booms.

'Gerald, this is Jordan,' I tell him.

'Jordan the DJ!' cries Gerald with glee. 'We'll be playing none of that rubbish in this house, but if it's trad music you're after, then you've come to the right place!'

Jordan politely shakes his hand, and Gerald announces at the top of his voice, 'Everyone, Dot's boyfriend is here!'

Red-faced, excitable Kellys gather round Jordan and bombard him.

'What do you study?'

'Are you a Catholic?'

'Do you like the Fureys?'

'Do you vote Labor?'

'What do you think about Dolly the Sheep?'

Before he can even begin to answer their questions, Julie Ann arrives. The circle around Jordan and me disintegrates.

'Oh Jules, I hope you're going to sing "Danny Boy" tonight,' says Aunty Christine-Paul.

'Ooh, yes! I've been looking forward to hearing it for months,' Aunty Theresa-May chimes in.

'Just a sec, I'll get my accordion,' Gerald says.

'How's all that jazz going?' Uncle Ted asks, in reference to a jazz band Julie Ann's joined.

While Julie Ann contends with the gushing Kellys, Dobbler takes advantage of the distraction to swipe some beer. Jack joins Jordan and me, laughing.

'You better think of some good anecdotes to tell them when they come back,' he warns Jordan. 'Or start loading the dishwasher.'

'Pardon?'

I guess Jordan wasn't listening the ten times I told him about my family's love of stories and contribution.

'Beer?' Jack tries again.

'No thanks, I'm driving.'

Even when he's not driving, Jordan rarely drinks. He's also the only DJ I know who doesn't touch drugs. There's something suspicious about that.

I leave Jordan with Jack and head over to Jade, who's serving drinks for ten bucks an hour.

'How's school?' I ask.

'Sluts College is beyond shit. I'm working on Mum and Dad to send me to Carnegie Secondary next year.'

'Really? Gerald used to use Carnegie Secondary as a threat on us.'

'Don't know why. You can do drama and art subjects there, plus you don't need to worry about wearing a stupid uniform or dumb-arse teachers interfering in your social life.'

'Cheers to that. Now, gimme a beer.'

I glance over at Jordan to see how he's faring. Julie Ann must be taking a break from her fans, because as well as Jack still dancing around him, Margaret's hovering, shoving a plate of hummus and pita bread in his face. Gerald's showing him his accordion, and Uncle Ted's pointing out the roulette table. Jordan resembles Prince Charles visiting a tropical island, the locals proudly showing him their culture, and he stands there awkwardly, nodding politely and looking like he'd rather be anywhere else.

Dr Ivanskiy lumbers over, asking Jade to top up his vodka.

'What the bloody hell did you do with your hair, Dot?' he asks, swigging his drink. 'You look like a little boy with your hair all short. Really, right unusual fashions these days.'

Jade and I roll our eyes, but it's with affection.

Dr Ivanskiy is oblivious and continues, 'Who is this Jordan fella?'

'Um…my boyfriend, I guess,' I reply.

'Your boyfriend? My goodness, never did I see a more mopey looking character. He stands around, all daft like former Stasi trying to blend in with ordinary people.'

'Well, he doesn't really know us, Dr Ivanskiy.'

'No Dot, he's a dud. Do you good to break up with him right away.'

Jade bursts out laughing, then asks, 'Do you have a girlfriend, Dr Ivanskiy?'

'No, I don't. Wasted all my time with silly women and then it was too late to find a decent one. So, I'm alone. Don't be daft like me, girls.'

His voice isn't as jolly as normal and he looks me right in the eye as he speaks. For some reason, I shiver.

Dr Ivanskiy returns to the roulette table and Jade turns to me, saying, 'Fuck, only Dr Ivanskiy can get away with telling someone their new boyfriend sucks!'

There's Jordan, still standing in the same spot with his hands in his pockets and his bad posture, nodding politely as Dobbler shows him the trick with the deodorant fire. Dr Ivanskiy has confirmed what I already knew.

TRACK 18 – ATOMIC

I'm curled up on the couch, having what I thought would be a cosy phone call with Cat, until she tells me her bad news.

'What the fuck d'you mean you're not coming to The Tube till exams are over?' I ask.

'Just for a few weeks. Then we've got the entire summer to party.'

'Can't you tell your parents to piss off? Or that you're studying all night with those nerdy students?'

'You know it's not as simple as that. Besides, I reckon I should *actually study*, seeing this is my final year and I want to get good marks.'

'Yeah well, I don't think it'd hurt to take one night a week off.'

'It's more than just one night though. It's the entire weekend getting ready for The Tube, going to The Tube and recovering from The Tube. Relax Dot, Jordan and the others will still be there.'

That's true, but I'd have a better time with Cat there too. From our grand entrance in our little dresses, Converse and glittery hair to our sign language pointing out losers, freaks and cuties, The Tube is a night for Dot and Cat, even since Jordan's been on the scene. Besides, Jordan isn't as much fun as Cat.

'Shouldn't you be studying too?' she asks.

'Technically...'

I look over at my textbooks, piled on the coffee table. They are not in the least inviting. The Vegetarian flutters around me, like a moth caught in a web.

'Gotta go, Cat,' I say. 'I think someone wants to use the phone.'

I hang up and sigh at my books. An old copy of *Gone with the Wind* is also lying on the table, which I pick up instead.

Our house is spotless since I keep finding things to clean rather than hitting the books. I wish I could somehow get my law degree without having to put in any effort. I'm over studying and I'm over feeling bad about not studying. There's not much else going on around here though, seeing the Vegetarian has requested the volume levels of a monastery while she studies. I manage to get a little revision in, plus some napping, and I read the entire works of Jane Austen.

On Saturday I go to The Tube alone and it's quiet, which shows how many students go here. None of the regulars are around; even Miss London and Jordan are away. Without people, the venue seems divey, and the flashing disco floor looks tacky. For the first time ever, I go home before closing.

During Sunday dinner at Glen Huntly, Jack laughs when I whinge about people who prioritise studying above socialising. 'Well, next week it's Julie Ann's gig at Bennetts Lane. Let's go there instead,' he suggests.

'Hmm…'

Jack bursts into an off-key rendition of 'All That Jazz'.

'All right, all right, as long as you stop singing!'

Julie Ann's at the Victorian College of the Arts and her jazz band is starting to get a few gigs. She may very well upstage Now and Then. She still delights us all with 'Danny Boy' at every Kelly family gathering, but I've never heard her sing jazz.

I meet Jack at Bennetts Lane and we're surrounded by family. Julie Ann's school friend, Helen, is also there and waves me over.

'Hi Dot,' she says. 'I knew I was in the right place when I noticed everyone had the same green eyes and olive skin. You can pick a Kelly anywhere. Except for you. Your hair looks amazing!'

I've put a bright orange rinse in my hair and gelled it into three triangles. The look I was going for was Vyvyan from *The Young Ones,* but Jack says I look more like a giant liquorice allsort with my orange hair, white face and lime-green dress. He's wearing an oversized Wu-Tang Clan tee-shirt and cargo pants, so what would he know about fashion?

There are so many family members here, there's hardly any room for Julie Ann's friends. Dr Ivanskiy is here too and buys Jack and me a vodka tonic.

'Ay yi yi, Dot! Your hair looks right daft, like a bloody pineapple.'

'You're not wrong, Dr I,' Jack chips in.

Dr Ivanskiy continues, 'And Jack, why you wear such baggy clothes like a scarecrow?'

'Really unusual fashions these days, hey Dr Ivanskiy?' Jack comments, just as I'm taking a sip of vodka tonic, which makes me laugh so much I spit my drink down my front.

'Another Kelly who can't hold her drink,' Jack muses.

'Where's that boyfriend of yours?' Dr Ivanskiy asks.

Who? Oh yeah, Jordan. 'He has to study,' I say.

We take a seat in the front row as Julie Ann's band starts up. I like Billie Holiday and Nina Simone, but think most jazz is pretentious, especially contemporary jazz. Shuffle, shuffle, shuffle go the drums; ooh la la goes the saxophone; and bippity, bippity bop sings Julie Ann. Despite the rest of the Kellys wetting themselves every time Julie Ann hits high C, I never thought much of her singing until now. She was always in tune, but her voice was so prissy I found it irritating. Tonight she uses a different voice; it's rich and a bit husky and has a lot more expression.

I enjoy listening to Julie Ann for the first few songs, but after a while I get bored by the self-indulgent instrumental solos that feature in every number.

I turn to Jack and ask, 'Heading down to Graceland this summer?'

'Don't see why not. Dobbler wants to try selling pot to the schoolies.'

'That guy's gunna end up in jail! He's a bad influence on the council flat kids he plays soccer with.'

'Ha!'

'Shush!' someone says.

'What the hell? Did I just get shushed?'

'Shush!' someone else says.

Jack and I look at each other and burst out laughing.

'SHUSH!!'

'Well, pardon me for having a chat and a laugh in a bar,' I whisper to Jack.

We listen to the rest of the show in silence, smirking every now and then at the thought of the shushers. I miss The Tube and I miss Cat, but it's fun hanging with Jack.

This is my last fun night out for a while.

♫ ♫ ♫

The following week is exams and I take mine wearing a little boy's school uniform I found in an op shop. The shirt is tight and I need to leave half the buttons undone, so it looks pretty sexy, especially with my Wonderbra. The rest of the students are wearing clothes so daggy it's depressing. What kind of twenty-one year old wears a Big W tracksuit in public? I'm really not looking forward to spending my entire working life with these people.

♫ ♫ ♫

Cat calls me as soon as she finishes her final exam. 'Ministry of Sound at Festival Hall! You in?'

'Hell, yeah!'

'Thank fuck those exams are over,' she says. 'This summer is going to rock!'

The night rolls round, and we turn up at Festival Hall in matching happy pants and boob tubes. We practically dance into the joint. Besides the sedate night at The Tube and Julie Ann's shushing gig, this is my first proper night out in a month!

I have mixed feelings about techno because there is a hell of a lot of crappy commercial stuff around, but when done properly there's nothing like it. If he's still out there, I'm sure the guy with the music would probably have a couple of good house albums in his collection. The music tonight is good, melodic and easy to dance to, with the same beat mixed all the way through. The DJs on stage have green laser beams shooting out from behind their decks and the place is going off.

The crowd is similar to that at The Tube, but with fewer mods. Cat and I stand on the edge of the dance floor for a moment, taking in the scene and letting the scene take in us. There are people with neon yellow safety bibs, pigtails, animal suits, wetsuits, dummies and so much glitter it looks like a million disco balls exploded. People are dancing wildly, running around like six-year-olds during playtime. Others are leaning against the walls in conversation, their mouths working overtime.

I line up at the bar to get some vodka tonics and Cat approaches a guy in a zebra suit who's doing star jumps. I look up at the stage and the laser beams turn from green to blue. I wonder if heaven looks like this.

'What were you talking to zebra boy about?' I ask Cat when I return with our drinks.

'Just bought some pills off him!'

'Serious?'

'Yes, why not? This is Ministry of Sound, I've finished my exams and I wanna let my hair down before my parents start nagging me to get a job.'

My history with drugs is limited. I've partaken in the occasional joint, but that's all. When I was ten, I saw a German film about heroin addicts on SBS and it scared the crap out of me. This man had three kids and they all became smackies; one died, one was a prostitute and the other injected into his toe. I couldn't sleep for days after.

Cat swallows one of the pills. 'Want one?' she asks.

'Um, I dunno…'

I'm curious, even though I don't want to try anything that gets me addicted so I end up a homeless, toothless prostitute with track marks on my toe; or anything that'll fry my brain so I end up jumping off a bridge and becoming special like Shane on *Degrassi Junior High*. Well, I won't take those sorts of drugs, but maybe pills are OK, as long as I don't OD on water. Cat dances around me, dangling the pill in front of my face. She seems all right.

'Ooh, go on then,' I say to her in a Yorkshire accent, and she shoves the pill down my throat.

'Jesus, it's working right away!'

It's like I'm hit by a bus full of pillows and flowers.

'Let's dance!' says Cat.

The laser beams shooting out from behind the DJ's deck are magnificent. The music is a siren's call, begging me to dance. All around me, people give me their most twinkling party smiles. Something in the air makes me feel safe, like being wrapped in a warm blanket that smells of flowers. I've been here before, I realise, but I can't remember when.

Everyone in the building is dancing; the floor's vibrating, the walls heaving. It's as though I was autistic my whole life, but now I'm finally able to connect with people. My heart is racing, I'm sweating like a pig and I can't stop wiggling my jaw around. Now what I want to do is talk and talk and talk.

I grab Cat's hand and say, 'C'mon, let's talk.'

We lean against the wall and I tell her about how she's my best friend and how much I appreciate her. I tell her about how bad I felt when I was too shy to keep up with her in high school and we drifted apart, how happy I am that we're friends again and about all the doors she has opened for me. I tell her I don't really love Jordan, I hate studying law and I'm not sure I want to be a lawyer after all, I actually just want to listen to music and go clubbing all the time. I tell her sometimes I feel so empty inside because all I care about is being considered cool and having fun. And I tell her about the guy with the music and how I've been waiting for him for so long.

'Where is he, Cat? He's the second half of my heart, but he's not here! Where the hell is he? And worse than him not being here is that idea that he doesn't even exist!' My tears must be making my aqua eye shadow and glitter mascara run, but I don't care.

'He's just around the corner, sweetie, I promise,' Cat says, and hands me a Chupa Chup. 'Here, have one of these.'

'Wow, this is sooo refreshing!' For some reason the lollipop is the best thing I've ever tasted.

Now it's Cat's turn to talk. She tells me how she thinks we'll be friends forever, no matter what. She tells me how it felt to be the only Indian kid in primary school and how she wouldn't have survived without me; she regrets drifting apart in high school, but she thought I thought she'd become vacuous. She tells me how glad she is that we're friends again and that we've discovered this world of clubs and parties together. She tells me about the pressure she's under to get top marks and a high-paying job, how she's never been able to have a proper boyfriend because her family won't accept anyone who doesn't share the same background, and how all the guys her parents introduce her to are old fobs, with bouffant hair and moustaches. She tells me how dirty she feels having to lie and sneak around all the time, just to have a normal social life. And she tells me she has to attend a twelve-hour wedding tomorrow and stand around after one hour's sleep, fending off old women who'll interrogate her about not being married.

We finish talking and it's daylight; the venue is emptying. We walk into the city to catch a tram home. Cat looks a mess, her hair is limp and her makeup's run all over her face so she looks like Barbara Cartland. She says I look the same. It's serene walking home. The pills are wearing off and I feel calm, tired and smelly – like how you feel when you've run around Albert Park Lake, I think.

'When did you take your first pill?' I ask Cat.

'I took one at the end of Year Twelve and when I went to the Big Day Out. This is my third.'

'Tonight was fun.'

'Yeah.'

'Next time, let's invite a bunch of people. Miss London can come and tell us how it's not as good as Brixton.'

'Well said, geeza.'

We walk the rest of the way to Flinders Street in silence. The city hasn't woken up yet and we don't want to break the tranquillity.

We sit together on the tram, not talking until we approach Punt Road and Cat says, 'I'm sorry we can't come down together, but I've got this all-day wedding. Try to get as much sleep as you can, then find a friend to hang out with. You don't wanna be sitting around by yourself coming down.'

'OK...'

'You'll feel better on Monday, then rough again on Tuesday – that's why it's called Ecky Tuesday – and by Wednesday you'll be back to normal. In the meantime, if you start to feel shit, try to chill out and remember all come downs are temporary.'

'Right, cheers. See you soon, I guess.' I stand up as the tram arrives at my stop.

'You will! I'll call you when I get back from the wedding, OK?'

We hug and I get off the tram. The fresh air is nice and I wind my way through the backstreets of Richmond, gazing at all of the little houses. Some are renovated spick and span, and some are scruffy and dilapidated. I like the scruffy ones best because they look more comforting. They keep the wary, come-down feeling on leash, and I head home to bed.

When I wake, it's early evening and everything's so quiet it feels like someone died. The calm feeling the little houses gave me has gone. I call out to the Vegetarian, but for once she's not here. I start to feel panicky, and it's the same feeling as when I have that dream about being stuck alone in Major Tom's capsule. I feel like there's been an apocalypse and I'm the only survivor. I feel like nothing fun is ever going to happen again for the rest of my life. I feel like I'll be studying law and working in a miserable job until I die. And I'll never find the guy with the music.

I take a few deep breaths and run through the list of friends I can call. Jordan's been getting on my nerves lately, and besides, it's hard enough explaining jokes to him, let alone explaining how I'm feeling right now. Miss London will have a thousand things to do and I don't have the energy for tagging along with her and all her friends. Amanda is anti-drugs after the joint-spewing incident, so I won't get any sympathy from her. Cat's at the wedding, and so in the end I call Jack.

'Ha ha ha!' he laughs. 'Well, I'm supposed to have a date tonight, but I was looking for an excuse to palm this chick off. Let's meet in Chinatown for dumplings, then go see *Happy Gilmore*.'

'That sounds exactly like what I wanna do. See you soon!'

TRACK 19 – I FOUGHT THE LAW

'In all honesty, I haven't studied properly in a year,' I tell Cat.

We're at Brunetti's sharing a bowl of gelato. In a couple hours, our uni results will be published and I'm starting to worry.

'Do you even *want* to be a lawyer?' Cat asks.

'Sure…I have since I was a kid. I wanna be a High Court judge making ground-breaking decisions, like legalising drugs and imprisoning bigots. Or maybe a QC, who drinks red wine at lunch, then defends the rights of the down-and-out.'

Cat doesn't answer; her mouth is full of gelato, so I keep talking, 'I thought after studying so hard in Year Twelve, I'd be able to cruise through my uni degree and tumble out the other end into a forty-grand job.'

'Not really like that though, is it?'

'Nope…'

What I didn't realise was that four years of endless lectures, tutorials, reading, writing, studying and exams were what was expected of me. What kind of person is able to read a hundred pages a day about Australia's Constitution or taxation without falling asleep? What kind of person enjoys taking four-hour exams that involve so much writing the skin on the side of your hand peels away? What kind of person spends a thousand dollars on interview suits, competing with a million other students, for a job in a law firm that won't even start for two years? People should be gagging to have me working for them and not the other way round!

'Clack, clack, clack,' I mutter.

Cat looks puzzled. 'Pardon?'

'The sound of people's IBM ThinkPads in the lecture theatre. There's no music to it…'

Jordan once told me he'd give his right nut for a laptop. I couldn't think of anything worse.

'Why don't you think about transferring to another degree?' Cat suggests. 'Something you're more interested in.'

I stare into space for a bit, then some unplanned words come out of my mouth, 'Music. I want to do something with music.'

'Such as?'

The wall of where to begin is insurmountable. 'Oh, I'm not sure. Do they have degrees in clubbing?'

Cat laughs, as I continue, 'But there are elements of law that interested me.'

I liked learning about the fingernail in the meat pie and the duty of care, and I liked learning about *mens rea*, but mainly because it reminded me of a man and his diarrhoea, which is funny. I also liked going to the Magistrates' Court and sitting in on committal hearings. I watched as ferrety men spoke about all the 'rips' they've done, or obese women told us about their speed labs.

'It's not enough though, is it?' Cat voices my thoughts.

'Nope. Come on, let's face the music.'

We walk over to Melbourne University; I walk so slow I'm practically going backwards. Except for the bits with uni in it, I love my life, but it can't go on like this forever. I can't be thirty and clubbing and taking pills and all that. I suppose I'll need to have some sort of career, but realistically I've no idea what I might like to do.

I picture myself working in a funky office, surrounded by gorgeous people who have champagne breakfasts, long lunches and business trips to New York. Every now and then, I might sit in front of a computer wearing lolly-pink nail-polish and type out a few documents. I'll go to client meetings, where one of my colleagues will explain all the details and the clients will check me out and think I look hot and then just sign the deal. I'll be known as a gun in my industry, but what actual work I'll be doing is a mystery.

We stand outside Union House, about to go in separate directions, Cat to the Commerce Faculty and me to the Law School.

'Meet you back here in fifteen?' Cat suggests.

'Sure.' My mouth is dry.

I find my noticeboard and it's surrounded, so I hang back a moment, wondering what to do about the crowd and my life. A pigeon flutters by, and shits within centimetres of where I'm sitting. In the end, I push through the crowd and scan for my student number.

There it is, for all to see. I've failed every single one of my subjects. *Wow, that's impressively bad.*

Instead of meeting Cat, I leave another way and go straight home. I can't think what to do, so I take a nap.

I don't sleep for long because the phone starts ringing. The first person to call is Cat. I apologise for bailing on her and she's sympathetic.

'Don't worry, Dot. Something will work out. Let's meet up for pizza and we can discuss Plan B.'

'Maybe tomorrow night. I just wanna hibernate tonight.'

'No problemo! Call me whenever!'

I forgot to ask Cat how she did, but I figure by her cheery voice that she did fine.

Then the family calls and the phone is passed between Margaret, Gerald and Jack, so I have to tell them my news three times.

'Never mind, now I won't have to worry about you developing fancy lawyer's airs,' Margaret says.

'Don't worry, Dot. You've got a lot of ability and something will come up,' Gerald says. 'You'll still be a contributor.'

'That's why I never bothered with uni. Want a job at the sports store?' Jack offers.

'I'll let you know.'

I go back to bed for a bit of a cry and a sleep, letting my hungry stomach gurgle away unanswered.

♫ ♫ ♫

I'm given one last chance in the form of a supplementary summer exam, and for the first time that year, I enter the library. I gather up a bunch of law journals and schlep over to the photocopier. It's being used by a man printing pages by the ream. He has his back to me, folding papers into little booklets, and he doesn't look like he's going anywhere fast. There are more photocopiers at the other end of the library, but Cat and Miss London are waiting in Lygon Street for cake and lattes.

Law degrees are prestigious, but chocolate mud cake is delicious. I dump the journals on a table and exit the building.

Outside, The Specials pop into my head and there's a spring in my step. I sing out loud about how every day I walk along the lonely street, trying to find a future, but fashion is my only culture. A voice from long ago pops into my head and tells me that the future's bright.

TRACK 20 – HEART OF GLASS

I'm lying on the couch, talking to Jordan. I've only just called him, but already the Vegetarian's materialised, signing to me that she wants to use the phone.

'What d'you wanna do tonight?' I ask Jordan, ignoring the Vegetarian.

'We could go see *Independence Day*,' Jordan suggests.

'Jesus Jordan, I'm not seeing a lame-arse movie on a Friday night! Why don't we go to that hip hop party with Jack?'

'I'll be too tired for The Tube tomorrow if we have a big one tonight.'

I wish Jordan would sleep during the days like the rest of us, instead of favouring sedate, early nights to keep energised.

'Well, *I'm* going to the party with Jack…so I guess I'll see you tomorrow.'

'OK then, see you later.'

I hang up, and the Vegetarian seizes the phone.

♫ ♫ ♫

I'm surrounded by white, middle-class kids who think they're black.

'Is it weird Jordan isn't bothered his girlfriend would rather hang out with her brother than him on a Friday night?' I ask Jack.

'At least he's not following you around like a puppy,' Jack remarks between Biggie Smalls' *uh-huhs*.

Jack's right, but I'm feeling whiney. 'All Jordan talks about are banks, how he's tired and needs an early night, and how it's better to go to a café with cheap, shit food rather than a café with nice, expensive food. I don't get him.'

'Plus he didn't appreciate it when I set my clothes on fire at the roulette party,' Dobbler shoves himself between Jack and me, sporting a shaved head and an eyebrow ring.

'How's it going, Romper Stomper?' Jack laughs.

'You're just jealous,' Dobbler says. 'Hey, can you guys spare me some beer? Mum's got her eagle eye on me, so I couldn't sneak any from home.'

As usual, a couple of council flat boys holding a soccer ball are hovering around Dobbler.

I hand him a stubby and say, 'One drink only. And you can share it with your mates.'

Dobbler's looking at me quizzically, trying to work out if he can get away with more.

'Aren't you boys in training for the World Cup or something?' Jack asks.

Now that his cooler cousin has spoken, Dobbler cuts his losses and heads off with his crew and one beer to pester the DJ.

I myself have a few drinks and snog a Peter Andre look-alike; totally not my type, but it's nice to be with a guy who has a bit of muscle on his arms. As we're embracing, I notice his shoulders are wider than mine. I'm about to get in a taxi with him when I recall that I have a boyfriend.

'Hey mate, I'm sorry but I think I'm just gunna go home by myself.'

I don't even bother mentioning Jordan as I close the door on Peter Andre and tell the driver to take me to Richmond. Peter stands there looking bewildered and pretty cute. I almost change my mind, but I feel like a skank, so I don't. I'm irritated with Jordan though. If it wasn't for him, I could be hooking up with an extremely hot guy right now.

Truth be told, it's been a while since I've had any action. Jordan never initiates anything and I only do after a drink. Lately even that has stopped happening. The thought of sleeping with Jordan is starting to make me feel queasy; not because anything unfortunate is going on, just that I'm not feeling the music.

When Cat comes over the next evening to get ready for The Tube, I ask her, 'If I married Jordan, would I have to do the deed with him once a week for the rest of my life? The idea of that is kind of a turn-off.'

'I know you're not in love with him, but do you at least like him?' Cat asks, as she applies purple lipstick. It's not the first time she's asked me this.

This is sad, but I have to think of my reply. 'Hmm, he's a nice guy, and he means well…'

My arms ache from twisting my hair into dozens of tiny buns. I take a break and shake out my hands. Cat's finished getting ready, and she waits for me to go on.

'Oh my god Cat, he's so boring! He's not even really into DJ'ing, he just does it for the money. And we have *nothing* at all in common! What kind of boyfriend would rather watch videos than go out? What kind of boyfriend has a lifelong dream to work in a bank? What kind of boyfriend has never once taken me on an actual date?'

'Then why're you with him?'

'Yeah, you're right…'

And then a pinprick of a thought drills itself into my head. *Maybe the next person to come along could be the guy with the music!* That's it, decided, then.

Now I just have to actually tell Jordan we should break up. I could ring him right now and do it, but already I feel the words freezing my throat shut. Maybe he'll break up with me instead. He doesn't exactly seem madly in love with me either. He's nice and all, but that's it. I don't expect to be showered with gifts, but I do expect to feel joy when I see him, and for him to feel joy when he sees me. Joy, as opposed to flatness. I decide to fizzle Jordan out.

'Let's check out the chill-out room,' Cat suggests, once we arrive at The Tube.

'You go. I'll say hi to Miss London.'

'Avoiding Jordan?'

'That's right, sister.'

♫ ♫ ♫

For the next few weeks, I go to The Tube but avoid Jordan and the chill-out room. Cat gives me looks that make me squirm, but it's like I've developed a terrible stutter and any words I need to say to Jordan refuse to come out. Finally he calls me.

'Hey, how's it going?'

'All right…' I reply.

There's a pause, then Jordan says, 'I'm well too, thanks for asking. I've got a second interview at NAB next week.'

'Oh, that's great.' I try to make my voice sound enthusiastic, but I'm struggling.

There's another pause before he continues, 'So, d'you wanna go see a movie or something tonight?'

Tell him, tell him, tell him! My internal dialogue is raging, but externally I just say, 'Um, that'd be nice, but I'm catching up with Cat tonight.'

'Oh OK, how about tomorrow?'

'Hmm, I think I'm seeing Amanda, and after that I'm going to Graceland for a few days.'

'Oh… Well, I'll give you a buzz when you get back.'

'Yeah, cool.'

'OK then. Bye, Dot.'

He hangs up, but rings back a couple minutes later. 'Listen Dot, when someone rings up for a chat there's no call to be rude, you know.'

His voice is calm and I feel like a kid caught picking her nose; I'm immediately on the defence. 'I'm not being rude, Jordan!'

Jordan's voice changes. 'Yes, you are! We haven't seen each other in ages, I ring up and ask you out, and hardly get two words from you.'

'What the hell? We're having a fucking conversation! What more do you expect?'

'What I expect is my girlfriend to come and say hi to me when she comes to the club where I'm working!'

'Well, you're not the boss of me!' *Is that the best I can argue? No wonder I could never be a lawyer.*

'Jesus! Maybe we need to take a break...'

'Maybe we should break up!'

'Fine then!'

'Fine!'

'You know, you can be a real cold bitch?'

'Whatever!'

We both slam our phones down, and it's done. I do feel like a bitch and I'm shaking from the argument. Aside from childhood bickering with Jack, this is the first proper fight I've had. Another thing I can check off. I feel slimy because I've upset Jordan, but also relieved we've finally broken up.

That night I dream I'm in Major Tom's capsule and I'm waiting for the guy with the music to arrive, but he doesn't and I'm alone.

♫ ♫ ♫

There's no fallout from the argument with Jordan, only silence.

I go to The Tube wearing a Union Jack tee-shirt and a fake, flashy smile. I don't go anywhere near the chill-out room, and I keep dancing so Jordan won't try to talk to me, not that he does. I wish he didn't DJ here.

'It's like The Tube is our baby and we're having a custody battle. I should win because I love it more,' I tell Cat. 'Oh, I feel terrible!'

Cat hugs me and says, 'That sucks, but you made the right decision. You and Jordan just weren't meant to be.'

I lean against her shoulder, enjoying being comforted, but there's also a creepy, snaily feeling in the back of my head. The Fairy comes over and hugs me too; she even offers me her wand for the evening. I don't especially miss having Jordan as my boyfriend, but people are acting like I do, and it's not all bad.

'You all right, love?' Miss London asks the next time she's taking a break from door bitch duties.

There's concern in her voice and I remember how she once snobbed me off for not going to a fancy school, but now she's a caring friend.

I say, 'Oh, I feel pretty shit, but I'm hanging in there…'

Miss London replies, 'Take care, innit.' She slips a few extra drinks cards into my hand.

'Chin up, Dot,' says Brian, the club manager, when he passes me at the bar later in the evening.

My chin was up, but I give Brian a grateful smile.

Finally, I peek into the chill-out room, but Jordan's busy DJ'ing and doesn't look up. Some plain-faced girls are hanging around his decks, and I start to feel like I miss him. I know we shouldn't get back together, but it's dawning on me that I'm going through a breakup and that I'm supposed to feel sad, and so I do feel sad.

For the rest of the night, I sit on a bar stool holding the Fairy's wand, and people come up and give me hugs. If this was a scene in a movie, 'Heaven Knows I'm Miserable Now' would definitely be playing in the background. Instead, they're playing 'Shiny Happy People'.

I spend the night dwelling on things, like how I was mean to Jordan and now I'm all alone and he'll never want to look at me again, and how I had a great opportunity to be a lawyer and save the world, but I failed, just because I didn't want to do a little bit of work. Also, the guy with the music isn't anywhere to be seen. Tears slide down my face, and I sit on the bar stool with Cat's arm around my shoulders. Half of me is actually crying, but the other half is admiring the romantic figure I cut. Bittersweet feels great.

TRACK 21 – UP THE JUNCTION

Boys R Us – MCG – 18th October 1996

What better way to end my association with this illustrious publication than with a review of what every teenage girl is calling the Concert of the Year. Yes indeed, I'm talking about Canadian supergroup Boys R Us. Last night I attended the opening night of their Australian tour, and it's a privilege to be able to share my thoughts with you on this underwhelming experience.

With only one album under their belt, it defies belief that five teens no one had heard of two months ago have managed to sell out the MCG four nights running. But we can't underestimate the force that is Boys R Us. Emerging from the obscurity of the Toronto church-band scene, these baseball cap-wearing lads are taking the world of pop by storm. Their saccharine harmonies, vacuous lyrics and synchronised shuffles are a thing to behold. The only good thing about this concert was the fact that the lads had just thirty minutes of material, so all the kiddies in the audience got to go home nice and early.

After three years dedicated to reviewing the likes of Boys R Us, a change of direction is required. Even if I didn't want to go, I'm sure to be fired once this wee article is unleashed. What prompted me to take these actions, just as I'm on the brink of becoming one of Melbourne's most celebrated music journalists, I hear you ask? Two girls singing 'Champagne Supernova' in Wellington Parade at the top of their voices early one morning. The delight in those girls' faces reminded me that listening to bands like Boys R Us will rob us of our radiance. We need to live, not exist!

So it's back to the grassroots music scene with me, starting with a project publishing zines dedicated to the 1970s post-punk movement (and by 'publishing' I mean photocopying everything myself in the Baillieu Library). Look out for my zines in Polyester Records. Boys R Us will not be featured. The future's bright.

Where's Your Head At, Can't Get You Out Of My Head, Handbags and Gladrags, Clint Eastwood, Have A Nice Day, Thank You, One More Time, Last Nite, Stan, Yellow, Fallin', Independent Women, Since I Left You, Hidden Place, Minority, Dead Leaves And The Dirty Ground, Harder Better Faster Stronger, Murder On The Dancefloor, Lady Marmalade, 19-2000, Ms Jackson, Freelove, Wish You Were Here, I'm Like A Bird, Teenage Dirtbag, Pyramid Song, Turn Off The Light, South Side, It's Raining Men, I Feel Loved, Girls Girls Girls, Cocoon, Get Ur Freak On, Sing, First Date, Hard To Explain, Caring Is Creepy, Take Me Home, New Born, Mississippi, The State Of Things, Bad Cover Version, It Wasn't Me, Hey Baby, Smooth Criminal, Frontier Psychiatrist, Because I Got High, One Step Closer, Bootylicious, Dancing In The Moonlight, Hero, Drops Of Jupiter (Tell Me), Family Affair, Ride Wit Me, Survivor, Romeo, Me Myself And I, Get The Party Started, Beautiful Day, Don't Stop Movin', Gotta Get Thru This, Somethin' Stupid, Shining Light, Dream On, Pissing In The Wind, Star 69, Juxtapozed With U, Crystal, In The End, Macy's Day Parade, Global A Go-Go, Why Does My Heart Feel So Bad, In Your Eyes, Stay Together For The Kids, Fever, Steal My Kisses, Renegades Of Funk, Trouble, All The Way To Reno (You're Gonna Be A Star), Knives Out, Warning, Is This It, Hotel Yorba, Powder Blue, Found That Soul, Kiss Kiss, The Trees, Someone To Call My Lover, Souljacker Part 1, Out Of Sight, Imitation Of Life, 60 Miles An Hour, 4 My People, It Began In Africa, American Dream, Here With Me, Mr Writer, Heaven Is A Halfpipe, Bohemian Like You, More Than A Woman, Ich Will, Fat Lip, Getting Away with It (All Messed Up), All I Ever Wanted, Agenda Suicide, Snowflakes, Buck Rogers, I'm A Slave 4 U, M!ssundaztood, Bad Ambassador, Lowrider, One Day in Your Life, Asleep In The Back, Stuck In A Moment You Can't Get Out Of, Boiler, Just A Day, There You'll Be, Essence, Don't Tell Me, Stock Exchange, Weapon Of Choice, All For You, Schism, Butterfly, Hanging By A Moment, If You're Gone, Superman (It's Not Easy), I'm Real, Again, Where The Party At, Jaded, Family Portrait, Concrete Angel, Island In The Sun, Loverboy, A Woman's Worth, Play, I'm Waking Up To Us, One Minute Man, F.E.A.R.

TRACK 22 – COOL FOR CATS

There are never any music jobs advertised online. I take temp job after temp job, waiting for my big break. I'm offered an interview for a permanent job at an IT start-up. It's not music, but I could use a bit of permanence, so what the hell.

The people interviewing me are a young man wearing a terrible mustard-coloured shirt and chinos, and an older woman who looks like she's about to fall off her fit ball. I know nothing about the role, but the office is bright and funky.

'So, any questions?' the man asks at the end of the interview.

'Why, yes,' I reply in my most professional voice. 'What's the social life like at this enterprise?'

The man and woman appear taken aback. I suppose I was meant to ask about the salary, career opportunities or how this start-up is faring since the dot-com crash.

The woman says, 'Well, we have a lolly jar…'

I look to the younger man for help; he sees where I'm headed and replies, 'Yes, and some of us go for Friday night drinks in the pub next door.'

Bingo, that's what I want to hear! Well, what I really want to find out is what the men are like here. I'd like them to parade their single, straight men in front of me and then I'll decide whether I want to work here.

A week later the man calls to tell me I've got the job.

'It was a tough decision. You don't have any useful experience, but I think you'll work hard, so congratulations!'

He's right about my experience. I know nothing about IT, but a couple years back I met a cute consultant who was working on the Y2K project. He told me I'd be good in IT, as I'm not stupid and nerds will listen to me because I'm not unfortunate looking. He also told me about the six-figure salary he was earning and the convertible BMW he was driving. Who am I to ignore the advice of a rich, handsome man?

I've had a few jobs in my time, all involving shuffling bits of paper around, tap, tap, tapping on a computer and talking to morons on the phone. These jobs are bread when I ordered cake, but I'm not sure how to acquire that cake. Oh well, I've negotiated a five-grand pay rise for this particular job, and maybe the BMW will appear someday. At any rate, it'll help out with the higher rent I'm paying for my new house. I ring Cat.

'Guess what, I'm an Operations Support Technician.'

'Woo hoo!' She pauses, then asks, 'Um, is that a good thing or a bad thing?'

'Well, I don't know what the actual work involves, but they have Friday night drinks, so *my* needs are met.'

'Kudos.'

I look over at Daz in the armchair opposite mine, to make sure he's asleep, before switching topics.

'Sooo, how did your date go?'

Recently, Cat's parents have been producing men and demanding she has awkward dinners with them.

'Oh, this one was *brilliant*. He had a massive rising inflection, so everything he said was a question? He spoke about himself the *entire* night, didn't ask me a single thing, then he actually forgot my name!'

I walk with the cordless phone into the kitchen to pour myself a glass of water, then settle back into my chair. 'Ha! Sounds like a winner!'

'Oh, yeah! But on a good note, he didn't have a moustache.'

'Did he have a quiff instead?'

Cat bursts out laughing, and it takes her a bit to compose herself before she can continue. 'He sure did, lady. But the good thing is, I just tell my parents I'm not interested and they take care of things. *I* personally don't have to have uncomfortable conversations with these fellows, just wait around till the next one shows up.'

'Maybe I'll ask your parents to help out next time I need to break up with someone,' I say.

'Ha! Oh, but there was fallout with the last one,' Cat says. 'Remember I had that massive project on and I was working sixty-hour weeks? The guy actually whined to his *mummy* that I wasn't replying to his emails fast enough, so then his mum complained to my mum!'

'What the hell!' My voice rises in shock, which stirs Daz. I pause while he settles back into sleep, then ask, 'But didn't you explain you were slammed at work?'

'Yup, but he reckons his future wife needs to prioritise him above all else! Even Mum agreed he was a muppet.'

'Bloody hell, Cat, you need to cut these losers loose so you have time to meet a normal man!'

'I know it. What about you though? Any potentials?'

'Nah...'

The guy with the music is nowhere to be seen. He's retreated behind a wall of Nickelback, Craig David, Westlife and Bob the Builder. Things are dire.

Our conversation is interrupted by an unearthly snort.

'What the hell's that?' Cat asks.

'Oh, just Daz, snoring in his chair as usual.'

'Tell him I said hi.'

'I will, whenever I get to meet him...'

My new housemate is a bicycle courier who spends his days on the edge of death racing through inner Melbourne's traffic. I've scarcely exchanged two words with him, because as soon as he's home he conks out, sleeping upright in the armchair. Daz is so easygoing he thinks my name is Doris, but it beats living with the Vegetarian. One shocking thing about Daz is that he's twenty-three, my first friend who's younger than me.

Younger people, ugh! I wasn't as devastated as I thought I would be when The Tube folded a couple years back, considering the club had started to become infiltrated by kiddies. These days Cat and I prefer bars, red wine, joints and foreign films to clubs, vodka tonics, pills and sleeping all day. We spend our evenings discussing life in Meyers Place, Spleen Bar or any other little place in Melbourne's laneways that's hidden from bogans.

I finish the call with Cat as I need to head out. Now and Then have a gig tonight. It's at a pub called the Bungalow up the north end of Nicholson Street, and when I arrive the place is full of Kellys. I spot Jack at a small table with his girlfriend Zara and a jug of beer.

'Hello, ladies,' I say.

'How's the coffee, cake, smoke and dope going?' Jack asks, grinning as I light up a menthol cigarette.

'Sweet,' I say. 'How's the babysitting going?'

Jack and Dobbler have recently started a project running soccer clinics for disadvantaged kids.

'Wicked! We've been asked to do two more schools next week.'

'That's great!'

I sit down and help myself to a beer. 'How's it going, Zara?'

Zara is the first girl Jack's really been keen on. She's quiet and serious, so at first I thought she was an odd choice for Jack, but it turns out they balance each other nicely. Besides, the world couldn't cope with two Jacks. Zara is a gun at loading dishwashers and making tea, so she meets the Kelly requirements. I smile at her and she smiles back.

'I'm well. I'm actually really looking forward to hearing your dad play,' she says.

'Me too. I can't believe I ever thought Now and Then were daggy. I'd far rather see them in this little pub than Kylie at the MCG.'

In fact, most of my live music these days is limited to Now and Then and Julie Ann's jazz band. Speak of the devil, Julie Ann arrives, a vision in baby blue and brown.

'Hey Jules!' We wave her over to our table.

'Hi guys, how's it going?'

'Sweet as.'

'How's all that jazz going?' I ask her.

'Pretty good, I've got a gig coming up at the Evelyn if you're keen.'

'As long as no one shushes us when we make obnoxious comments.'

Julie Ann's expression hesitates between annoyance and amusement; in the end she settles with a laugh.

'There's the Doc!' says Jack.

Dr Ivanskiy lumbers through the gathering crowd and stops at our table, staring pointedly at my tee-shirt worn over a long-sleeved top.

'Dot, why do you put your clothes on back to front inside out? Ay yi yi, I dunno about these fashions.'

I'm about to reply that I'm just a right unusual character when I spot Aunty Christine-Paul hovering, and I remember the childhood lecture I received about making fun of people's accents. Instead I say, 'How about a drink, Dr Ivanskiy? My shout. I've got a new job.'

'Put your bloody money away.'

I don't think Dr Ivanskiy's ever let anyone buy him anything in his life, even when he was a penniless refugee from Ukraine. I'm torn between wanting to buy him a drink and defaulting to receiving gifts from him.

The band's tune-up sounds stop and a hush falls over the pub.

'G'day, we're Now and Then,' says Dave, the singer.

'Whoooo!' The Kellys cheer so loud you'd think we were at the Kylie concert. A few non-Kellys in the audience look uncomfortable, but we ignore them.

'Let's get cracking!' Dave says, and they're off with 'It's a Great Day for the Irish'.

'Grand craic, to be sure!' Jack whoops, grabbing a bemused Zara by the hand and dragging her to the dance floor.

The other Kellys are all soon up and dancing. Even Grandma picks up her skirt and wobbles around.

Dr Ivanskiy yells at me excitedly, 'You and me, Dot! You and me!'

He picks me up, but can only manage a few steps. Either he's getting on or I've put on weight. I do a bit of Michael Flatley-style dancing and everyone cheers. I blush, but I'm happy. Soon I'm surrounded by intergenerational green eyes and olive skin, and we're shouting out the lyrics to 'Whiskey in the Jar' so loud that the band can hardly be heard.

Dad jumps down from the stage, grabs Julie Ann, shoves her towards Dave and the two sing together.

Oh, Danny boy, the pipes, the pipes are calling,

From glen to glen, and down the mountain side,

The summer's gone, and all the roses falling,

'Tis you, 'tis you must go and I must bide.

We all join in, more jubilant than mournful, so our singing doesn't really suit the song, but it doesn't matter.

Anyone who came to sit and quietly appreciate some trad music must be sorely disappointed. One man is rushing out and almost crashes into Dr Ivanskiy and me.

Above the ruckus I can hear Dad's foot tapping.

TRACK 23 – LIFE DURING WARTIME

The people who sit near me have left work for the day, so I give Cat a buzz to chat about my new job.

'Do you know what an Operations Support Technician does yet?' she asks.

'Not really. Some sort of nerd stuff. I help out when the servers go down on each other.'

Cat giggles, then asks, 'Dot, is this really the job for you?'

'Yes, Cat, this is the job for me. And the reason being is that everyone here is under thirty and up for going out any night of the week. Plus, we're about to sign a massive account which means huge bonuses and blow jobs for all. Who cares about the actual work! Anyway, I gotta go, it's beer o'clock.'

This company, with its plethora of single men, is my El Dorado! I am a little concerned that I have no clue how to do my actual job, but Rebecca, the girl I'm replacing, has some helpful advice, which she dispenses during her farewell drinks in the pub next door to the office.

'Be nice to the systems administrators: smile at them and show interest in their World of Warcraft stories. If the customer service team nags you, tell them to fuck off. Don't be good at mundane tasks, because you don't wanna be stuck with them. Demand a promotion every six months, whether you deserve one or not. Ensure you make at least one work-related call on your mobile a month, then expense the lot. And most importantly, when you're out for drinks, the senior person always pays.'

We're sitting side by side in a booth, crammed with half the company, and Rebecca's talking low so they don't hear. I lean in to listen above the din.

'Thanks, great tips,' I say. 'But I'm still none the wiser about how to do my job.'

The systems administrators show up, clutching whiskey and cola beverages. Most of them are a little tubby and don't fit into the booth, so they stand beside the table. I'm sitting on the edge, so smile hello at them.

'What're you talking about?' this guy, Ian, wants to know.

'I'm hoping I'll be able to do my job once Rebecca leaves,' I reply.

'Oh, just ask us whenever you're stuck,' he says.

'Thanks! You guys are awesome.'

'Do you play World of Warcraft?' Ian asks, swigging his brown drink.

'Ah, no…should I be taking it up?' Computer games aren't my forte; I'll have to ask Jack. My drink's empty, so I stand up to head to the bar.

'Nah, don't worry, you're a girl,' Ian says.

I'm about to arc up when the account managers arrive and I'm lost in a blur of business glamour. I'm standing awkwardly between the table and bench, but I don't move as I watch the guys make their way towards us. They make me feel the same way Martin Jones once did. They're so handsome, with their laptops slung over their shoulders, business cards in their pockets, trips to Sydney and loud-voiced conversations about all they've achieved. They're the golden boys of the company, allowed to get away with eccentric behaviour and piss-taking because we're all depending on the deals they sign.

'Where's Trev?' they boom at us.

Speechless, I point out a booth at the other end of the pub where the alpha account manager, Trevor Cook, is holding court. He's been there since three, flirting with girls and minding a seat for his buddies. Trevor is chasing the company's Moby Dick: the Eksnep account.

Trevor is bald and stocky with a hoop earring and a gold tooth; he wears a *Simpsons* tie and has a silver Nokia clipped to his belt. He's allowed to do whatever he likes, because he's going to get this account over the line and he's the one who has to sacrifice his personal life, flying all over the world, 'bending over and parting his cheeks' to the Eksnep execs. No one bats an eyelid when Trevor shows up at work drunk, stomping around yelling at people, calling Management a bunch of pencil dicks and insisting he will only report to the CEO.

One of the systems administrators is saying something to me about World of Warcraft, but the pub band starts playing so I can't hear. I hit the dance floor with the customer service mob, and bop along to some pub standards – 'Brown Eyed Girl', 'You're the Voice', 'Sweet Home Alabama', 'Under the Bridge' and 'Mister Jones'. It's dire, yet I enjoy it. I enjoy it because I'm full of Carlton Draught and because sometimes I don't want to be all alone with my cool music in Major Tom's capsule.

I dance until the band takes a break, drink another drink, then slide into a spare spot at Trevor's booth. He hasn't budged the entire evening, not even to go to the toilet.

'D'you know how much I earn?' Trevor asks, slurring slightly.

I assume he's talking to Jake, the other account manager sitting there, but when I look up, he's staring right at me. I feel my face go red.

'Um, no...'

'A hundred and twennie grand, including bonuses. Is that enough for all I do?'

'That's three times my salary!'

Trevor doesn't hear and starts talking at Jake. I sit back, sipping my beer, observing him. He's wearing acid wash jeans and a chambray shirt, and I'm pretty sure he votes Liberal. Trevor lights up a cigarette and orders Jake to fetch him another bourbon and Coke. He puffs away, then notices me sitting quietly.

'What's your name again?'

'Dot.'

'What do you think of me, Dot?'

'Um, I hardly know you.'

Trevor finds this amusing and laughs loud. Then he leans in and whispers, 'I'm a very insecure man.'

His glazed blue eyes water up a little and I frantically think of something to say. 'Maybe you need a holiday?'

'Maybe I do, maybe I do. You know, you're an interesting person to talk to, Dot.'

This time I definitely can't think of a reply, so I take a gulp of beer. Jordan never mentioned I was interesting.

Jake returns with Trevor's drink and I'm ignored for the rest of the night.

The next week in the office, Trevor winks at me when he passes by, and allocates me shitty tasks, like printing out his presentations because he hasn't worked out how to connect to the colour printer. He thanks me by making the same noise people make to gee-up a horse. How can a person be so uncouth yet so intriguing at the same time? The more I know of him, the less of him I can work out. I like the mystery.

Finally, after a lot of swaggering, ranting, bending over and personal sacrifices, Trevor signs Eksnep. He grins like a little boy and thanks everyone for their help, even me, so I guess all the printing paid off. I feel happy to see him happy. We cram into the boardroom for the company announcement and cartons of UDLs are produced.

I drink UDLs, spilling one on the boardroom table, and listen and nod as various colleagues tell me their thoughts.

'Trevor's the bomb, he's kept us all in a job for the next five years,' says Jake.

I wasn't worried about losing my job, and yet I feel grateful to Trevor.

'Trevor's kind of a cutie, isn't he?' Petra, the receptionist, says.

He's the cutest unattractive man I've ever met.

'Who cares as long as we get free drinks and on-call allowances,' says Ian.

I like free drinks, but hope I'm not asked to go on-call.

'It's going to cost us more to support this client than any revenue we'll ever earn from them,' Maxine, the financial controller, says.

I don't know what that means.

Trevor bursts into the room and shouts, 'I'll get a first class trip to America out of this!'

'Um, yeah cool,' I say, and grab another drink.

Once we finish the UDLs, Trevor announces there's a party back at his place.

I'm not sure if I'm invited, but as I'm shuffling towards the door Trevor catches my eye and says, 'Where d'you think you're going, young lady? We need pretty girls at this party, otherwise it's just me and these cunts.'

I blush at his language: the c-word and calling me pretty. It feels like I've been shot right through like a bolt of blue.

We tumble out of taxis into Trevor's house, which is full of IKEA furniture. There's a mirror lying flat on the dining table and a cabinet full of liquor – Jim Beam, Bundy and Jack Daniels. The only mixer Trevor has is Coke, which I won't drink because of the teeth and gut-rotting.

'You got any beer?' I ask.

'Check the fridge.'

The fridge is full of beer. In fact, I can't see any food in there except a forlorn slice of pizza. Everyone else is mixing drinks – the Coke and alcohol smell like cashed-up boganity. Trevor's running around, waving the Eksnep contract in his hand.

'Woo hoo! *It's the dawning of the Age of Aquarius!* he sings.

'Dude, you got any music?' someone asks.

'Yeah, it's all on the computer. Dot, you know about music, make us a playlist.'

Wow, he noticed I like music! Frankly, if Trevor noticed I had a pimple I'd be flattered. As I look through Trevor's MP3 files I realise it's doubtful that he's the man with the music. I compile a playlist of the least offensive pub standards, kicking off with 'Khe Sanh'. Everyone's singing along, and I realise these boisterous men in their flashy suits are just like my family.

I soon find out what the mirror is doing on the table, when Trevor beckons me over. 'Have some speed?'

Powder has never entered my nose, but if benign old truckies can do it, then I'm sure it'll do me no harm. Trevor cuts a couple of lines with his corporate Amex and hands me a rolled up hundred-dollar note.

'Ladies first.'

It takes me a few snorts to finish the line, but at least no one laughs at me. I stand back to analyse the effect, but can't feel anything other than the buzz of UDLs and beer. I add 'My Generation' to the top of the playlist to see if that'll get me in the mood, but I'm feeling nothing.

'Um, is this shit?' I'm reluctant to ask in case it's the best stuff ever and I've made a public embarrassment of myself, but blame the alcohol for making me blurt the question out.

'Of course it's shit!' booms Trevor.

'Next time I'll just have a coffee,' I venture a slight joke.

He roars with laughter, then whispers to me, 'I wouldn't know what to do with substances of any real quality…none of this is real, you know.' Trevor gestures around the room and tosses the Eksnep contract on the table. *Wow, he's so smart!*

'Like *The Matrix?*' I ask.

He laughs again, and I raise my eyebrows and grin. He winks back at me and I feel like swooning, but not from the speed.

♫ ♫ ♫

Trevor's one of those people who talks a lot outside work; he tells me about what he's doing, work gossip and what he thinks about people. According to Trevor, most people are living proof that you don't need a long neck to be a goose. He's not very talkative in the office though. Oh, he'll talk if he needs something, but he doesn't like to chat, not even when I join him for a cigarette break. He's got his mobile phone glued to his ear most of the time anyway. He's the most interesting person I've ever worked with.

Signing Eksnep was the achievement of the decade for our company and our competitors are majorly pissed off, but the comments made by Maxine at the celebratory drinks turn out to be accurate. The entire company is constantly stressed, trying to meet the client's impossible demands.

If their emails sit there for a second longer than the agreed time, Trevor will stalk into the room, red-faced with the muscles in his neck twitching and yell, 'You're all a bunch of cunts and I quit!'

Jake and the other account managers have to calm him down, which generally means buying him drinks.

After working more overtime than I care for, I work out ways to fudge the Eksnep response requirements. I tell them their issue is in the process of being resolved, escalated, whatever. I send them half-completed answers to their questions, surrounded by flowing prose and technical terminology I've found on Google. My emails are so mystifying it takes them a couple of days to realise I haven't addressed the problem, but that buys me time to actually resolve things.

Just as a grey doubt is starting to shade my work days, the client emails Trevor to tell him I'm the bomb. Trevor thanks me by giving me a stack of stickers with the Eksnep logo on it. As soon as I've been here six months, I'm asking for that promotion.

TRACK 24 – ONLY THE GOOD DIE YOUNG

As I walk home from work, weaving through the crowds, I hear a voice. 'Excuse me, do you have any spare change?'

'Nope.'

I don't look at the person, but as I'm continuing on my way, he calls my name. I turn and notice he's familiar in a long-ago way, a child's round face distorted into an adult's. An adult who doesn't know what to make of this world.

'Remember me?'

It's Zack from primary school.

'It's Zack. From primary school,' he says.

'Zack…How's it going?'

He's shapeless, in a fleecy green tracksuit, but he doesn't have that greasy sheen homeless people have, so I wonder what he's doing begging for money.

'I'm well. I have been looking in a comic book shop and now I would like to catch my train home, but I've lost my Metcard. I live in South Yarra with my mum.'

'Ah, that's a shame you lost your ticket.'

'Yes, it is. Do you have any hobbies and interests?'

Zack is a close talker, his big nose almost touches my face. 'Um…' I edge away, but Zack draws in even nearer.

'I enjoy drawing and reading comic books,' he says.

'Cool, that's nice.' I take another step back.

'Do you want to keep in contact?'

'I'd like to, Zack, but I'm moving to England.' I rummage around in my purse and produce three dollars. 'Here, buy yourself a ticket home.'

'Thank you. Bye-bye.' And away Zack goes, hobbling down Flinders Street like a man three times his age.

Why do I always tell Zack I'm going to England? Is it more than just trying to get rid of him? 'London Calling' has been the soundtrack to my life since before I even had a memory. Should I listen to the call?

I shrug it off and as I continue walking, I SMS Cat.

Guess who I saw?

Robbie Williams

LOL! Zack from skool

OMG! Cute?

Nah. Bad clothes, still weird

LOL!

Bar Open 2nite?

Yep cu there @ 9

I seem to be in a bar every night of the week. Well, what would I do at home, watch television? In fact, when our television blew up, Daz and I didn't bother to get a new one. *Oh wow, I'm sooo cut up about missing all those* Big Brother *episodes…* When we're home, Daz sleeps in the armchair and I sort out MP3s on my computer. To be honest, when I'm at home I don't feel that good. With only Daz's snoring for company, I get that same feeling as when I have the dream about being abandoned in Major Tom's capsule. It's blank and empty and my heart palpitates. I throw pillows at Daz to wake him up for a talk, but he just grunts in his sleep. That's why I go out.

When I arrive at Bar Open, Cat's already there, nursing a small glass of red wine. We heard they drink wine in water glasses in Paris.

'House red in a small water glass and a bowl of wasabi peas,' I tell the bartender.

'Whaddup, bitch?' Cat asks when I sit down opposite her.

'Nothin' much. Went for a run around the block after work, but two hundred metres in and I was spent. How was your date?'

'Oh my god, Dot, this guy was such a fool. He wanted to meet in Starbucks, for fuck's sake! Who does he think I am?'

I'm shocked on Cat's behalf. 'What a jerk! He could have at least taken you for a *noice Choinese.*'

Cat laughs. She doesn't worry too much about the string of unfortunate men she dates, and she takes the arguments with her parents in her stride.

'Something will come up at some stage and it better be a hot man's dick!' she says.

We swivel our heads, scanning the bar to see if there's anyone here worth talking to, but there's not.

'So how's Trevor going?' Cat asks.

I sigh as I feel my heart rate go up at the mention of his name.

'I can't stop thinking about him, Cat. He's so loud and crass, but when he talks to me I feel like he can make all the shitty stuff go away.'

'But he's a prick…'

Cat believes if someone is a prick, then they should be terminated from your life, no questions asked. I don't think she gets those alone feelings of being stuck in space.

'Has anything ever happened with him?' she asks.

'Nah…I hover around at the end of the night, but he seems more interested in talking about work than hooking up. Maybe if I jumped on him something would happen…'

'I reckon you can do better, Dot.'

Cat doesn't really know Trevor, though.

Every now and then I go on a date with some guy I meet at a bar or a party.

They're nice guys, gentlemen who open the car door and pay for the meal, but they're meek and wishy-washy. Trevor is the only guy on the scene who has oomph; he's the only guy who'll admit to playing the game even though none of it is real. There's a planet somewhere where the real Trevor lives. If I can work out how to fly my space capsule properly, I could find him.

Cat says, 'I don't think he's The One, Dot.'

I shrug French-style and light up a menthol, just to avoid speaking for thirty seconds. On paper Trevor isn't The One, but what if I do fly over to that planet and find the real Trevor? The real Trevor is probably comfortable in his own skin and cares about other people; the real Trevor doesn't need an Eksnep account or bottles of booze to feel happy and the real Trevor would probably love a person like me.

I doubt Cat will buy this, so instead I say, 'It's just a crush. It'll pass.'

♪ ♪ ♪

I dream about being in Major Tom's capsule again, but Trevor and his planet are nowhere to be seen. As I'm peering out my window, searching for him, I'm jolted back to Earth by the *Grange Hill* theme. I open one eye and check my mobile; Cat's calling.

'What's wrong with you, sister? It's fucking seven thirty in the morning!'

For some reason Cat's voice is small, like how she spoke when we were five. 'I just got off the phone with Fleur.'

'Oh, how's engaged life?'

Fleur recently got engaged, or as she put it, 'I'm dropping out of the workforce, I've bagged me a lawyer!'

My question goes unanswered. 'Remember Martin Jones?'

'Of course I do! I had the biggest crush on him, but, alas, my one chance of love was ruined by Jack tagging along on our date.'

'Well, he's dead. He took his life.'

Where did he take it? 'What?!?'

'He slit his wrists in the bath.' Cat's crying.

I picture a young man lying motionless in a bath of blood. I can't reconcile this with the smiling boy in his 501s and white Bonds tee-shirt, who was too polite to play Spin the Bottle. It must be a joke.

I arrange to meet Cat after work in St Kilda. At work I'm on autopilot, scarcely responding, even when Trevor says hi. I answer my emails and get out of there as quickly as I can.

Martin Jones is dead and now I know how it feels to be core-shocked. Dead, what is dead? I've never known anyone to die. Grandpa Kelly went before I was born, so although it's left a legacy on my family, I wasn't around for the actual death part. Do dead people go to heaven, are they born again, do they rot in the ground, do they walk around talking to Haley Joel Osment, or are they floating up there in space all alone in a capsule?

The weather's still nice, so I meet Cat at St Kilda beach. She's got a bottle of red wine and a joint.

She gives me a watery, wintery smile, hands me the joint and says, 'I thought this might be in order.'

I take a drag and ask, 'D'you know what happened?'

'Not really. His mum found him. He hadn't really done much since university, so maybe he was depressed and all.'

'Did he think about what that would do to his mum, finding him in the bath like that?'

'I guess he was so caught up he probably wasn't thinking.'

'Had you seen him since school?'

'Not really. I saw him at the five-year reunion and he seemed just the same – charming, handsome, a little distant.'

'I had such a crush on him.'

It's a weak thing to say, but what isn't in these circumstances? So tragic, taken so young, heartbreaking, no one saw it coming. These are just platitudes.

'I can't picture him as anything other than a fifteen-year-old kid who liked *The Lost Boys*, Public Enemy and skateboarding,' I say.

'Me too, but he always was kinda aloof, wasn't he? I mean, he was sociable and talked to everyone, but if it was up to him, I've a feeling he'd rather be left alone and not talk to anyone, even back then.'

'Like how he never indulged in Spin the Bottle antics or had a girlfriend?'

'Yeah, and he was like that at the school reunion. No hint of a girlfriend, or boyfriend. Everyone else was excited to see each other, but Martin Jones seemed like the Queen, smiling and chatting with everyone, but not really fussed about being there.'

We pass the wine and joint back and forth, our lips growing stained and our eyes red.

'He was very smart though,' I remark.

'Yeah, dux of the school and then getting into medicine. I don't think he felt any pressure though. He didn't have to do much to do well.'

'Maybe everything came too easily to him? Sports, the academic stuff, being good looking and popular. Maybe he never found something to struggle against?'

'At the end of the day, we don't know. We didn't know him at all,' Cat says.

'Imagine him taking a razor and slicing open his wrists, vertically cos he wasn't mucking around, then lying in the bath watching the water turn pink, then red. Feeling pain, then cold, then numb and then just falling asleep forever.'

Cat's eyebrows wrinkle. 'Dot, you're getting a little descriptive.'

I imagine Martin Jones, stuck in his space capsule, looking out the window and seeing everyone waving and talking at him. He could work out what they were saying by lip reading, but when he answered, they smiled and nodded but they couldn't hear what he said. How long can you go on with nobody able to understand you? Martin Jones flew his capsule farther and farther away, until one day we lost all contact with him.

Cat's crying, but I don't have any tears. I feel empty. I stare at the flat, grey water stretched across the bay and I know why Martin Jones did it.

A man walks past with his dog and asks, 'Are you girls smoking pot?'

We revert to fifteen-year-old schoolgirls and say, 'Nooo!'

'Come on, let's get something to eat,' I suggest, and we turn our backs on the grey sea and thoughts of Martin Jones.

We find a little place on Acland Street that's transitioning from coffee and cake to dinner and booze. It's packed, and Cat scouts for a spare table while I fumble in my bag for my cigarettes. Someone taps me on the back.

'Take my table,' he says. 'I'm leaving.'

'Cool, thanks,' I say.

He has a kind voice that's somehow recognisable. There's something about him that makes me look up, but he's already gone.

It's inevitable. That night I dream of Major Tom's capsule and wake up sweating. If only my television wasn't broken, I could stick on a DVD to relax myself. I think of *The Matrix*, which reminds me of Trevor. If Trevor was mine, all these scary thoughts and dreams would fly away and our life would be full of music.

TRACK 25 – EVER FALLEN IN LOVE?

Amanda's getting married and the engagement party is at the Train Tracks Hotel. The pub's changed since I was a kid; it's now slick and full of cashed up bogans.

I buzz Cat to discuss. 'D'you reckon we have to go?'

'*I* don't, but isn't Amanda one of your best friends? C'mon Dot, it'll be fun!'

'I'm not so sure. The Train Tracks is full of douches and the music's crap.'

'Oh, it's not that bad. Besides, it'll be good to take a break from going to cool bars to drink red wine and judge people. Let's go to a daggy bar to drink red wine and judge people.'

Maybe Cat has a point. Much as I enjoy going to bars that are too hard for suburban people to find, it could be fun to try something different. Besides, how would I like it if someone didn't go to my engagement party just because they didn't care for the venue? Well, if I got engaged everyone would be so amazed they'd all show up out of sheer curiosity.

I arrive and scope out the front of Train Tracks. The crashing train is gone and the façade is painted a clean white that covers all character the old building once had.

I hear Cat's voice from behind. 'Geez, you have wicked taste in clothes!'

We're wearing virtually identical outfits: low-rise cords, halter tops and glasses with pink lenses.

'So do you, my dear,' I reply. 'So do you.'

Inside, we're surrounded by striped polos with popped collars clutching frozen margaritas. We weave through these personages to the back, where Amanda has a couple of tables reserved. I peck her on the cheek and congratulate her. It might be one of the last times I see Amanda before she's lost to the suburbs, two kids and an oversized four-wheel drive. When I look down the years, I can see that her destiny was set out from an early age, with her mild-mannered desire for early nights and not doing anything too controversial. Amanda will get married in a church, change her surname and make sandwiches for her husband to take to work. I try to alter this trajectory by offering her a menthol cigarette.

'No thanks,' she says, taking a sip from what appears to be a glass of Coke with no alcohol.

Cat raises her right eyebrow and I look in that direction to see a group of clean-cut yet good-looking guys. I nod my approval, and as more of Amanda's guests arrive we inch towards the group of guys. Once we're within striking distance, Cat gives them a big smile so they know it's safe to talk to us, but before they can, I feel a tap on my shoulder.

'Excuse me ladeez, but I'm getting an awkward vibe from one of youse,' says a character in a black Adidas tracksuit.

'Oh!' I say, taken aback that he'd be allowed entry in such an outfit.

He continues, 'You see, I'm a part-time psychic and I can tell that one of you had a bad experience a couple years ago.'

I pretend to cough.

'Wow!' says Cat, her lips twitching. 'That's amazing you can tell that!'

'When you think about it, everyone's had a bad experience at some point in their lives,' I say.

'I'm Terry,' the man says, unperturbed by my scepticism. 'So, what do you ladeez do for a living?'

'I work for an insurance company,' says Cat.

'I work in IT.'

'Interesting,' says Terry, even though it's not. 'How much do youse earn?'

'Excuse me?'

Cat can't control herself any longer and bursts out laughing. I'm shocked. Telling people how much you earn is like telling people about a poo you've done; some matters are strictly private. Trevor talks about how much he earns, but because I like him, I don't mind. As for Terry, I wish he'd buzz off.

'Well, whatever youse earn, I'll double it. I'm gunna open a nightclub in Sydney Road with three exciting levels. The first level will play hip hop and R&B, the second will play eighties classics and the third will be a VIP lounge with a spa. If youse work there, I'll give ya a company car. Mercedes.'

We raise our eyebrows.

'I'll buy youse a drink,' Terry says and staggers off.

'What the hell is with this guy?' I ask Cat.

'Who knows, but I've always wanted a Mercedes,' she laughs.

'And what exactly does he expect us to do in his VIP spa? Cheeky bugger!'

Terry returns, drinking from a jug of beer. He catches my eye and stumbles. The jug flies out of his hands and beer splashes onto my crotch, making it look like I've pissed myself. Cat hoots with laughter. A bewildered Terry is on his knees, way too close to my crotch area, but before he can stand, one of the good-looking guys appears beside us.

'Sorry to interrupt, but do you girls need rescuing?' he asks.

'Yes, please!' we say.

The guy leads us to the dance floor and says, 'I'm Raj.'

'Do I know you?' Cat asks.

They work out that their dads are old uni mates, so they would have run into each other at various family functions.

'How come my parents didn't try to set you up with me?' she asks.

'Oh, they probably did, but I've been worming out of those blind dates.'

'Well, you missed out!' Cat laughs.

Raj laughs too. So that's what it's like when you meet someone and you click right away – easy, funny and comfortable. I have beer spilt all over my pants by Terry and Cat meets a great guy like Raj. Yet for some reason, I don't mind. At school, I was devastated when Cat announced she was going out with Joshua Hawkins, but tonight I'm happy for her, especially after all those terrible dates she's had to go on.

'Can't Get You Out of My Head' comes on, and Cat, Raj and I do the synchronised dance moves, much to the horror of Amanda and her pals. Terry stumbles to the edge of the dance floor, but he's too drunk to manoeuvre past the crowd. We spend the rest of the evening chatting with Raj and his friends, who are all nice, but I have Trevor-coloured glasses on.

At the end of the night, Raj asks Cat for her number, which she gives him, along with a little peck on the cheek.

'How come you didn't snog him?' I ask when we're in the taxi.

'Because I want this one coming back for more.'

The Steps version of 'Tragedy' comes on the radio.

'Poor Terry, he really was a tragedy,' Cat laughs. 'I wish him all the best with his nightclub endeavours though.'

'If he's a part-time psychic, surely he knows we won't be working in that club.'

We both giggle.

♫ ♫ ♫

Raj does call Cat and they go on proper dates. They go out for nice dinners, not just coffees or a drink in the pub. Raj isn't a total metrosexual though; he's also up for coming out for a beer with us. He's affable and slots into our circle quickly.

Before I know it, they're officially an item. I thought Cat would become gooey and spend less time with me, but she's just the same.

♫ ♫ ♫

It's Friday night, and I meet Cat and Fleur at this new bar in Flinders Lane. The brown and orange décor is designed by Edie, who's moved from fashion to interior design. There are no doors, just beaded hangings. With that and the lounge music playing in the background, the place gives off the vibe that Austin Powers will burst through the entrance at any moment.

'Raj is a great guy, innit,' says Fleur, who's still keeping up the pretence of an English accent.

Cat replies, 'You know, I feel really happy with Raj and I'm pretty sure he's The One, but I don't feel butterflies. Why d'you think that is?'

'Maybe because you know where you stand with him, you don't need the butterflies?' I suggest.

Cat thinks for a bit. 'Yeah… You know what, I think I'm gunna tell my parents.'

'You sure?'

In Cat's family, that's a big deal. Once you announce you've got a boyfriend, you're pretty much expected to get married. I know then that Cat's life is about to change forever. There's a certain path that most people follow. I thought Cat might be different, but she's not. It's only me who's different.

I feel like we're running down the platform at Flinders Street Station, and Cat, who's just ahead of me, makes it on to the train, but I miss it. It's peak hour though, and another one is coming soon.

Although, lately I've been wondering which platform my train departs from. Sheets of sameness surround Melbourne and my crush on Trevor is going nowhere. I keep thinking about London. It's still calling. Maybe I'll go there and hang out with Clive James, Kylie and the other expats. Maybe the guy with the music is over there. At any rate, I can pick up a new accent and a new lease on life, like Fleur did.

♫ ♫ ♫

It's unclear whether Cat's parents like Raj or whether they're just relieved she finally found someone, but she has their blessing and arrangements are made. Less than six months pass from the day she met him till the day a wedding is announced, but no one feels like it's too fast.

'Things won't change,' Cat assures me. 'We'll still go out and stuff. More so, cos I won't be living with my parents.'

'Yeah, I know,' I reply. 'The thing is, maybe I'm going to go overseas for a while. To London. I sort of want to shake things up a bit.'

'Oh? I'll miss you!'

'Come for a visit?'

'You know I will, sister.'

♬ ♬ ♬

Cat wears four different saris on her twelve-hour long wedding day, and in each one she looks like a princess and not at all like herself. Not at all like the little girl in her blue-and-white chequered uniform, not at all like the wild teenager experimenting with anything she could lay her hands on, not at all like my clubbing and drinking buddy and my best friend.

'I'm still here,' she tells me, from underneath layers of makeup and gold jewellery.

'I hope so!'

We hug and stay like that until one of Cat's aunties moves me along.

♬ ♬ ♬

I don't see much of Cat for the next few months, as she's involved in post-wedding, honeymoon and house-purchasing activities. She and Raj buy a friendly-looking weatherboard in Preston.

We stand out the front of her new house. It's flat and square, but it gives off a welcoming air of barbeques, polished floorboards and gardening.

'Is Preston the burbs?' Cat asks, slightly worried.

I think for a moment. 'Well…it's not that far away. It's a nice house and it's yours, so who cares where the hell it is.'

'True point. Come over for a barbeque?'

♬ ♬ ♬

It turns out that Raj is an excellent barbequer and consummate carnivore.

'Jesus Raj, where are the salads?' Cat asks.

Fleur, Edie and I are staring at a table laden with chicken skewers, steak, sausages, a small bowl of olives and loaf of bread.

'Salads?' Raj is confused. 'We've got to keep up our iron levels, girls!'

He also has a well-stocked selection of beer, and I select something from a local brewery to help wash down all the meat.

The Saturday nights that were once devoted to The Tube now become Cat and Raj's barbeque nights. Every week they invite over a selection of people to try some marinade that Raj has concocted. I'm present for all these occasions, and I've developed a new practice of driving home before midnight, after no more than two drinks. Life is calm, but I feel something brewing.

On a quiet night at home, I rifle through the files of MP3s I've downloaded from Napster. My music collection is immaculate, but I don't know what to do with it or who to show. I'm bored, so I go for a walk instead. I walk down the laneways and along the narrow streets, gazing at the little workmen's cottages. At first I'm walking briskly, but soon I slow down and take everything in. Something about these old houses makes me feel like I can breathe properly. I continue walking, contemplating my next steps.

TRACK 26 – LONDON CALLING

Two aeroplanes crash into the Twin Towers and everyone is in shock. Except me. I'm too excited because I've booked a one-way flight to London.

The people at work wish me well, but don't offer me a promotion in an attempt to make me stay. Trevor doesn't even show up at my leaving party. I pack the giant jar of Vegemite and Discman they gave me in my suitcase.

Mum, Dad and Jack see me off at the airport. Mum cries, Jack doesn't make any jokes and Dad says nothing about contribution. I wonder if I've made the right decision and I open my eyes wide so that water doesn't drip out.

'You'll have a wonderful time,' Mum says.

'Yeah, you will,' Dad and Jack echo.

I hug the three of them tight, but I no longer feel the urge to cry.

I sit on a plane for twenty-four hours, watching movie after movie. I've never been this far from home before and it feels good to sit in a cocoon, devoid of time and place, so that I can emerge hazy but ready for a new life.

As the plane lands at Heathrow Airport, I look out the window at the ground staff waiting in their gloves and beanies. The intro to 'London Calling' plays in my head and I smile. Fatigue hits me as I shuffle towards arrivals, but I don't feel as tired as the passport control staff look. It's like I was at a pretty good party the night before. I'm slightly hungover, but there's an even better party tonight. The combined grogginess and excitement have the same effect as a milky alcoholic drink.

Swaying slightly with the imaginary White Russian in my system, I follow the rainbow of nationalities to the Tube, absorbing accents I've only ever heard on television. The sight of the London Underground logo pushes some of my grogginess away.

♪ ♪ ♪

The train emerges from the tunnel and I blink at the bright grey sky. Row after row of brown terrace houses flash by. Everything looks so familiar, but it also feels like I've arrived on a different planet. I look around at my fellow passengers grinning, but they refuse to meet my eyes. They're already wearing coats, but not with beanies and gloves yet. I hope my Melbourne clothes are warm enough until I get a job.

I navigate my way to a share house I saw on Gumtree. All the houses are the same as those I saw from the train, brown brick boxes with garbage bags on the side of the road. I find number 172 and watch a rat sniff at the rubbish. Even from outside I can hear *The Simpsons* theme, so I bang on the front door as hard as I can. It's opened by a guy my age dressed in board shorts and a tank top. *Great, I've flown halfway across the world and the first person I meet is a bloody Australian.*

'Hi!' His voice is cheery, so I forgive him.

'James?'

'That's my name, don't wear it out.'

'Ha! I'm Dot. I emailed you about the room.'

'Sweet as. Come in and take a look.'

James shows me through the house, which is a dusty warren of small rooms. The stairs are narrow and the carpet balding. The walls are covered in posters of the crooked Nirvana smile, surfing scenes and paintings by someone who's not quite a painter. I take off my jumper, as they've set the central heating to stifling. In each room, someone comes to the door and we're introduced.

'How many people live here?' I ask.

James counts on his fingers, then says, 'Eight. Oh, and the dosser in the lounge room. Nine. Ten with you.'

He shows me a tiny room crammed with a single bed, chest of drawers and wardrobe. It's clean though, and someone's left bedding neatly folded on top of the drawers.

'Nice,' I say.

'Yeah,' James agrees. 'This is the good room. It's the only room that people aren't sharing.'

'People share rooms this size?'

'Sure. Anything to save money for travelling. London's expensive.'

We head back down the stairs; they're so steep I wonder if I'll be able to navigate them when I'm drunk. We crack open a Stella and drink it in the kitchen.

'Any questions?' James asks.

'Yeah. Are the people who live here a sociable bunch?'

'We sure are, mate. We leave messages on the noticeboard if anyone's doing something fun, and whoever wants can tag along. Check it out.'

The noticeboard's full of messages and invitations, much nicer than the notes the Vegetarian used to leave. Something catches my eye, like a gold coin on the footpath.

'You're going to see Joe Strummer and the Mescaleros?'

James sips his beer then wipes his mouth with the back of his hand. 'Yep. Never heard of 'em, but one of the guys got tickets. It's not for a few months, so you could prolly still get one.'

'Wow…' I breathe.

'So, you keen on the room?'

'Yeah, but I guess you're interviewing other people?'

I was planning to stay at a hostel tonight, but I really like the possibilities of this house. I fiddle with the tab on my can. The jetlag and beer have taken their effect, and I hope I don't need to venture out into the cold again.

'Don't worry.' James strolls into the hallway and yells, 'Should we let Dot move in?'

'Yes!' a chorus replies.

♫ ♫ ♫

The next morning I'm out of my new house early. London is grey and green, an exciting new colour scheme compared with Melbourne's blues and yellows. At last I've come to where the music is. The first thing I do is find an internet café and buy a ticket for the Mescaleros concert. I want to be there right now, but I'm also enjoying the delicious anticipation.

I send Cat and Jack emails to let everyone know I've arrived safely and glimpse at a couple of job sites. I can't concentrate on the mundanity though. In a drum beat, I'm out on the street and into the nearest Tube station. I study the map on the wall to find out how to get to the source – the place where music and fashion and trains crashing out of walls began. I go to the Kings Road.

At first glance, nothing is left, just bland boutiques and gastropubs, but if I half shut my eyes so everything is out of focus, I can see them – the punks, the teddy boys, the beautiful people. The man with the music is with them too, beckoning me onwards down the road. A sour-looking teenage girl brushes past me and I'm pretty sure I can hear Nelly emanating from her Discman. I turn on some music in my head to block him out. Johnny Rotten sneers at Nelly as I cross the road humming 'Anarchy in the UK'.

I still can't believe I'm actually in London. All the music I care about was born in this city. I grin to myself and for some reason I start running. I run to the beat of every world-changing song that was created here. They're all playing in my head at once; it's almost too much to bear. And when I stop to catch my breath, I spit discreetly, a communion for the punks.

♫ ♫ ♫

At night, my new housemates take me to the local Irish pub for 'welcome to London' drinks. They shout me a pint of something called a snakebite. It's revolting, and yet I nod my head appreciatively in time with the Gorillaz, who are playing through the speakers.

I return the round and am shocked at the price of a few pints.

'Best not to convert,' James says, as he sucks away on a cigarette. 'Our western pacific pesos aren't much good here.'

'Guess I better get a job pretty quick,' I say, sipping on my snakebite. 'Mmm, maybe this drink isn't so bad after all.'

♬ ♬ ♬

I've been called in for an interview. I'm not sure what the job entails but that doesn't matter, as long as it doesn't infringe on my spare time, which I plan on dedicating to music. The guy interviewing me looks and sounds like Hugh Grant. I can't believe real people actually talk like this.

'You'll be working in a colourful team,' Hugh tells me. 'Do you think you can handle that?'

'How do you mean?'

'Well, there's Todd, who spends his working days online gambling. Don't ever lend him money. Then there's Freya, who takes a day off every time she has a fight with her boyfriend, which is at least once a week. And there's Aaron, who goes to the toilet at three every afternoon and emerges talking a hundred miles a minute, if you know what I mean. Do you have any questions?'

'Yes. What's the social life like at this place?'

'Friday night drinks are mandatory.'

After my first day, I'm taken to the local Wetherspoons for more welcome drinks.

'Why not get the whole bottle?' suggests an advertisement on the toilet door. Why not, indeed? Freya and I buy a bottle of wine each.

♬ ♬ ♬

I'm constantly meeting someone new, whether it's housemates, people at work or randoms in the pub. People I've only just met invite me to see gigs, go to parties, fly to Europe for a weekend, or participate in threesomes. I don't say yes to all the invitations, but it's flattering to be asked. There are no quiet moments where I can stop and ruminate, and even in my sleep I'm too busy to dream about Major Tom's capsule.

I push through grim-faced crowds wearing dowdy anoraks. I ignore them and work my way deeper into the music. It keeps me warm as winter arrives. My excitement mounts, and for the first few months my clenching stomach won't let me eat anything aside from pappadums and lime pickle.

There's The Good Mixer in colourful Camden, where art students invented Britpop. There are the fashion boutiques of Chelsea, where a Fagin and his Nancy turned their gaggle of urchins into a punk band that set the universe alight. There's the riverside, where Terry and Julie fell in love, and where Joe Strummer lived. London is calling me from every pub, chip shop and grotty terrace house. I don't need to look for anything, I just need to consume.

The history and the music soak into me, mixing dreams with reality. Everywhere I go, I hear a hundred thousand guitars and drums and voices that don't need to sing with an American accent. All my time, all my money, is devoted to music. I catch glimpses of the man with the music everywhere, but he's elusive as always. I don't mind, though. He shows me all he has to show and I store it away in the part of my mind reserved for precious treasures.

As the weather gets colder and my layers of clothing increase, I'm caught in such a buzz that I almost forget about Joe Strummer and the Mescaleros, but a week or so before the gig, I remember, and it's all I can think about. I've seen amazing musicians in Melbourne – Blur, Oasis, Portishead, Radiohead – but this will be my first hero gig, the first time I hear someone who created music that sits so deep inside me it's cemented to my soul.

The night has arrived and I'm beside myself. I bundle into the venue with my housemates, depositing coats, hats, scarves and gloves in the cloakroom.

'Have a good night, innit,' the girl on the door, a clone of Fleur, says.

Unlike my Tube days, I don't make a grand entrance with my friends. They head to the bar and I dash away to find a spot in front of the stage. After an aeon the support act comes on, but I hardly even hear them. I stand with my shoulders straight and feet wide apart so no one can shove me from my spot. It's like I'm unaware of my surroundings and am frozen with anticipation.

I don't move through the changeover. The roadies are excruciatingly slow. The crowd pushes in behind me, but I don't budge. I'm counting down, it's about to happen, it happens. I'm almost in tears, like those girls from 1960s footage of Beatles concerts. I'm metres away from Joe Strummer. The first chords strike up and I switch everything off, except that primordial part of my brain. I remember a party long ago, when someone first told me about this man, tattooed him onto my subconscious. It's like I'm not even me. I'm one with the music, the band, and the audience.

Hours later, someone taps me on the back.

'Dot? It's time to go,' James says.

I turn and face him.

'Wow, you were in some kind of trance,' he says.

We stand in the cold as James argues with a mini cab driver. My housemates are all drunk, singing 'Hey Baby'. I shiver at the thought of the gig being over and wish I had some alcohol in my system to keep warm.

The mini cab driver parks in front of us and opens his doors.

James punches me lightly on the arm. 'Don't worry, Dot, there'll be other gigs. I call shotgun!'

Echo and the Bunnymen sang that nothing lasts forever. Maybe they're wrong though.

TRACK 27 – COMFORTABLY NUMB

Now and Then – The Bungalow – 20 January 2001

Thanks for dropping by. You're reading the first post on a brand new website dedicated to the best music in town that you've never heard of. I want to give you an insight into what's really out there music-wise. I want you to see the magical and majestic things that are being created right here in Melbourne. If a band has been playing gigs every month for the past twenty-odd years and draws a crowd of double figures every time, then they're too good to read about in the mainstream press. You'll only hear about them here.

Now and Then is a local Irish folk band who can only be described as raucous. They play the kind of music you dance to when dancing gives you the same feeling a whizzy dizzy did when you were a child.

I caught one Now and Then gig at the Train Tracks Hotel in the late 1970s, even though I was more into nihilistic punk at the time. Their high-energy gigging style hasn't changed one bit since that time. The only thing that's changed is the amount of grey in the musicians' hair.

When you want to fling everything that holds you back off a cliff, when you want to hear music without ego, music that invites you to relax and remember that you're you, music you can get up and dance to without a skerrick of self-consciousness, music played by people who love their instruments, who love to look their audience in the eye, who wouldn't know how to market themselves in a pink fit – that's when it's time to see Now and Then.

Now and Then is not a band for a mellow night, sipping red and nodding appreciatively at the violin solos. They're a band for a bare-bones pub that sells beer by the jugful, a pub that doesn't mind if the audience takes over the gig.

This particular concert disintegrated into an off-key rendering of 'Danny Boy' by the entire audience, so loud that if Danny himself was sitting in the leafy suburbs, he'd hear the call, jump into his Ford Falcon, whizz down the South Eastern Freeway and burst into this pub, heart beating proudly to hear so many people calling his name.

I watched the gig from the side — the jubilation of the band and audience confirmed I'm on the right road. My only criticism was that the crowd was slightly too tight-knit for me to feel like joining in. At any rate, I enjoyed this gig so much I almost forgot I had another band to review on the other side of the city. As I dashed out, I bumped into a young woman dancing with an old fella. It was that kind of intergenerational gig.

So this is my new calling, bringing this music to you, to give you a taste of what's out there, if only you get up out of your chair and venture into Melbourne's all-embracing music scene. The future's bright.

Electric Feel, Back To Black, My People, Paper Planes, American Boy, Don't Hold Back, That's Not My Name, Viva La Vida, Kids, Poker Face, I'm Yours, Dance Wiv Me, 4 Minutes, Shut Up And Let Me Go, Nine In The Afternoon, Miss Independent, Talk Like That, Moving To New York, Rehab, Grace Kelly, Big Girl (You Are Beautiful), When I Grow Up, Ready For The Floor, So What, Single Ladies, Untouched, Dream Catch Me, No One, Great DJ, Chasing Pavements, Valerie, 2 Hearts, In The Ayer, Walking On A Dream, I Kissed A Girl, Got Money, I Don't Care, Sex On Fire, Pork And Beans, Sweet About Me, All I Want To Do, Need U Bad, Back When I Knew It All, Sun Goes Down, Just Dance, Mrs Officer, Low, Pumpkin Soup, Gimme More, All Summer Long, Shake It, Hot N Cold, Black And Gold, Crank That, Bubbly, Closer, Running Back, Use Somebody, Apologize, Perfect, Work, White Noise, Take Me To The Floor, The Geeks Were Right, Lollipop, Sensual Seduction, Conquest, Time To Pretend, Whatever You Like, Something Anything, Alive, A&E, This Boy's In Love, Stop And Stare, Free Things For Poor People, Sober, The Age Of Understatement, Violet Hill, I Never Liked You, Kansas City, Shadow Of The Day, Foundations, Party People, Happy Ending, Wow, M79, Clumsy, Like You'll Never See Me Again, Two Doors Down, Hold On, Sweetest Girl (Dollar Bill), Hearts On Fire, Superstar, Run, Just Fine, The Boss, Now You're Gone, Rule The World, Bluebirds Flying High, We Are The People, This Is An Emergency, Relax (Take It Easy), Flux, Paparazzi, My Destiny, Chasing Cars, Cassius, Ruby, Jump In The Pool, Waving Flags, NW5, Sunshine In The Rain, Get What You Want, The Beginning Of The Twist, Nude, Lights Out, Look For The Woman, Radio Heart, Runaway, The Shock Of The Lightning, My Mistakes Were Made For You, Infinity 2008, I'm Outta Time, Stuck On Repeat, Blue Ridge Mountains, The Rip, Dance Dance Dance, Courtship Dating, I Know UR Girlfriend Hates Me, Oxford Comma

Streaming

TRACK 28 – PUBLIC IMAGE

I wake up in my share house in Camden and realise seven years have passed. I'm bloated with music and kebabs. There's a shoebox full of concert tickets sitting in the back of my wardrobe, but little else to show for my time here. I'm working the same job, friends come and go, but there's no one significant and I hardly ever leave the city. I roll out of bed onto the floor. I'm late for work again, but I don't stir until the cold snakes into me. I move in slow motion, as if that could hold back future years.

Trudging to work, I pass a café and although I'm really late at this point, I go in for a cup of tea. I smell sizzling bacon and order a full English breakfast. I sit there, pushing my eggs around, and let cracks of realisation that I can't do this forever enter my mind.

I grew up in a family who were always the last to leave a party, but maybe it's better to leave a party at its high point, rather than the drunken, half-remembered fug stage. Gig after gig, party after party, bar after bar, at some point the merry-go-round speeds up and everything becomes too blurred to enjoy.

London has grown stale. It's Jabba the Hutt wearing a bikini, a giant city whose infrastructure can hardly support it. Despite the music, this place is not my home.

I call the office to tell them I'm sick and start walking. I search for the cutting-edge style that once came out of swinging London, but instead I see suits with pink ties and overweight teenagers in tracksuits.

The river is grim. I look for the beauty Terry and Julie saw as they walked over the bridge. Instead, I see a dead rat. Waterloo Station is too crowded to enter and smells of Ginsters Pies. Carnaby Street doesn't heave with bright, groovy folk dancing around Austin Powers; instead, herds of tourists mill about, heavy with Topshop bags. There are no punks on the Kings Road, only rugby fans in polo shirts pouring ten-pound vodka tonics down their throats.

I can spot Australians from fifty metres away by their casual saunter and well-worn Billabong clothes. They're Jafas, Just Another Fucking Aussie, and they're everywhere – in the parks playing hacky sack and cooking sausages on miniature barbeques purchased from Argos; on the couch enjoying *Simpsons* marathons; at the pub at five am watching the AFL Grand Final; in the clubs of Brixton, peaking far too early after guzzling three-pound pills; driving around Europe in decrepit vans, singing about a land down under until their voices grow hoarse. I realise these people have started to delight rather than disgust me. I'm homesick.

Back in my room, streaming internet radio, a song worms its way into me. It's the original version of 'Shivers', performed by a bunch of boys from Melbourne, laughing at the angst of adolescent crushes. The discordant guitars echo and echo, sending ripples across the ocean to me. I can feel crazy, fluctuating weather; I can smell wet laneways and coffee; I yearn for Mum and Dad, Jack and Cat. It's time.

♫ ♫ ♫

I land at Melbourne Airport, expecting it to be village-like compared with Heathrow. Instead, it's buzzing with noisy people and flashing cameras. Cat's waiting for me, a smile splitting her face. She grabs me in a bear hug that almost cracks my ribs.

'Trust you to arrive the same day as Tony Mokbel,' she says, still clutching me tight.

I have no idea who that is, but I hope he's as happy as I am to be back home.

I rent a little place all to myself, exaggerate my London achievements, take a grown up job with no social life – not even a lolly jar – and search my hair for greys. One minute I'm a bright young thing, a regular on the gigging scene, and the next I'm usurped by Gen Ys with asymmetric hair who call me 'honey'. As compensation, I get paid well. Still not enough for that convertible BMW, but enough to feel like one of the *Sex and the City* women.

Cat and I resume our friendship, plastering it all over Facebook. We make sarcastic comments on each other's statuses and chat about how boring our old friends have become.

> *Hey Cat, does Amanda even exist? Every status update is about her bloody kids. If I wanted to know about them, I'd be their Facebook friends!*

> *If she's got nothing interesting to say, why are you friends with her? So, dinner this Wednesday???*

> *Yeah...but I have to work late and now that you have kids don't you eat at five? :p*

> *Fuck off, I'm not Amanda. Just come round whenever you finish. Looking forward to seeing your head!*

I stare at Amanda's smiling profile picture, enjoying a moment of nostalgia, before clicking the unfriend button. It's been too long since we've had anything in common, and I don't want photos of infants I have no emotional connection with cluttering my newsfeed.

All of a sudden, children are everywhere. I guess people really needed that baby bonus to buy a wide-screen TV. Everyone I work with is married with kids – which explains the shocking lack of social activities – and all my friends have bred. Cat and Raj now have Rita and Anita, two cheeky and self-assured girls, clones of the Cat I met in primary school. And then there's Coco, who Jack and Zara produced in my absence.

Sunday lunches at Glen Huntly are resumed, and Coco pushes his chair closer to me than any grown man would.

'Why Coco?' I ask Jack. 'It makes him sound like a middle-aged drag queen.'

Coco picks the vegies off his plate and dumps them on Jack's.

'He didn't like his real name, so he chose this one himself,' Jacks says proudly, eating a piece of Coco's carrot.

'Hmm, maybe that's a hint not to name any more Kelly men Colin,' I say.

I reach over and grab one of Coco's beans from Jack's plate. I look at Dad to see if he's mad that Coco isn't eating his vegetables, but instead he's smiling indulgently at the boy.

'No more Colin!' Coco shouts.

I lean in and whisper to Coco, 'When you're older, I'll take you to Disneyland.'

'Thomas there?' he asks.

I've no idea whether Disney has franchised Thomas the Tank Engine or any of his friends, so I say, 'We'll have to go there and find out.'

Jack's green eyes shine back at me from a small, round face.

'Dot, can you take a look at something in the computer room after lunch?' Dad asks.

We head into the music room, which is also now the computer room. Dad has only just joined the online world, but he's embracing it, spending time analysing his superannuation fund, downloading music from iTunes, watching Irish bands on YouTube and checking out real estate.

'What's happening, Dad?' I ask.

'I can't get into my bloody Hotmail. This thing's bullshit!'

'It's still logged into Mum's account. Click sign out then log in again with your username and password.'

'Ah…just a sec.'

Dad leaves the room, shuffles around in his bedroom, then returns wearing glasses and carrying a small notebook. His username and password are written down and he types them in with one finger.

'You OK now?'

'Yep, I'm in!'

Mum enters with a tray of tea cups.

'When your father's finished, I want you to show me how to use Ancestory.com,' she says.

I give her a hug and say, 'It's good to be home.'

TRACK 29 – I KNOW WHAT BOYS LIKE

Trevor Cook sends me a friend request on Facebook. It's been years since I've seen Trevor, but apparently my old crush has been lying dormant the entire time, because when I see the little red icon with his name next to it, my heart somersaults. He only just sent the request, so I'm going to leave it for a bit before responding. I look at his photos; he's a little fatter and more lined. There are a couple of photos of him at the races and the rest are from work functions. To my satisfaction, no girlfriend-like figures can be seen.

The next day I accept Trevor's friend request and send him a message.

> Hey Stranger,
> Good to hear from you. I just got
> back from a 7-year stint in the
> UK and it's awesome to be back
> home! What's happening with you?
> Dot

There are a thousand things I want to say to Trevor, but I don't want to overwhelm him. He always did have a gnat-like attention span. He replies, surprisingly quickly.

> Hi Miss Dot,
> Looks like your time in the UK did
> you good, going by your photos.
> I wouldn't mind a few years
> overseas myself, but it's pretty
> hard getting savings together

*with this fucking economy. I'm
still an account manager, different
company, but I'm working on a
big deal similar to the Eksnep
account, and when it closes later
this year I'll be rich enough to hire
ten high-class hookers to wipe
my arse with hundred-dollar bills.
As long as all these cunts at my
company give me the support I
need, that is. Tell me more about
you. Your Facebook posts are
hilarious, by the way ;)
Trev*

*Good to hear you're still in the
account management game. You
always were a gun at it and I'm
sure you'll close a sweet deal
soon. So what's all the old crew
up to these days? I guess a lot
of them are married with kids
now? Seems to be the trend at
the moment. I'm pretty much the
only single person in my whole
company, but it does have its
upsides, as I can safely say
I'm the coolest person who
works there!*

I don't know I'd call it a good thing
still being an account manager,
but it's what I know and I don't
want to start again in another role
on some shithouse salary until I've
paid off my credit cards. One day
though! Yeah, most of the boys
have a missus and kids these
days, which puts a dampener on
pub nights, but usually someone
comes out for a bit and for the
other nights I have my Xbox.
Not like the old days though,
eh? Naturally you're the coolest
person in your office, you always
were a babe ;)

So you're thinking of a career
change? What would you like to
do? My dream job is to be a
music journo!

You'd make a great music journo.
I remember the time you ripped
apart my music collection at that
party! Once I pay off my credit
cards, I'd like to be a teacher,
help kids etc. Join us for drinks
on Friday?

As soon as work finishes on Friday, I rush to the pub to meet Trevor, wearing my Cue dress and red tights. I try to visualise the Dot that Trevor would have seen last, but she's gone.

'Hello, gorgeous. Look at you, all grown up!' Trevor booms.

He doesn't get up, but he kicks out a chair for me. I sit down and give him a pat on the arm.

'Oh shush, I'm just old,' I blush.

'Good to see you, Dot,' says Jake, Trevor's account manager buddy.

So I'm back with the old crowd. It's even the same pub and the same band is there playing the same set. *Ah, 'Brown Eyed Girl', I missed you!*

Most of the guys are mellower versions of themselves. They talk about their kids and no longer retire to the toilet for a cheeky line. Trevor's the same though, knocking back drinks and eyeing off the girls behind the bar.

Trevor and I talk for hours. The others leave early, and it's not just because they need to get home to their families. Trevor tells me about how he feels unfulfilled in his job, but he's tied to it for financial reasons. He tells me about his plans to become a teacher; he feels he knows a thing or two he can teach the kids of today. He tells me about his struggles to give up smoking. He tells me how he feels a little lost. And he tells me how he's ragingly insecure.

I like his words, but Trevor stubs out his cigarette in such a confident way, I question exactly how insecure he is. He grins at me like a kid who's helped himself to two biscuits instead of one, and I wonder if I'll ever get to see the insecure gem that lies under his skin.

In turn, I tell Trevor about how it feels weird to be back home after so long, because everything's the same and everything's different and no one's interested in my travel tales. I tell him I'm finding it hard to adjust to being in my thirties, surrounded by Gen Ys. I tell him I still don't have a clue what I'm doing at work and yet I keep getting promoted. And I tell him sometimes I feel so insecure I must have some sort of disability. Then I stop talking, and drain my beer.

'Everyone feels the same, Dot,' Trevor says. 'Everyone's the same.'

'Yeah I know…but I forget that sometimes.'

'Let's have another drink!'

'OK, but one more no more,' which is the same thing I say to Coco.

Trevor winks at me and goes to the bar. I feel like swooning, but not from the alcohol.

At the end of the night, I assume Trevor's going to invite me home, but instead he stumbles into a taxi and slurs, 'Take it easy,' as he's driven away.

Take it easy?! I should know better than to expect anything from Trevor, but I'm disappointed.

♫ ♫ ♫

A few weeks pass and my life now centres on interactions with Trevor. If he makes a comment on my Facebook status I have a good day, and I start engineering my posts so they're something he'd find funny and want to comment on. I accept every one of his invitations, and he accepts none of mine. I don't care, I'm hooked.

Despite all our deep conversations, Trevor hasn't made the slightest move, which I'm finding increasingly frustrating. The next time I'm at Cat's, I raise this with her.

'I'm not sure what his problem is. I know he's not seeing anyone. Does he have something wrong with his penis, or is it possible I'm not as hot as I think I am?'

'Not possible!' cries Cat. 'Maybe he doesn't know you're into him.'

'Does he need a written fucking invitation? I'm out with the guy every week!'

'Why don't *you* make a move?'

'Who does he think I am? He's the bloody man!'

Cat shrugs. 'Try it, you've got nothing to lose. If he isn't interested, just say you were drunk and it was a mistake, then go back to being friends.'

We're interrupted by sniggering.

'Girls!' shouts Cat in a fake, stern voice.

Two little girls trail into the lounge room where we're sitting. I still can't believe that Cat has produced walking, talking offspring; yet here they are. I wink awkwardly at them and they giggle again.

'Were you eavesdropping on Mum and Aunty Dot?'

'Nooo!'

'I hope not, because sometimes grown-ups want to swear and talk about things little girls don't need to hear. Now go play in the garden.'

'Aunty Dot loves Trevor,' I hear them laugh as they skip away. I blush.

I am going to have to do something about this Trevor situation though. I think about him all the time and the preoccupation is irritating.

♫ ♫ ♫

Next time we catch up, I drink more than usual and rush through our conversation. At the end of the night, when Trevor's flagging down a taxi, I look into his glassy eyes, grab his shirt collar and kiss him.

'Hmm,' is all he has to say. 'Hmm.'

Oh shit, he's not keen and I've made him feel awkward! I want to die, but instead I say, 'Oops, guess I just got caught up in the moment.'

'Oh, it's cool,' says Trevor. 'I've been waiting for that to happen for a while.'

'Then why the hell didn't you do anything about it?' I snap, relieved and embarrassed at the same time.

He smiles, looking like a grown-up version of that little boy statue on the corner at Caulfield Park, waiting for his space capsule to come pick him up.

'Do you want to come home with me?' I ask.

'Yes,' says Trevor, and takes my hand.

♫ ♫ ♫

In the morning I feel like Scarlett O'Hara did after that night Rhett Butler carried her up the stairs. It was a moment of thundering orchestra music, but the other moment, sitting in the taxi with Trevor holding my hand, was the best thing that's ever happened to me.

I don't hear from Trevor for the next few days and I feel sick. It's a cold feeling of dread, as though I'm being stabbed by the liquid metal of the T-1000 from *Terminator 2*. I have a deadline at work, but can't concentrate. By Thursday, I'm so far behind I have to work late. I go home exhausted and watch a repeat of *Sex and the City* before falling asleep on the couch. In the morning, there's a text from Trevor asking me to join him and the boys for drinks.

I turn up at the pub, and it's the same as every other night, Trevor and the guys talking about their grand plans. The conversation seems stale, as I wait quietly for everyone to leave.

'Why didn't you call me?' I ask Trevor, as soon as his last buddy has left.

'Why didn't you call me?' Trevor echoes. Then he puts his arm around me. 'Don't pout, Dot. You look a lot prettier when you're smiling.'

I go back to Trevor's house that night, and every Friday night from then on. Just being in his presence makes me feel magical. With his dubious tastes, such as enjoying commercial radio, Trevor's not the man with the music, but maybe there is no man with the music. Maybe that doesn't even matter.

TRACK 30 – TOO DRUNK TO FUCK

So how's your dream bf?

It's a Saturday afternoon and Trevor and I are lying on his couch watching repeats of *The Sopranos*. We're four episodes in and I'm getting bored, so Cat's text is a welcome interruption. I untangle myself from Trevor's arms and move onto the armchair to reply.

*Great! We're having a cosy
arvo watching TV.*

*Fabulous...but tell me
about him.*

I look over at Trevor, who's scratching his nuts. He's doing it more in an absent-minded little boy way than a creepy old man way.

He's like a lovely cuddly teddy.

*Sounds to me like he needs
more substance, Dot.*

*There's substance to him. I
just need to uncover it.*

OK.

*Everyone has substance,
when you get to know
them...don't they?*

Trevor hoists himself off the couch and opens the sliding door, not taking his eyes off the television the whole time. He stands in the open doorway, hypnotised, smoking a cigarette. When he finally catches my eye, he winks.

'I swear, you're the last person I know who still smokes.' I smile at him with affection.

Trevor shrugs and turns back to Tony Soprano, puffing away. I think about the past months with him. I watch as he pushes the replay button on the same night, distracting himself with another drink, another computer game, another DVD. Trevor is a twentieth-century boy, lost in this new millennium of smoke-free zones and two standard drinks per day.

There's substance to Trevor, though. It's like there's a piano concerto playing in the background when we talk for hours about his plans and ideas. He's started asking me about mine a little less, but I like seeing his eyes light up when he talks about paying off his debts and becoming a teacher.

There isn't much conversation today, though. Hours pass and I'm arranging Trevor's remote controls in order of size. *The Sopranos* is still on, and Trevor has opened his laptop and is poring over the Excel spreadsheet he uses to track his finances.

'You should move in here,' he says. 'We'd both save on rent and you're here pretty much all the time anyway.'

'Does that mean you want us to be a couple?' My mind races with the next fifty years of possibilities, the remote controls forgotten by my side.

Trevor closes his laptop and lies back on the couch, which makes a thumping sound under his weight.

'Sure,' he says, and pumps up the TV volume.

I sneak a peek at his face, searching for something more, but it's as though he's reflected in one of those mirrors at Luna Park, compressed and distorted.

♫ ♫ ♫

I move in with Trevor, paying double rent until I find someone to take over my old place. I haven't told him yet, but I'm in love with him. It's a continuation of the crush that started back in 2001, only more intense now that I have him. I feel calm when he's around and frantic when he's not. Every so often, a thorn of concern pricks up, like I didn't realise exactly how much he drinks. I thought he just had those big nights on Fridays, but it's more like every second night, and on the alternate nights he'll lie on the couch watching DVDs or playing his Xbox, nursing a hangover like other men his age nurse their newborn children.

I'm not sure if Trevor's saving much money since I moved in, but I'm not. For one thing, his power bills are way higher than mine thanks to all the appliances he uses. Not to mention the internet he's constantly jacked in to, searching for friends on LinkedIn and Facebook, shopping on Amazon and eBay, playing Fantasy Football and, according to the browser history, looking at a bit of porn. When bills and rent are due, Trevor's often short, so I cover the difference. Still, it's worth it for the big hugs he gives me almost every morning.

♪ ♪ ♪

I get home from work just after eight and Trevor is there in his tracksuit, playing on the Xbox again. He's become quite overweight; possibly obese, if I go by the medical definition. I squeeze the soft muffin around my stomach and feel queasy at the thought of all the takeaways we've been eating. Trevor swigs from a bottle of red. The sight irritates me, but I push the thought away. If Scarlett O'Hara could think about it tomorrow, then so can I.

Every light in the house is on, the television in the bedroom is on – I never dreamed I'd live in a house with a television in the bedroom – both the computer and laptop are on – one of them streaming classic eighties rock – the air conditioner is on and the Xbox is on.

'You cooking tonight?' Trevor asks.

'Can't be fucked.' I'm exhausted from work and from the noise of Trevor's appliances. 'You want to cook?'

'Can't be fucked.'

I order pizza – vegetarian, to be healthy – and go wait in the garden to escape the overstimulation of the house. I look at Trevor through the sliding door, but he doesn't budge. It's a pretty garden: a little paved courtyard shaded by tropical plants. I should invite friends over, but I'm wary of the inevitable piss-up session that would ensue. Lately I've had enough of heavy drinking. Tired of the headaches. For every additional drink Trevor consumes, I seem to have one less. Now I'm virtually a teetotaller, and starting to wonder if Trevor has a problem, like a proper problem.

Eventually he comes outside for a cigarette. I sit opposite, willing him to start up some sort of conversation.

'What?' is all he has to say, in an irritated voice I'm hearing more often.

My throat muscles clench, preventing me from saying anything confrontational or meaningful, so I say nothing and go back into the house.

♫ ♫ ♫

We've been living together for eight months and Trevor still hasn't met my family or Cat. I go to lunches at Glen Huntly alone and make excuses for him. Finally, one Saturday I take a chance and start with Cat, inviting her and Raj over for a barbeque.

The day begins with promise. Appreciative of the microbrewed beers Raj brings, Trevor is in good form, charming everyone with his stories and not drinking too much in front of Rita and Anita. Maybe I imagined the morose, Xbox-playing figure.

This afternoon I remember all the reasons why I love Trevor – his gift of the gab; his booming laugh; the comicality of his swaggering bravado that he thinks hides his vulnerability, but in reality just accentuates it.

'Nice to finally meet you,' Cat says to him as they're leaving.

'Thanks for an awesome day, Trevor. Looking forward to catching up again,' Raj says.

'Great, Raj. We should organise a boys night soon,' Trevor says.

He has his arm around me as we see them off, and I'm content. It doesn't last long though. His arm mirrors their car pulling away, then he walks back into the house to his Xbox.

'Your Indian friend is a hottie,' he says, as he settles onto the couch.

I stand away from the couch, wondering what to do. Have I reverted to the silent Dot in the corner? There's a mess of dishes in the kitchen, but I take a nap instead. I've been napping a lot lately. The more computer games Trevor plays, the more I sleep.

'You know sleeping so much is a sign of depression?' he comments when I emerge a couple hours later.

'Piss off,' I say. 'I've got a big week at work coming up.'

'Suit yourself.' He returns to his game.

♫ ♫ ♫

Another night, another pub, I watch Trevor get drunk and talk about the Eksnep account again and again. When his drinking buddies go home, he glues his phone to his ear, calling everyone he knows until he finds someone else to go out with. All the while, I sip my orange juice, watching and waiting. When we're home together, I take fourth place behind the Xbox, laptop and DVD player.

Something's going to change, though; something's just around the corner. The affectionate, talkative Trevor who welcomed me back from London will shrug off his slump, cut back on the alcohol and tell me he loves me. He'll turn off his noisy appliances, allowing music to return, and my life will be perfect.

♫ ♫ ♫

The annual roulette party is approaching. Jack and my cousins are all bringing their partners. The week before, I remind Trevor about the party at regular intervals.

'Yeah, yeah,' he says. 'I'll be there.'

'Do you promise? I really want you to meet my family.'

'Sure.'

'How about we take it easy on Friday night, so we're nice and fresh for the party on Saturday?'

'OK.'

On Saturday morning, Trevor has a hangover. Going to the roulette party tonight will break his pattern of boozing one day and lying on the couch the next, but he did promise me he'd go. I let him rest until late afternoon.

I stand between Trevor on the couch and the television, so he's forced to pay me attention.

'You'll be right for the party tonight, won't you Trevor?' My voice comes out small and squeaky.

'No alcohol for me tonight, Dot.'

'Cool, you don't have to drink, but you're coming, aren't you? This is important to me.'

'Some other time. I won't be good company tonight.'

'Please! My parents have been asking about you. They're starting to think you don't exist.'

Trevor doesn't notice my small joke. He's looking in my direction, but not at me.

'Not tonight. We'll have them over for a barbeque soon,' he says.

Trevor can't be budged when he's made up his mind, and I've already nagged him more than usual, so I go to the party alone.

'And where's the amazing Trevor?' Dad asks when he opens the front door.

'Um, he's sick…but we're going to have you over for a barbeque soon.'

Dr Ivanskiy is standing behind Dad, looking at me, but I can't think of anything to say to him.

After months of teetotalling, I need a drink, so I tell Mum I'll sleep in my old Norsca-green bedroom rather than drive home tonight. I drink a bottle of pinot gris and hit the roulette table. I put my money on red and win a hundred dollars, but I don't feel victorious.

'Come out for a smoke, Dot,' says Dr Ivanskiy.

'I don't smoke anymore.'

'Me either. Come out for fresh air.'

I stumble outside, giggling as I correct my footing. Dr Ivanskiy and I sit in my childhood garden and look up at the stars. Mum is in the kitchen making tea, the others jostling each other to be first in line for a cup.

A possum scurries along the side fence and we watch it for a bit, then Dr Ivanskiy sighs and says, 'Dot, I only say it because no one else will. I don't want to make you right angry, but I have to tell you this.'

This is the first time I've seen Dr Ivanskiy hesitate. I feel my heart rate increase, on alert for whatever it is he's about to say.

He sighs again, then resumes, 'That Trevor's not a good man. He's not for you, little Dot.'

He's right, you know, a small voice whispers, but I ignore it. I spot a shooting star in the sky, or maybe it's a satellite, or a space capsule.

'Oh, he's just going through a rough patch, Dr Ivanskiy. He's sorry he couldn't be here tonight. He's really a great guy.'

'Whatever he is, he'll do you no good.'

'I'm happy with him.'

'Are you? Bloody hell, take a look at yourself! I've never seen you dress so scruffy, even when you were a thunder-faced teenager.'

It's true. I still wear my Cue suits to work, but the rest of the time baggy jeans and hoodies are my uniform. They're comfortable and don't cut into my slightly pudgy waist when I'm taking a nap. I examine my fingernails.

Dr Ivanskiy shifts his weight and continues, 'Who are you, Dot?'

I'm feeling super awkward now. 'Dot Kelly, daughter of Gerald and Margaret, palest of the Kelly clan.'

Dr Ivanskiy doesn't laugh. I start to feel panicky; the only thing worse than losing Trevor would be losing myself. A tear escapes from my eye and takes a ride down my face. Dr Ivanskiy enfolds me in a bear hug. It's been a while since I've felt so safe.

'I'm sorry, little one. I don't mean to upset you. Ignore me, I'm an old fool,' he says.

'No, no. You're right. But I'm so scared of being alone.'

'You're not alone! Same as I'm not alone. Look behind you.'

I peer through the window into the kitchen. Everyone is drinking tea together, and Jack catches my eye and waves. In the background, I can hear Julie Ann singing 'Danny Boy' and I swear I feel the vibrations of Dad's tapping foot.

♫ ♫ ♫

I arrive home the next morning feeling rough. Trevor's sitting on the couch in his tracksuit, fiddling with his Excel spreadsheet. I snuck a look at it a couple days ago. His credit card debt hasn't decreased at all. Somehow my savings have been drained though.

Angry guitars play in my head, the first music I've heard in ages. I wanted a lover like any other, but what did I get?

TRACK 31 – LOVE WILL TEAR US APART

I eliminate gut-rotting, brain-rotting soft drink and junk food from my diet and join a gym. I can't do more than slowly jog a kilometre on the treadmill, but a speckle of pride starts to form in my heart. What I sweat out is heinous. God knows which toxins have been lurking within my body. I shove my gym gear in the washing machine before it has the chance to stink up the entire house. No sign of Trevor, so I text him.

Where are you?

Pub.

Trevor's grown too lazy for bar hopping. Now he spends all his time at a pub next door to his office, a once inviting old building, newly fitted out and stripped of life. His married buddies have slipped off the scene, but lately he's acquired a new following of guys fifteen years his junior, ready to worship and match him drink for drink.

I arrive at the pub. Trevor and his cronies are in full conversation about someone they reckon is a wanker. He raises his eyebrow at me in greeting but doesn't stop talking. I buy an orange juice at the bar, calculating how many hours it'll take before I can drag him home. The only thing worse than yet another night like this would be to go home to the empty house.

Sober and bored with the bombastics, I go outside to get some fresh air. I look up at the stars and wish I was in my space capsule, far away from this large, noisy person, who's become more of an addiction than a lover.

'Cheer up,' says a man who's walking down the street. 'The future's bright.'

He has a nice voice, and I start to say something, but he's already turned the corner. Whoever he is, he's right; my future doesn't have to be drenched in alcohol and disappointment. Dr Ivanskiy is right too.

I hail a taxi, leaving Trevor at the pub.

♫ ♫ ♫

I keep up with the gym and get used to living a different sort of life from Trevor. He'll follow my example soon. In the meantime, we're strangers sharing the same house, civil with each other, but my stomach is tight with anticipation. What I hope will happen is that Trevor will emerge from his cocoon and start acting like he loves me. In the meantime, I bury myself in work and the gym.

Cat texts me.

> *How ru lady?*

> *Great! Just busy with work n stuff. Let's catch up soon!*

> *Yes! Call me ☺*

I have an important client presentation at work. I hate giving presentations; talking in front of people makes me feel like a phoney. I practise a couple of times in front of the bathroom mirror. Trevor is out, so I walk about the house answering questions out loud I imagine the clients will ask. I go to bed feeling more confident, but I can't sleep; it's past midnight and Trevor still isn't home. I pull out my old copy of *Pride and Prejudice* and comfort-read myself to sleep. Just as I'm dozing off, Mr Darcy's antithesis arrives, swearing and crashing about, reeking of booze and cigarettes. He can't just go to bed, so the television and all his gadgets spring to life at full volume.

In the morning, Trevor's still lying on the couch watching television. Something inside me is smouldering, and as Trevor shifts his body to fart, it catches alight.

I stand over him with my arms crossed and my brows drawn.

'Nice one, dickhead!' I snarl. 'I've got a massive presentation to deliver on no sleep whatsoever, thanks to you!'

Trevor's face flickers with irritation at being interrupted. 'Sor-ree!' he snaps and turns around on the couch, presenting me with his back and arse crack.

I feel my face grow hot. 'Jesus Christ, this is bullshit!'

Trevor sighs, then says flatly, 'Just move out, Dot. We both know this isn't working.'

'Fine then, I will!'

'Good.'

Trevor hasn't turned around this whole time. And then, he actually falls asleep! It's the site of his arse crack, the only thing he can be bothered showing me, which makes me come to the realisation that, no matter how much I love him, this is all I'm ever going to get from him. Waiting and hoping are a waste of my time.

I stand there, undecided for a moment, before shifting on to autopilot. I go to work, deliver my presentation, come home early, ignore Trevor on the couch, pack my stuff into my car and drive to Graceland, which is empty for the winter. I call the office and tell them I'll be working from home for a week. And then I log on to Facebook, defriend Trevor, untag myself from every photo I'm in with him, remove my relationship status, delete his number from my phone and erase our entire text message and email history. He's gone from my life in under an hour.

I hide away in Graceland, crying, with only the squawk of parrots to keep me company. I don't contact anyone. It's like Trevor threw a bucket of boiling water on me, then walked away. At first I was in shock, then pain and now I'm just trying to hide the burn scars from everyone, in case they're repulsed.

Eventually I go back to work, driving from Graceland every day. I explain my swollen eyes with hay fever and don't mention a thing about Trevor. I drive along the highway in my capsule of a car, waiting for numbness to cover up the pain.

Finally, when I think I can get through a sentence without crying, I call Cat.

'Hey, babe,' she says.

I can hear the girls giggling in the background, the same sound Cat and I made almost thirty years ago. The sound of children's voices is something that'll probably never be heard in my house. I can't even get a word out; the girls' laughter and Cat's familiar, cheerful voice sets me off, howling like a baby.

'Dot, what's up? Is it Trevor?'

I'm surprised how quickly she guesses.

'We broke up…' I cry some more, trying to remember the last time I really sobbed like this. When I fell out with Cat at school is the only time I can think of.

'Oh Dot, I'm so sorry. Come over?' She's talking to me in the same voice she uses when her girls are upset. It feels nice.

'Soon,' I say. 'I just want to be alone for a little bit.'

This is the first time Major Tom's capsule hasn't filled me with dread.

'OK…but if you're feeling really terrible, call me. You can scream if you like.'

'Yep…'

I don't scream and I don't sleep. Instead, I spend each night lying on the couch, listening to The Smiths because heaven knows I'm miserable now. My stomach is a knot so I live off Vita-Weats, the only thing I can eat without gagging.

Trevor moves on; I hear that he's dating some chick in her twenties. Despite my expungings, Facebook worms a photo my way. I stare at Trevor's large, beaming face next to some girl I've never seen before. I hate her, but I can't bring myself to hate him. I text Cat.

> *Can u come to Graceland?*
> *Need to discuss T's new gf.*

> *Prick! I'll be over right*
> *after work.*

I haven't smoked for years, but I buy myself a packet of Peter Stuyvesants and a bottle of red. I'm sitting on the couch drinking wine out of an old Vegemite jar and ashing directly onto the floor by the time Cat arrives.

'Oh, honey!' she says and hugs me.

'He never even loved me, did he? I was just useful for splitting bills.'

Cat sits there with her arm around my shoulders. She doesn't say anything.

'It's not that it's over and he's met someone else at the speed of light that's upsetting… Well, it is, how dare he! But what's worse is that the person I loved never really existed… I wasted all that time with him and now I'll probably never have a baby and those space capsule dreams will never stop… I thought we'd get through this rough patch and then we'd get married and have kids, like every other bloody person in the world. It's not fair! I always thought there was more to Trevor, someone only I saw. I was so sure that the real Trevor was about to appear at any moment… It's fucking annoying to be wrong about that. I'm so stupid! Everyone was right… All there really was under that bravado was a big, fat turd.'

Cat pours herself a glass of wine and I continue babbling, tears and snot running down my face.

'And what the fuck gives him the right to move on so quickly?'

'He's not moving on, he's stuck on a merry-go-round that he'll probably never get off, but you're moving forward, even if you don't feel like you are.'

I'm in a swimming pool of grief, but Cat has jumped in with me. She's got her arm around me and my head is on her shoulder. We're the same age, but right now it's nice to feel like the child.

The crush I've had for half my adult life is up in flames; but that's all it was, a crush, a chemical reaction that can be replaced with something else or kept at bay with distractions. It was never the love like they talk about at people's weddings – the love that is patient and kind, and not jealous or arrogant. I sit up straight.

'You might feel shitty for a while, but it'll get better. I promise,' Cat says.

'How do you know?'

She takes a sip of wine, 'Oh, it's what they say in the movies.'

TRACK 32 – DANCING WITH MYSELF

I'm sitting in a café with Trevor. He sips a black coffee as I stare at him with the angriest face I can muster. The only reason I agreed to meet him is in case he wants to get back together. He should, if he had any taste. Then I can tell him no, and he can be just as disappointed as I was.

After minutes of stony silence, Trevor slides an envelope my way. There's about five hundred dollars inside.

'What the hell's this?' I ask.

'According to my spreadsheet, it's what I owe you for bills.'

I crinkle the envelope and money in my fist, debating between throwing it in his face and shoving it in my bag. I opt for the sensible rather than the passionate.

Trevor would never be able to get that amount of money together, so I snarl, 'Did *that girl* give you this?'

He doesn't reply, but I can tell by his expression that she did.

'I'm going to AA,' he announces, after a couple more minutes of silence.

'Oh, great!' I feel my face heat up with anger. 'I have to endure over a year of your alcoholic shit, but you'll get sober for some dumb *kid* you've known two seconds!'

Trevor fiddles with the packets of sugar on the table. I do not feel appeased that he looks ashamed. He's not the person I wanted him to be.

'I think you're a beautiful person, Dot.'

'I don't give a fuck what kind of person you think I am,' I reply, and walk out of the café, without turning around once.

♪ ♪ ♪

I lie in bed at night stewing, balancing on the edge, in the same position I've slept for the past year. But then, one of my arms flops across the mattress, and slowly I wriggle around until I'm stretched out in the shape of a star.

My time brooding at Graceland writing mournful poetry has come to an end, so I return to the inner city, this time renting a place in North Fitzroy.

The hoodies are gone and my wardrobe bursts with single-shoulder dresses, fitted jackets, sweater dresses, pencil skirts and large sunglasses, all purchased at the vintage market in Daylesford. I see a picture of Katie Holmes with a fringe, and go to a hairdresser to get the same style. I feel classy and receive compliments from Gen Y girls.

I get my nails done, and as I admire my shiny new coat of shellac, I realise that's what I've become. I'm brighter but tougher; I wonder what of myself I've lost.

♫ ♫ ♫

I go round to Glen Huntly for lunch and find Mum frowning at the computer.

'This Ancestory.com is too hard to use, it drives me mad,' she tells me.

'Why do you bother with it, then?'

'I enjoy learning, Dot.'

I sit down next to Mum and show her how to use the site, talking slower than I did the first time I showed her. She sits with one arm around me and the other taking notes. Mum is learning something new; it's inspiring.

For the first time in years, I wonder how my life would've turned out if I'd finished my law degree. Would I have been on my way to the High Court? While Mum makes tea, I research enrolling in law as a mature-age student, but the fees are prohibitive. I wonder what I can do instead. There's only one answer.

♫ ♫ ♫

I bring the music back. I search the airwaves for new singers who emerged in my absence. I'm surprised how much I missed, and am immediately besotted with the cheerful new electropop sound.

Jade pops by with a six pack. We sit in my tiny lounge room, drinking beers and listening to music. The only furniture that fits in here is a couch and a bookshelf full of CDs. Jade shuffles through my CDs, with a raised eyebrow.

'Your music collection is awesome, but why do you bother with CDs? Get vinyl, if you want something retro,' she says.

'I don't have room for a record player. Besides, CDs will be retro one day, and when they are, I'll have a fabulous collection ready to go.'

'Nah, it's all gunna be streamed,' says Jade.

I think about the glitter-and-dust covered CDs I stacked on my bedroom floor when I first left home. I played them till they stopped working as I got ready for The Tube, for parties, for my life.

'I like CDs,' I say.

Music blows away the cobwebs in my brain and I take it with me everywhere. I play MGMT loud in my car as I drive down the coast to Graceland and I feel shouty happy. I play The Presets before meeting friends at a bar and I feel sexy. I listen to The Ting Tings on my iPhone on the tram to work and laugh at the sullen suits. They think I'm one of them, but I'm not. The post-punk and Britpop in my collection are happy to share space with The Faint, The Fratellis, The Killers and LCD Soundsystem. The synths are still there, as are drum machines and jangly guitars.

♫ ♫ ♫

'I think it's time I start dating again,' I say to Cat. We're in the stairwell of a new restaurant, waiting for a table we're told is forty-five minutes away.

'Oh goodie, you're going to have so much fun and I can't wait to hear all your cool stories!'

'Look at you, in your ivory tower of marriedness.'

'I do like a good story,' Cat admits. 'A girl from work did all this internet dating. Her stories were hilarious! She ended up meeting some guy online and getting engaged, so that could happen to you too!'

It could indeed, and when I get home after dinner I create myself a profile on a dating site.

I browse through pages and pages of men. Some of them contact me and we go on dates. They are not what their online personas claim, though. I narrow my searches, avoiding men under five foot ten, men who don't have cars, men who like cats, men who live miles away, men who talk about their exes, men who talk about how busy they are and men who say that women are too picky.

Cat calls me after a date for the lowdown. She questions me à la Macaulay Culkin and John Candy in *Uncle Buck*.

'What did you do?' she asks.

'Had a drink at Cookie.'

'What did you wear?'

'Black pencil skirt and green fitted jacket with matching ankle boots.'

'What did he wear?'

'Dark blue jeans and woolly jumper his mum knit.'

'Which celebrity did he most resemble?'

'A craggy version of that guy who was in *The Man from Snowy River*.'

'Tom Burlinson. What did he discuss?'

'Four wheel driving and loneliness.'

'Who had better taste in music?'

'Me. He mentioned John Farnham.'

'Who was taller?'

'Him…just.'

'Who was better looking?'

'Me.'

'Pash?'

'Nope.'

'Second date?'

'Nah.'

Cat hoots with laughter, but it quickly fades.

'Everything OK?' I ask.

'Can we catch up tonight, just you and me? Somewhere quiet-ish so we can chat.'

We meet in a bar in the foyer of a hotel. It's soulless, but at least they give us a small bowl of rice crackers to go with our drinks. Cat's unusually quiet, picking out wasabi peas from the crackers, instead of chattering about some fool at work, Raj or the girls, like she normally does. My chest feels tight.

'So, what did you want to talk to me about?' I ask. My voice comes out sounding ten years younger, but not in a good way.

After a pause, Cat says, 'Remember when you went to London?'

I know what she's about to say, and 'Don't Go' by Yazoo starts playing in my head. 'Ye-es,' is all I can say.

'Well, it's my turn now. The office has given me a transfer for a year.'

'Oh.' I look down at my lap, then ask, 'What about Raj and the girls?'

'They'll come too.'

I poke around in the bowl for a bit. 'Sounds cool. You'll have a blast. London's amazing.'

She nods, both of us are quiet, alternating fishing crackers from the bowl.

'It's only for a year,' Cat says eventually. 'Two, tops. You know Mum won't cope if I'm away any longer.'

Me either. I don't say it out loud though. Instead I take a sip of wine, followed by another and then another. I can't stop drinking. Cat mustn't know what to say either, as she hoes into the crackers, frowning with concentration as she pops them one after the other into her mouth. Something in my neck tics, remembering the hurt I felt when we fell out at school. Guys may come and go, but I can't lose my best friend.

I put my glass down and say, 'We'll miss each other.'

Cat pushes away the empty bowl; her eyelashes are wet. 'Yeah...'

'I might come visit.'

'You better.'

TRACK 33 – EMOTIONAL RESCUE

Standing in the work toilets, I re-apply my mask of makeup and examine myself in the mirror. A well-groomed, professional-looking woman is staring back at me, but my eyes are wary, like an underage kid who's snuck into a nightclub and is afraid of getting caught. I put on my Jackie O sunglasses and leave the office.

I arrive at a bar next to a dumpster; flashing fairy lights distract me from the smell. Cat and Edie are already here with a thin girl wrapped in a pashmina.

'Hello! I am Laure,' says the girl, kissing me on each cheek.

'We work together,' Cat explains. 'Laure hasn't been in Melbourne long and she wants to check out some local scenes.'

Laure's nose wrinkles in the direction of the dumpster. 'This scene certainly is intriguing,' she says.

Like me, Laure is recently single. 'I came here with my ex-Australian boyfriend, and when we broke up I thought why the fuck should I leave, so I stayed. Now I'm ready to explore this city for myself, with you, my awesome new friends!'

I give Cat a grateful little pinch on the elbow.

♫ ♫ ♫

A few weeks later, we're at Cat's for yet another farewell barbeque, but Raj's meat lies untouched next to the remains of Laure's magnificent yet stinky tartiflette.

'That was a-maz-ing!' I say. 'I swear I ate a whole block of cheese.'

'You probably did,' says Laure. 'There were four reblochon cheeses in the recipe. Take some more white wine to help you digest.'

Cat's checking something on her phone. 'Apparently one of the old Tube DJs has opened a club called the New Tube.'

'Really? Is it Jordan?' I ask.

'Nah…the guy who played all the Britpop.'

'Oh, cool! We should check it out.'

'Bummer, it's the day I'm leaving… But you go. You might meet someone there!'

'What is this Tube?' Laure asks.

'Oh, it's the club that Cat and I used to frequent back in the day. They played the best indie music and we danced our pants off!'

'And snogged half of Melbourne,' Cat adds.

Raj appears to clear away the meat and rolls his eyes. 'Can't have been anyone quality, seeing I never went there.'

We ignore him.

'Any trip-hop in this club?' Laure asks.

I remember Portishead, Morcheeba and Massive Attack being played around, but I'm not sure if it was at The Tube. I want Laure to come though, so I say, 'Yeah, they'll play anything nineties. As long as it's not Aqua or something.'

'Awesome! I'm in!' Laure says.

'Can we come too?' Rita and Anita are never far away, listening in on our conversation.

'Of course you can,' Cat says. '*When* you turn eighteen!'

The girls poke their tongues out at Cat and run off. She catches me looking at her. 'What?'

'Just that if I ever had my own family, I'd want it to be like yours. You guys have fun together, but you're not enmeshed. Still, the idea of a baby growing inside me, then sucking on my boobs makes me feel kind of queasy. And as for changing shitty nappies, I couldn't think of anything more vile.'

Cat laughs. 'Well, you better get a nanny, Lady Muck.'

'I'm with you, Dot,' Laure says.

♫ ♫ ♫

The day comes by too soon, and I'm at the airport with Cat and about ten members of her family. We sip chai from flasks while Raj tries to stop the girls from running off.

They glide along in shoes with inbuilt wheels and flashing lights, yelling out improbable things such as, 'Shine yer shoes, guvnor,' and, 'Cor, blimey!'

Cat and I watch the girls, laughing. I can't decide if I want to be them or to have them.

'We've said goodbye to each other a couple times now, haven't we, Dot?' Cat says.

'Yeah, but we're amigos para siempre.'

'Girls are *amigas*!' says Rita with a roll of her eyes, and skates away before we can reply.

I turn back to Cat and say, 'Please don't come back with one of those fake accents like Fleur did.'

Cat laughs, 'I won't, but I can't make promises for the girls. Sounds like they already have one!'

Anita skates up to us at top speed. I have to reach out and grab her to stop her from running over my toes.

'Toodle pip!' she says.

I'm first in line to give Cat, Raj and the girls a goodbye hug. Relatives queue behind me.

'Be good,' I say to the girls.

'You're not the boss of us,' they say. 'But we'll send you an email, innit.'

'If you need decent meat, Waitrose has New Zealand lamb,' I tell Raj.

'Thanks for the tip.'

'Don't stay forever,' I say to Cat, hugging her extra long.

'Of course she won't!' says Cat's teary mum, who's standing next to me.

'You heard Mum,' Cat says. 'Look after yourself, Dot.'

I step aside to let Cat's relatives say goodbye. Then we watch the four of them file through the departure door, the girls gliding ahead on their wheelies.

♫ ♫ ♫

It's the New Tube night tonight, but I'm not sure if it's a welcome distraction or a reminder that Cat won't be around for a while.

I meet Laure and her friends out the front, and as we walk upstairs to the club, the familiar music slithers into my ears and zaps my brain. I can feel my neural pathways firing up.

The music's the only thing that's the same, though. The place is now overrun with Gen Ys. I say hi to the balding DJ and he shows me some old photos. There's Cat and me, apple-cheeked and bright-eyed, nothing to indicate the amount of substances we consumed. Nowadays, I can't drink more than a couple glasses before my eyes glaze.

Laure and I line up at the bar to buy a jug of beer for the group.

'Seventeen dollars for a jug? You're having a giggle!' I say when the bartender rings up our bill.

'Huh?' The kid serving us probably hasn't come across cheaper beer.

'Come on, Dot. Just because you're back in your old club does not mean they have their old prices,' Laure says.

'I swear jugs were ten dollars.'

'Maybe last century.'

We sit around drinking beer until we hear 'Parklife' playing, and hit the dance floor, shoving Gen Ys out of the way as we go. There are no girls in fairy costumes, no flashing lights on the floor and my knees hurt a little when I jump, but the music makes me forget for a moment.

After a few more songs, I head to the bar to get a glass of water and hear the clearing of a throat by my side. I turn to see a young guy, fiddling with his black-rimmed glasses.

'D'you come here often?' he asks.

I laugh. 'Gee, I haven't heard that line in ages!'

The guy looks confused and I notice that he's terribly young, so I answer his question instead, 'Nah, just thought I'd do something different with the girls. What about you?'

'Yeah, I come here with the boys pretty much every week. We love hearing the old tunes.'

Old tunes?!

'Awesome…so, are you at uni?'

'Yeah, I'm doing law.'

'Really? I used to study law too! I dropped out though, and now I'm in IT.'

'Cool.'

Why am I talking about such boring things? The boy seems interested though and keeps talking. Laure and the others are still dancing, so I stay with him. We talk about nothing, keeping the conversation going for a decent amount of time before we leave together.

We sit side by side in a taxi.

'How old are you?' he asks me, in the way kids still ask each other that question.

'Um…thirty-six.'

His eyes light up at the possibility of bagging an older woman, I assume. Then he remembers his manners and says, 'Oh, you totes don't look it. I'd say you're twenty-eight max.'

'How sweet!' I'm all buttered up and saucy now. 'And how old might you be, young man?'

'Twenty-one.'

I should be the one who's twenty-one, not thirty-six! I take the boy home anyway because I've never been a cougar before, so I can check that off my list, and because I don't want Trevor to be the last man I've slept with.

In the end, it was just the idea of it, plus bragging rights with the girls, that makes it worthwhile. I wake up the next morning with a throbbing head and the taste of beer still in my mouth. I peek at the sleeping boy next to me. He's weedy and not even good looking. Back in the original Tube era I wouldn't have given him the time of day. Oh god, I don't want to turn into a piece of dog poo – the older I get the easier I am to pick up. Next time I hook up with someone outside my age pool, they're going to be hot and ripped, otherwise I may as well hang with the balding, beer-bellied guys my own age.

TRACK 34 – BRASS IN POCKET

'Did you ever come across a pyramid-shaped penis?' Laure asks.

I clamp my mouth shut with my hand, to prevent myself spitting masticated brie all over her pristine balcony. 'Is that a thing?' I ask once I can talk.

'Well, I've seen a couple,' Laure replies. 'What the fuck do these guys expect me to do with them?'

'Same thing every other man expects,' I say, grabbing a handful of olives.

'What's with those guys on dating sites who want to chat online for hours on end? Agree to meet for a coffee and be done with it! I don't have time to sit in front of a computer all night, chatting with socially inept fools,' Edie says.

'And what's the deal with every one of them saying *Shawshank Redemption* is their favourite movie?' I wonder.

'Maybe they think it's an intelligent choice of film that would impress women,' Laure suggests.

'I'd be more impressed if their favourite movie was *The Lost Boys*,' I say.

'I hate how they lie about their height,' Edie adds. 'Online they say they're almost two metres, but when I meet them, they're midgets!'

'Would *we* ever lie about our weight like that?' I ask.

We pause for a moment to think, simultaneously yell out, 'Yes!' then burst out laughing.

It's been three years of these cheese nights on Laure's balcony. Cat's still not back, but I'm enjoying life.

There's a group of geeky-looking guys on the balcony next door to Laure's. They turn around at the sound of our outburst, which makes us laugh even more. We've been talking pretty loud, so they must have heard everything we said.

Edie ignores them, and says, 'Well, I've been out with this guy about eight times and he still hasn't slept with me. I've invited him back and all, but he always has some excuse.'

'Clearly he has something wrong with his dick,' I conclude.

'Yes, that is a more reasonable assumption than the possibility he's not into her,' Laure says, pouring herself another glass of wine, her mouth twitching.

'Well, I met his exact opposite,' I continue. 'We went to this pub on Southbank for a drink and within twenty minutes he'd moved his seat next to mine and started groping me.'

'Maybe he's a sex addict. A proper one who should be in therapy,' Laure says.

'You know how I can tell when I like a guy?' Edie says. 'When he brings me flowers and I'm not repulsed.'

Evidently the guys next door are repulsed, because they give us a look then go inside, slamming their sliding door behind them. We laugh so much we can no longer talk.

♫ ♫ ♫

The weekend is on fast forward and the next thing I know, it's Monday morning and I'm in a taxi at an uncivilised hour on my way to the airport. Work has started sending me to exotic places such as Canberra, and seeing I don't have many commitments, such as children, I go. I quickly learn that travelling for work purposes is far from glamorous. My shoulder aches from carting my laptop around and the early mornings give me the same feeling a hangover does.

My interstate colleagues seem to think it's fine to go home right after work and leave me without a social life. So I go to the hotel gym for a bit, then retire to my bland room to work some more.

My mind wanders and I reminisce about my time in London. Even with Cat there, I couldn't go back, just like I couldn't go back to Trevor. But the music in London bulked up my soul.

I shut my eyes and remember what it was like to hear Joe Strummer singing live for the first time, only a year before he passed away. The beat of that music carried me over the river, above the terrace houses and across the sea back to Melbourne. Quiet or loud, it's been with me ever since. The light from my laptop screen beckons me.

Music is the home you keep returning to, I type onto a blank screen.

I continue typing.

I get up from my desk to stretch my legs and am shocked to see that three hours have passed. I don't even know what I wrote, I was that entranced. I read it back and think it could be OK. It's not a proper music review; instead it's a cavalcade of the senses that sweeps me back. For people who don't care about the playlist or the band's latest album, what I wrote might be of interest. If they want to know what it was like, I can tell them about the time when, for an unguarded moment, I was one with the music, the audience and the band. When all it took was the beat of a drum and the twang of a guitar to lift us up.

Maybe I can start a music blog. Maybe this will fill the emptiness.

♫ ♫ ♫

Back home, my workload increases and the time I thought I had for music-writing vanishes. I like being noticed by the sorts of people in the office who eight years ago I could only admire from a distance. I like being heavily involved in closing the naughties Eksnep, and I like the bonuses that hit my bank account. I use the money for things that can only be described as material, but they furnish my house nicely. As usual, the actual work I'm doing isn't filling me with music. It would be OK if it was just a nine-to-five job, but these days a forty-hour week is a rare thing that only slackers and public servants can enjoy.

I push nagging thoughts out of my head and carry on; my hours aren't as bad as Cat's in London, and my pay isn't as bad as Laure's. Maybe that's all there is and maybe that's not so bad.

I have a lot of work to do today, but I can't focus. My boss, Irene, glides past, staring at me. She's an emotionless, intimidating woman. I can't say she seems overcome with joy to see me, so I focus on my laptop and type as fast as I can. Once Irene moves on, I open Facebook and scroll through my newsfeed, looking for something, although I'm not sure what it is.

I walk home from work, but when I get to my street, I continue walking. I walk past the little houses and gaze at them. The scruffy but inviting workman's cottages still make me feel calm. They make me feel like I'm home, even though I don't live in them. I walk around and around, still looking for something, but I'm not sure what it is.

I'm starting to feel tired and hungry. Maybe it's time to stop looking. Maybe a house needs a brick wall in front of it, so no one like Trevor can get in. I head home.

It's still early, and without any plans tonight or work trips tomorrow, I sink into my blog, letting words and music swirl me around. I'm in zero gravity as I write and write and write. I've heard of people being able to live off blogs, but I'm not sure how. Still, I picture myself in a hammock on a tropical island, typing away and sipping a drink from a coconut shell.

It's not until a few months later that I feel like I've written all I can, my forearms stiff with typing. I create a WordPress site and publish all of my writing. I'm live! I take a shower. The thought of some kid reading my posts, and feeling the same joy about music as I do, fills me with excited anticipation. If we share the joy of music, surely all the bad things in the world will disappear.

After my shower, I check to see if anyone's made comments. There are none. I go to bed and in the morning I check again. No comments. I check every day for the next week. Still no comments. In the movies they say that if you build it, they will come. But for me, they don't.

I scour my site for ways to improve it, but I can't see how. I share the blog's link on Facebook, and still no comments are made. I contact music magazines and people who run similar blogs, and they answer me with silence.

'Why isn't anyone interested in my blog?' I ask, during a family lunch at Glen Huntly.

'Maybe it doesn't contribute,' Dad suggests.

'But it does!'

He raises his eyebrows and I say, 'Take a look.'

Dad puts his glasses on and we head to the computer room. He reads while I hover, shifting my weight from one leg to the other.

'Well?' I ask after he's been reading for five or so minutes.

'It's well written, but I don't know any of this music. Who are Television? You'd have to write about Irish music to get my interest, to be honest.'

'But doesn't a love of music transcend personal taste?'

Dad stands up and squeezes my shoulder, 'Find the people who share your interests. Now, let's have a cup of tea.'

He leaves the room, but I remain on the computer. I find 'London Calling' on YouTube and have a listen, hoping the clang of the guitars will cheer me up. My foot refuses to tap, my head refuses to nod. I play the song again; still nothing.

The man with the music has abandoned me.

TRACK 35 – SHIVERS

I sit at my desk, crossing and uncrossing my legs. There's plenty of work to do, but I can't be bothered. I stick in my earbuds and listen to some Blondie, forcing my foot to tap, but I'm out of time and feel no better. I can't wait for Jack to cheer me up tonight.

Mensaje! shouts my phone, in a Speedy Gonzales approximation of a Mexican accent.

Dennis, in the adjacent desk, jumps. I switch my phone to silent and read the text.

> *Hey sis, can't make it*
> *tonight. Coco broke his arm,*
> *waiting in the emergency*
> *room surrounded by people*
> *with fake coughs.*

> *Oh that's terrible! Want me*
> *to come and wait with you?*

> *You're too kind but already*
> *got Mum, Dad, Zara, her*
> *parents and Kurt. No room*
> *left in the waiting room.*

I shove my phone in my bag and slam my laptop shut. Dennis jumps again. *Man, he's delicate!*

'Oh, I forgot to tell you that Irene wants to see you,' he informs me.

Irene never has anything to say to me. I don't think she likes me. 'What about?' I ask.

'She didn't say.'

Irene is sitting in her office, her long nails making the sound of a train as they clatter across her keyboard.

'You wanted to see me?' I'm annoyed with how small my voice sounds.

Irene looks up but doesn't smile. 'Oh, hi. Yeah, are you available for a meeting with Felix, Eric and myself tomorrow morning?'

Why do HR and the Managing Director want to speak to me? My role never crosses lines with them. *I haven't done anything bad, have I?* I travel all over the countryside for this job and I get my work done, even if sometimes I'm a little late and occasionally leave a little early. Maybe they're more anal than I thought. Maybe that's why Irene is never friendly.

'What's the meeting about?'

The phone rings and as she moves towards the handset, she says, 'We'll talk tomorrow. Meet us in Eric's office at nine.'

'Is it good news or bad?'

Irene picks up the phone, shooing me away. *Damn her for being so inscrutable!* Even though it's not quite five, and it's potentially another black mark against my name, I leave the office.

I stomp down the street ruminating, almost bumping into people. Colleagues in the past have been summoned to mysterious meetings, never to be seen again. Surely Irene would have been more talkative if she didn't have bad news for me tomorrow.

Jack's in the hospital surrounded by family and I'm alone in the city surrounded by strangers. Cat will be on the Tube now, rushing to work, and Laure's on holiday in France. No one to call, no one to comfort me. My social life has been hectic for most of my adult life, but suddenly I realise I only really have two friends. As a child, my family were always the last people to leave the party, and now I'm the last of the last. I picture a tragic diva, all alone on the dance floor, her mascara running and the lights casting shadows in the crevices of her face. The Bee Gees version of 'Tragedy' plays in the background.

I walk down Little Bourke Street. People hurrying home from work are replaced with people hurrying out to dinner. Chinese students stand outside restaurants; their desperation to attract patrons makes me uncomfortable. It's still too early for the smell of dumplings to be tempting, so I turn into a small laneway.

I squeeze past a parked delivery truck and hear music coming from a little bar. The front wall is nothing more than a pane of glass with a gap for a door. Inside I see wood panelling and Scandinavian furniture. Just one nice, crisp pinot grigio should chase away my worries.

I order a glass of wine and some wasabi peas. A kid with a Ned Kelly beard stands by his turntables. He's playing 'Sugar Man' and then slides into 'The Passenger'. I love those songs, and yet I feel nothing. Maybe the volume is too low, so I move closer, but my brain's asking for silence.

Back on my stool, I pop wasabi peas into my mouth, but with each mustardy explosion, I think of yet another area of my life that's not quite right. I started by flunking out of uni, and now I've failed at my blog, my relationships and my career. I'll probably have to go and live with my parents until I find another job, and who knows how long that will take. I can't think of one thing I'm really contributing to. A mortified tear pools in my eye, so I take a big gulp of wine to rush it away.

Crow-like noises emanate from the street. I look up and see a group of men in suits, the loud type who sit with their legs wide open on the tram. The types who never have to worry about failing at anything. *Please don't let them come in here*, I pray to the conscious atoms that apparently fill the universe. That theory must be bullshit though because the suits walk right in.

They fill the bar, their voices drowning out everyone, including Iggy Pop. I glug my wine and slide off the stool, glaring at the men as I walk by. One makes eye contact, and I freeze. He's handsome, immaculately dressed and presented. He could be Martin Jones, all grown up. I'd forgotten that real people could be this good looking. He doesn't give off the same overbearing insecure bravado as the other men. I assume quiet confidence is what he has.

My face releases itself from its grimace and my cheeks heat up. I realise I've been standing here like a twit for seconds, but as I turn to leave, the man speaks.

'Dot?'

How does he know my name? Is he Martin Jones' ghost come back to taunt me with his dreamlike inaccessibility?

'You're Dot Kelly, aren't you?'

'Um…yeah.' I can't bring myself to meet his eyes now. Great, because my teenage crush has reappeared, I've reverted to my gormless teenage self.

'I guess you don't remember me? Jordan Gregory.'

One of the other men taps him on the shoulder and asks him what he wants to drink. As Jordan answers him, I use the time to collect myself. *Holy shit!* Jordan is unrecognisably hot. He's the only person I've met who's actually improved with age. The skinny dork I dated at uni is gone. This Jordan is well built, distinguished and somehow taller. By the time Jordan finishes answering his friend, I'm standing straight with my chest pushed out.

I look him right in the eye and say, 'Why, of course I remember you, Jordan. How have you been?'

'Pretty good. I hope you weren't leaving because of us. We're out celebrating. I just got promoted to Director.'

I'm twirling my earrings. 'Well, congratulations, Jordan.'

His friend appears with a pot of beer, which is swallowed by Jordan's hand. I don't see a wedding ring. I glimpse at his shoulders and they are definitely broader than mine. Jordan introduces me to his colleagues, who have toned down their boorishness.

'Don't let us hold you up, though,' he says.

I'd forgotten I was leaving, and look outside to see that it's raining. Maybe the universe had been listening, after all.

I beam at Jordan. 'I suppose I could wait until it stops raining.'

♫ ♫ ♫

A few hours later and we're in a taxi together.

'It's good to see you again, Jordan,' I say.

'It's good to see you too, Dot.'

We smile at each other and I try to remember why I dumped him all those years ago. The taxi pulls up out the front of my place, but I don't open the door.

'D'you wanna come inside for a cuppa tea?' I slur.

'I don' drink tea.' Jordan is also slurring a little.

I'm not sure if he's taking me literally or he's not interested. Either way, I'm disappointed.

As I reach for the door, Jordan puts his hand on my leg and says, 'I'd like to come inside, though.'

TRACK 36 – NEW LIFE

It's the morning and Jordan is gone. I roll out of bed and lie on the floor for a moment, trying to think up arguments for not being fired. In the end, I decide to let my career die with dignity. I dress in my smartest suit, abandoning my usual makeup routine for the more subdued tones that Irene uses.

It's nine o'clock precisely when I get to Eric's office. I'm the first one here. I sit near his EA, feeling the same way I did at school waiting outside the principal's office. I place my hands in my lap, but they jump up to smooth down my hair and straighten my collar. Then they scratch my face and finally they settle on picking my nails, which is what I'm doing when Eric, Irene and Felix show up, brandishing their takeaway coffees.

'Morning,' Eric says. 'Shall we?'

We sit around the table in his office, and for a moment no one says anything.

'I expect you're wondering why you're here?' Eric eventually asks me.

'Yep,' my voice comes out in a squeaky whisper. I definitely am that schoolgirl again, and I can't meet the principal's gaze.

Irene speaks, 'Well Dot, we've all been impressed with your work lately.'

She pauses and Felix continues, 'We'd like to offer you a promotion.'

I clench my muscles to make sure I don't wet myself with relief. They tell me about my new role, but I'm hardly listening. All of a sudden these people are the nicest beings that ever existed and this is the greatest company I've ever worked for! They want me. Could this be another new Tube? People weren't interested in my blog, but they're interested in my work. This is my chance for substance.

♫ ♫ ♫

Over the next few weeks, I immerse myself in my new role. I've become the company writer; all documents are given to me to either edit or create from scratch. Aside from my disastrous blog, this is the first time I've written since I left university. It's like hearing Cat's voice on the phone, familiar and easy, and I slip right into the task. Small layers of my personal life are peeled away as I sink in deeper. I become one of those people who bustle about the office, important with meetings, workshops and interstate flights. This is something solid and adult-like; being professional and more mature might be fun. The bustling seems to suit me too, as I'm feeling bosomy at the moment, for some reason.

♫ ♫ ♫

Jordan still hasn't called, and my stomach churns with disappointment. Coffee tastes bad, and I try to remember the last time I felt ill for reasons that weren't alcohol related.

I'm dreaming I'm in the capsule again, but this time it's a rough ride. Thrown from side to side, I wake up nauseated and lie still, waiting for the feeling to subside. Instead, it grows worse. I jump out of bed and bolt. My toilet must be surprised to be presented with my face instead of the usual rear end, but the sick feeling vanishes right away. By the time I'm cleaning my teeth, I'm fine.

♫ ♫ ♫

Eric has asked me to write a report for a client. I read through the incoherent pages colleagues before me have written and tweeze out splinters of useful information. Delicious possibilities of words and sentence structures sprinkle over me. I hardly move from my desk the whole day and it's well after eight when I send Eric my finished document. With a certainty that's unfamiliar, I know I've done a good job.

The next morning I'm sick again, and today the feeling doesn't pass after I've thrown up. The face I see in the mirror of the office lift would make Procol Harum pleased, with its whiter shade of pale. I'm looking forward to sitting at my desk, motionless, with only words for company. They're becoming my friends, just like the music was.

Something is coming; I feel it. Maybe that's why I've been sick. Maybe I'm just excited about change. I've even stopped stressing about Jordan. I'll either hear from him or I won't; it is what it is. I also shut away thoughts of the man with the music, that childish dream that came out of a speck of an event from aeons ago. Words are here now, and they provide for me. I breathe deep, and step out of the elevator into the foyer, almost bumping into Irene.

'Morning, Dot. Everything OK?'

'I'm fine. My stomach's a bit unsettled, but nothing a cup of tea won't fix.'

'Maybe you're pregnant,' she jokes.

I laugh too, 'If I was ten years younger, I'd be worried now.'

I make a cup of tea in the kitchen, chat with a few people, head to my desk and switch on my laptop. As I watch my emails downloading, I think about that night with Jordan. *Oh…shit!*

A couple hours later I'm in the work toilets, staring at the plus sign on the little white stick. This does not happen to women like me, women who've decided to be serious and career-oriented. This is the sort of thing that happens to irresponsible schoolgirls. I feel my cheeks redden as I recollect just how irresponsible Jordan and I were that night.

I wash my hands with soap and water for about five minutes, because I can't think of what else to do. The door opens, and I see Irene's reflection standing behind me.

'Still not feeling well?'

'Um…not really. Do you mind if I go home?'

'Sure.'

I can't tell if she minds or not, but I leave anyway. I walk past my tram stop and keep walking. Once I'm out of the CBD, I hit the side streets, where it's quieter. The twitter of birds and rustle of leaves slows me down, and I can finally start thinking. I'm having a baby. Do I want to have a baby? I like the promise of my new life, with this new role at work. Would this other new life ruin all that? If this had been ten years ago, I'd be straight off to that clinic on Wellington

Parade. I'd stare down those crazy protesters out the front, then exercise my rights over my own body.

I love Cat's girls and Jack's boys in a small doses kind of way, yet I don't know how I feel about children in general. The cherubic heads plastered all over my Facebook newsfeed don't make me feel maternal at all. I stop on a street corner and place my hand on my stomach; I don't feel anything.

I shudder at the thought of my body growing fat, of developing a waddle. Who's going to look after this baby when I'm at work, at the gym, on a date? Who's even going to want to date me, with a screaming baggage in tow? What if it has foetal alcohol syndrome or a personality I don't like? What if it's a conservative?!? And what will Jordan think? We haven't seen each other in years and now one passing encounter binds us together forever. I'm secure in the support and acceptance my family and friends will provide, but if only they had leanings one way or the other, my decision might be easier. I can no longer let life just flow.

Alone on the street corner, I need to talk to someone and think about who to call – Cat, Laure, Jack, Mum, Julie Ann? My choice surprises me, but I call right away.

'Hello?'

'Hi, Dr Ivanskiy, it's Dot.'

'Dot? Bloody hell, you never phoned me in your life. What're you up to?'

'Dr Ivanskiy, should I have a baby?'

'Of course you bloody should! Think about when you were a kid. You should give someone else the same magic. Don't become a lonely old bugger like me.'

As I hang up, I hear the creak of swings and the seagull voices of small children, and find myself turning the corner. I reach a park full of kids and even fuller of adults. I stand to the side, watching them, knowing I stand out in my smart work clothes and discomfort with the screechings. I'd come to the park to see the children; instead, I'm observing myself. I'm glamorous and aloof, I'm

Jocelyn, and I'm alone. My stomach somersaults with the same feeling as when I have my dream.

A woman walks past me, bent with the effort of pushing a kid in a stroller through the grass. Although he's in a stroller, he's at least five years old and when he stands up, I notice he's wearing a nappy. As he runs to the equipment, the woman turns and smiles at me. There's a dreamy quality to her. It must be tough, raising a disabled child.

The woman pushes her pram back to me and says, 'What a glorious day.'

Her movements are languid and I wonder if she's a mother with a little helper. 'Yes,' I reply, even though it's not.

She looks over at her son and then turns back to ask me, 'Which one's yours?'

'I don't have one.'

'Oh?'

'I'm pregnant.'

Sunshine breaks out across the woman's face. She touches my arm, saying, 'Congratulations! That's wonderful.'

'Mmm…'

'Oooh, you'll love being a mummy. It's a divine journey you're starting. Life changing.'

She sounds like one of those girls who went to Earthcore, back in the day.

'I'm not sure I'm ready to change my life in this way,' I tell her.

'Oh, you are.'

Her knowingness irritates me, so I change the subject. 'How do you do it, raising a special needs child?'

Surprise flicks across the woman's eyes. 'Orbital isn't special needs.'

I look at the boy, pushing over a child half his age, his nappy bulging through his pants.

'Oh, sorry! I just thought because he's still in a stroller and nappies… But he can't be as old as I guessed. Sorry, I know nothing about kids.'

The woman doesn't seem offended, and she turns towards little Orbital, enrapt. 'He's six. He'll choose when he walks and uses the toilet.'

Not knowing how to reply, I look again at the equipment where the children are trying to play, but they're all tangled up in the limbs of parents who won't leave them be. If I do have this baby, I'll be doing things differently.

TRACK 37 – MAKING PLANS FOR NIGEL

This time I'm sick in the work toilets. When I leave the cubicle, Irene is standing in front of the sinks holding a glass of water.

'Thanks,' I say, and drink it in one go.

I wash my face, sneaking glances in the mirror at Irene's reflection watching me. I'm going to have to tell her at some point and I wonder how she'll react. Deadpan, probably, but I wonder what she'll think.

'Dot?'

'Yes, I'm pregnant,' I snap, as I rummage in my bag for the toothbrush I've taken to carrying everywhere.

'Congratulations.'

'Thanks…'

I clean my teeth and still Irene stands there. I wish she wasn't so hard to read. This job is the only thing that's certain in my life; it's the ledge I cling to in a turbulent pool. I need it so much I'm vulnerable.

'This isn't a problem for the company, is it?' *Why did I blurt out such a servile question?*

'Of course not.' Irene stretches her mouth into a smile. 'I was sick every day for three months with my first. So you have my sympathy.'

'I didn't know you had kids.'

'A girl and a boy. They're both in high school now.'

The unreadable Irene is gone.

'Tell me about them,' I say.

Her stretched smile relaxes as we talk about her kids. It's the longest conversation I've ever had with her.

When we've exhausted that topic, she says, 'I didn't realise you were in a relationship.'

I glance at her neatly tied back hair, charcoal suit and gleaming wedding ring. 'I am,' I reply. 'He's a director at a bank. Jordan Gregory.'

'Well, you know that after the next planning day there's a dinner, and partners are welcome.'

I nod. Irene smiles and places her hand on my arm. 'Congratulations again,' she says.

When I get back to my desk, I check my phone and there's a message from Jordan.

Hey lovely lady. Sorry I
haven't been in contact but
I had to go overseas and
since then I've been flat out
at the office. How about
dinner one night this week?

I sit in my chair, heavy with relief.

I'd love that. How about the
day after tomorrow?

Great! Let me know where
you'd like to go.

It would have been nice if he'd suggested a place, but at least he's interested enough to want to catch up. I visualise my wardrobe and wonder what I'll wear. I'm mentally selecting my shoes when I remember the news I have to tell Jordan. I have no idea how he'll react, or even what I want from him, but tell him I must.

♫ ♫ ♫

Jordan and I sit in a bar, picking at a ham and cheese platter. Everyone else here is excited in an after-work way. I wish I'd suggested somewhere quieter to meet, but under pressure of choosing, I defaulted to one of the usual trendy haunts I go to gossip with Cat and Laure.

We make small talk, but my heart is beating out of control the entire time. Jordan's placed his phone on the table corner, and I keep looking at it, rather than his face. I don't know how to bring up my news, and the longer we talk the harder it seems.

Jordan finishes his beer and asks, 'Another?'

'Mineral water again, please.'

He raises his eyebrows but doesn't say anything. While he's at the bar I conclude that I need to do this in the same way Mum used to tweezer out my splinters; one quick movement and deal with the whinging after.

Jordan returns with my mineral water and a brown drink for himself.

'What's that?' I ask.

'Coke.'

I check his teeth for signs of rot, but they're nice and white.

He continues, 'I'm not much of a drinker, really. The other night was an exception. But what's the deal, Dot? This is the first time I've seen *you* not drink. Have you changed so much?'

OK, go tweezers! 'Yes, no, I mean, I don't know… But there's a reason I'm not drinking tonight. You see…well, it turns out, actually, that I'm pregnant. Um, from the other night?'

Bloody hell, why do I have to make life-altering announcements à la Hugh Grant in a Richard Curtis movie?

I watch Jordan's face turn from tan to white to red.

'Oh,' he says.

And then his phone vibrates. We both look at it; someone called Peter From Work is calling. Jordan stares at the phone for an eternity; then he looks back at me, before pressing decline.

I stir my ice blocks with my straw, waiting for him to say more, but he doesn't. *I've told him, now it's his turn to talk. Why doesn't he talk?* I have to admit Jordan looks pretty cute when he's shocked; there's a boyish confusion about him that I'd never noticed all those years ago.

'Jordan?'

He takes a sip of his drink. 'Hmm. So, what do you want to do?'

'Well, it'd be ridiculous for a person of my age not to keep it.'

'Yes, of course.' I wish he wasn't so quick to agree that I'm a 'person of my age'.

'What do you want from me?' He's not accusing, just curious.

'I don't know. I just wanted to tell you. I mean, I hope this isn't the last time we see each other, but the main thing was to tell you. I'm still processing this myself.'

'Yes, of course,' he repeats, then stands up. 'Excuse me.'

At first I think he's leaving, but instead he heads over to the bar. He returns with a beer, which he proceeds to drink quickly for a person who doesn't drink much. I wait for him to speak, playing with my ice blocks in the meantime.

Eventually he sighs and says, 'Dot, I'm not going to be a jerk to you, but I need some time to think this over. Can you give me some time?'

'Yes, of course,' I echo his own words.

We stand outside the bar. *Should we be kissing, shaking hands, or what?* I hear the whirr of Jordan's phone from his pocket and he takes it out to show me that Peter From Work is calling again.

'Um, I have to take this. Let's touch base in a few days though.' He pecks me on the cheek, then stalks off into the night, phone at his ear.

On the tram, on my way home, I get a message from Cat.

Hey babe, how's it going?

I debate for a bit before replying.

Pretty good. How's London?

Cat and I chat about London, and I don't tell her. I need to sort things with Jordan first, whatever that means.

♫ ♫ ♫

Just as I'm thinking I'll never hear from him again, he messages me.

> *How about you come to my*
> *place for dinner tomorrow*
> *night? We can talk better*
> *with no other people around.*

I agree, and Jordan texts me his address. It's in a place called Wintergate Gardens.

> *I thought you lived in*
> *Melbourne.*

> *I do.*

I look up this Wintergate Gardens place on Google Maps. *Jesus, it's in the middle of nowhere!*

There are no nearby train stations, so the next day I'm forced to drive down the freeway for what feels like forever. When I take the Wintergate Gardens exit, I notice all the houses are massive rendered creations, gardenless and identical. Just the kind of area I hate. *But why do I hate it?* I can't think of a reason, other than the fact that I decided outer suburbs were daggy when I was about fourteen. Maybe there's nothing wrong with them though. Maybe it's time to stop being so immature. I like little houses, but some people might like big houses, and there's nothing wrong with that. I decide to give Wintergate Gardens the benefit of the doubt.

I pull my scratched Barina into a double driveway next to the biggest, blackest car in the world. I pause to behold it and can't decide if it's a car or a truck or a spaceship.

Jordan answers as soon as I ring the bell. He's wearing jeans that are a shade too blue and a cream shirt. He's still a version of Martin Jones, but he looks better in his work clothes.

'Hey,' he says and gives me an awkward peck on the cheek. 'Come on through.'

This is the largest house I've been in, bigger even than Fleur's childhood home. Jordan leads me through to what real estate sites call the open-plan living space.

'Wow, you have a corner couch!'

I can't help myself – I take a running jump onto the couch. It's leather, so the landing isn't as cloudlike as I'd imagined.

'Be careful,' Jordan, who's still standing in the doorway, says.

'Oh, sorry. I didn't get my shoes on it.'

'No, I meant be careful of yourself…in your condition.'

'Oh.' I'd forgotten that I was in a condition.

Jordan shows me around and I have to admit his house is pretty schmick. Nice to be somewhere without rust stains in the bath.

He cooks a stir-fry and we sit at his dining table. He offers me a Coke.

'Nah, I don't fancy liquid Drano today.'

'Pardon?'

Jordan gets cute crinkles around his eyes when he's confused.

'Never mind,' I say.

We eat dinner, making small talk, skirting around the topic. When we're done, we retire to the corner couch with a bowl of ice cream each. Jordan flicks on the television.

Some inane reality show is on, so I say in a loud voice, 'I guess we should talk about this situation.'

He turns the television down, but not off. 'Yes, of course.'

I spoon ice cream into my mouth, then start. 'I hadn't really thought about having kids before. But now that I am, I'm going to proceed. It might be fun.'

'OK.'

'And what do you propose your involvement will be, Jordan?'

A flicker of hurt shoots across his face, so I continue, 'What I mean to say is, I'm fond of you, Jordan. I think we're both more mature now, and capable of behaving better than we did back in the day. Besides, I find you attractive…'

Jordan smiles a bit. *Wow, he is attractive.*

A whirring noise comes from the kitchen counter: Jordan's phone. We both look over, but Jordan doesn't move to answer it. Instead he says, 'I like you too, Dot. I always did. I'll support you, regardless, but maybe you and I have something more, what with our history and all.'

Jordan's hand is on my knee now.

'Maybe we do,' I say, as I lean in towards him.

♫ ♫ ♫

I'm walking down my street on the way to work. I hear a booming noise and as I round the corner, who should I see but Trevor. His big bald head and his laughing mouth make him look like the Luna Park entrance. Standing slightly behind him is a woman, younger but plainer than me.

'Dot! How's it going?' Trevor leans in to give me a hug, but I step back. The plain woman grabs hold of his flailing hand.

'What are you doing here?' I ask.

'We live here now.'

'What? You can't live here!' *How dare Trevor move to my neighbourhood, how very dare he!*

'It's a free country,' he replies, laughing.

'So, are you a teacher now?' I ask.

'Not quite. It's still the dream though. Just gotta pay off those credit cards.'

I shake my head and walk away. I bet he hasn't completed AA either, since he's never tried to make amends with me.

'Come round for a barbeque,' Trevor calls after me.

I walk as fast as I can through the narrow streets and little houses. They've suddenly lost their appeal.

TRACK 38 – (KEEP FEELING) FASCINATION

Futures Bright @mowyourlawn1960   21 Oct 2011
Anyone need their lawn moving? Music lover and handyman,
that's me #OddJobs #MusicChats

Futures Bright @mowyourlawn1960   30 Oct 2011
Cropped grey hair, lawn mowing muscles and outdoorsy tan
make me look like aging rock star turned vegetarian #NotBad

Futures Bright @mowyourlawn1960   1 Nov 2011
Last of the tar and beer chemicals have coughed themselves out
of my lungs. #FeelingGood! #PoisonFree

Futures Bright @mowyourlawn1960   2 Nov 2011
2 new gigs to accompany lawn mowing, washing high-rise office
windows and hosting insomnia community radio program on
#111FM #MusicInTheSky

Futures Bright @mowyourlawn1960   3 Nov 2011
Maddie concert this Thurs at the Betty Ford Bar in Northcote.
This kid is special, you need to hear her sing #VoiceOfAnAngel

Futures Bright @mowyourlawn1960   6 Nov 2011
17 years old and already she sings of road trips, sunsets and
love gone wrong #MaddieGig

Futures Bright @mowyourlawn1960   6 Nov 2011
Her voice murmurs of adventure, guitar lulling you along for the
ride, drums are but a gentle swish in the breeze #MaddieGig

Futures Bright @mowyourlawn1960   6 Nov 2011

Maddie shy and awkward, can't work a crowd, but when she sings we all shut up #MaddieGig

Futures Bright @mowyourlawn1960   6 Nov 2011

I hope this kid has enough success to earn a living but not enough to tarnish her soul #MaddieGig

Futures Bright @mowyourlawn1960   15 Nov 2011

1st program on air! Been working on my playlist all week. Tune in tonight for jangly guitars #111FM

Futures Bright @mowyourlawn1960   15 Nov 2011

Presenting my own music program feels like going home after being lost for centuries #111FM

Futures Bright @mowyourlawn1960   18 Nov 2011

Fascinating views while cleaning in the sky. Ant people in street below and close ups of office drones #AnalyseThat #RearWindow

Futures Bright @mowyourlawn1960   22 Nov 2011

Sitting at a radio console whispering musical secrets into a furry microphone, sharing my hopes n dreams with the world #111FM

Futures Bright @mowyourlawn1960   23 Nov 2011

Walk in Caulfield Park. What's the bronze statue of the boy waiting for? I'm waiting too, but good waiting #WhatAboutMe

Futures Bright @mowyourlawn1960   25 Nov 2011

Spring in the air, as am I! Cleaning windows, saw into the soul of a woman checking Facebook in her office. Somehow familiar #Atomic

Lazarus, Hello, Burn The Witch, Duele El Corazón, WTF, Bol Do Na Zara, Alarm, Your Best American Girl, This One's For You, Drone Bomb Me, Hymn For The Weekend, Cold Water, Just Like Fire, When We Were Young, Dangerous Woman, Papercuts, Low Life, All The Way Up, No Money, Die A Happy Man, Down In The DM, Heathens, Pop Style, Cruel, Wherever I Go, The Ministry of Defence, Everything You've Come to Expect, Somewhere On A Beach, Work From Home, Daydreaming, Bobo, Came Here To Forget, Hotter Than Hell, Wobble, Same Old Love, On My Mind, My House, Used To Love You, Can't Stop The Feeling, Into You, Send My Love (To Your New Lover), I Hate U I Love U, Cake By The Ocean, Birds, In My Blood, Controlla, Blackstar, You Don't Know Love, Sex, We Don't Talk Anymore, Panda, I Took A Pill In Ibiza, Wolves Of Winter, Closer, The 1975, All In My Head, Kill Em With Kindness, Cleopatra, Piece Of Me, Give Me Your Love, 7 Years, Starboy, Cheap Thrills,

Lean On, Girls Like, Cake By Money, A Of Dreams, That Girl, Don't Let

Vinyl + Download

Light It Up, Be Alright, The Ocean, Head Full No Woman, Final Song, Me Down,

Broccoli, Fast Car, Faded, All My Friends, One Dance, Stressed Out, Secret Love Song, Love & Hate, When The Bassline Drops, Adventure Of A Lifetime, Hands To Myself, Middle, Get Ugly, Treat You Better, This Girl, Never Be Like You, Home, No, 1955, Here, Army, Dancing On My Own, Uber Everywhere, Gamma Knife, Am I Wrong, Black Man In A White World, Hype, Strange Torpedo, Below, It's Just A Pop Song, This Is What You Came For, First Day Out Tha Feds, Shine, Stitches, In Common, Lake By The Ocean, Say You Do, Apple Cider I Don't Mind, Boyfriend, Chandelier, In Flight, You're The One, Woman Is A Word, Perfect Strangers, Aviation, The Community Of Hope, Swipe Life, Only Girl, Money Longer, Soundcheck, Destroyed By Hippie Powers, Bored To Death, Keep Singing, Animal Style, Violet, Mean What I Mean, 1 Of 1, Freak Like Me, Come Down, Lockjaw, Rush, Morning Sex

TRACK 39 – ONCE IN A LIFETIME

Pattie watches me observing myself in the mirror. I've spent a fortune at the gym, but I have my figure back. It's sinewed, like Madonna's.

'Where're you going, Dot?' Pattie asks.

'Out.'

I watch her expression from the mirror to see if she minds, but her eyes are like Kalamata olives – black and glossy, but unreadable. Does she wish on the first star at night that she could go to a party?

'Remember, only half an hour of screen time.'

'Daddy lets me have more.'

Jordan comes into the bedroom, scratching his belly which has grown round over the past few years.

'Jordan, Pattie gets only half an hour of screen time, OK? And that includes television, laptops, Wii, iPads, iPhones and iFarts.'

I look at Pattie to see if she laughs at my joke; she doesn't.

'Yeah, yeah,' says Jordan, as he changes out of his work clothes.

I open my mouth to give further instructions about not giving her junk food, cleaning her teeth and putting her to sleep in her own bed, but his phone vibrates from somewhere in the house and he walks off to answer it. Besides, I don't want to be a nag.

I sweep into my walk-in closet to select some shoes. Our house is big enough to sweep around in. This is the fanciest house I've ever lived in, but it's come at a cost and that cost is Wintergate Gardens. Flat, full of gardenless McMansions and streets lined with oversized cars, my enthusiasm for living somewhere new soon faded. I can't believe I've been here over five years.

Despite the absence of footpaths, I take Pattie on long walks and all we see are houses, houses and more houses. No little cafés to stop off at for a cold drip coffee and a Fair Trade hot chocolate, no boutiques to try on gorgeous clothes made by funky local designers and no bars to enjoy a cheeky, mid-week glass of shiraz. I look for a community I can be part of, but everyone is too insular and too busy paying off their exorbitant mortgages to be a community. You need to do more than name a suburb after a Jane Austin-sounding English estate to give it life.

My Barina recently died, so tonight I'm forced to use Jordan's monstrous SUV, now decorated with My Family stickers.

'I don't see why you have to have such a big car,' I say to Jordan, who's come back into the bedroom. 'It's impossible to park, terrible for the environment and is against everything I stand for.'

'We have a child, Dot.'

'In my day, kids were bundled into the boot of a station wagon. Besides, we could fit a car-seat in the back of a two-door Barina.'

'Small cars aren't as safe. Besides, we might have more than one child.'

I set my mouth into a thin line.

♫ ♫ ♫

Cat and I meet in a bar in St Kilda.

'How's life?' she asks, as she nibbles on pistachio and yoghurt cake.

We're trying this thing where we order one cake and one drink to share. Metabolisms become stupid around this age.

'Comme ci, comme ça,' I reply.

Cat hasn't been back from London long, so I'm still filling her in on years of gossip. London has faded her complexion, so she's not much darker than me now, but her Australian accent survived.

Cat's eating, so I continue, 'I'm ticking all my boxes, so shouldn't things be a little better than so-so?'

'Depends on the boxes, I guess.'

I break off a piece of cake and pop it into my mouth. 'Isn't a nice big house, good career, husband and a kid everyone's boxes?' I ask.

'Who's everyone?'

'Well, that's what you have and you're happy.'

Cat shrugs. I look out at the street, where the SUV is parked, blocking the view. 'Do you like SUVs?' I ask her.

'I don't really have an opinion one way or the other.' She sips from the glass of wine and looks at me quizzically.

On paper we have similar lives, but there's something vibrant about Cat's, with Raj with his barbeques and their noisy, cheeky girls, that's absent from mine. Cat and Raj talk to each other like teenagers sharing secrets. When he's not on the phone to the office, Jordan and I talk about household chores and Pattie. Rita and Anita are precocious and their bedrooms are pigsties, but they're lovable and fun. Pattie is polite and neat as a pin, but she's serious and guarded.

I change the subject one more time. 'So now it's Fleur's turn to move to London? Again.'

'Yep. I guess her faux-cockney accent ran out and she needed a top up. You hear from Amanda?'

'Only that one time when I first had Pattie, which was awkward, seeing I'd previously deleted her from Facebook. All she wanted to do was talk about kids. People who don't retain their own identity once they've had a family depress the hell out of me.'

Why is everything I say such a mood-drainer? Cat comes to the rescue and switches the conversation to lighter things, such as her confusion over the popularity of Pokémon Go and an argument she's having with a Gen Z at work.

'Jesus, they're even worse than the Millennials,' she tells me. 'This girl's always taking *personal days,* even though I've told her countless times there's no such thing. And she insists on texting me when she's sick, despite the fact that I keep reminding her it's company policy to call. Once she even tweeted that she wasn't coming in!'

'Is that the one whose mum came with her to the job interview?'

'The very same. The mum negotiated an exorbitant salary for her too.'

'What does this girl even do?'

'Fucked if I know, Dot. Something to do with social media, but I suspect the only online brand she's managing is her own.'

I pop the last bit of cake in my mouth and say, 'Ha! Reminds me of the time I asked for my first promotion.'

'Remind me.'

'Remember? I'd been in the job only a few months when I marched up to my boss and demanded a promotion. When he asked me what I'd achieved, I said nothing, but I'd been there three months so felt like it was time.'

'Oh, yeah…' Cat laughs. 'Did he promote you?'

'Nah. He told me to piss off.'

'I guess all young people are obnoxious, whatever the generation,' Cat says.

When I get home Jordan is in the lounge room, gazing at his iPad. I tell him the funny story about Cat and her younger colleague, but he doesn't take his eyes off the screen.

'Don't you think that's funny?' I prompt him. 'We're complaining about some of the things we also did back in the day.'

'Oh, young people aren't that bad,' Jordan replies. 'I relate to the guys at the bank pretty well, and they love it when I tell them I used to be a DJ.'

Jordan's DJ stories last longer than the period he actually was a DJ. Besides, it depresses me when he talks about 'young people' as it makes him sound like an old fuddy-duddy and, by implication, me too.

I go into our bedroom to change. Pattie is asleep in there.

I return to the lounge room. 'Jordan, why is Pattie in our room? She needs to sleep in her own bed.'

'Oh relax, Dot. She's not doing any harm in there.'

Jordan turns his attention back to his iPad and that's the end of our conversation for the evening.

I go back to our bedroom, scoop up Pattie and carry her to her room. She wakes up, grizzling. 'No-oh!'

'Yes, Pattie! You're sleeping in your own room. No nonsense!'

'No!'

'Pattie, this is your warning. If you don't go to sleep in your own bed you're not going to the park tomorrow.'

'Who cares! Dumb Dot!'

'Whatever. Now give me a kiss and get to sleep.'

Pattie gives me a kiss that doesn't touch a single part of my body. She wriggles out of my grip and crawls into her bed unassisted, presenting me with her back.

'Night night, Pattie,' I say.

She doesn't reply.

TRACK 40 – PSYCHO KILLER

It's still warm and light when I get home from work, so Pattie and I have time for a pre-dinner walk. Luckily she's inherited my lean frame, but with childhood obesity what it is these days, I'm not taking any chances. We walk every day, play in the park and only ever have junk food for special treats. I don't want her teeth and guts rotting away.

Pattie is outside on the trampoline with the safety net I had removed so she can learn to monitor her own risk-taking. I've never seen a child bounce so stiffly. I want to give her a cuddle, but can't face her wriggling away from me again.

'Come on, Pattie, let's go to the park,' I call out, as I change from my work clothes into a stripy dress.

'No! I want a biscuit!'

'Well, you're not having one. We'll have dinner when we get back, so you're not filling yourself up on crap.'

'Hungry!'

'Then have some fruit. Mmm, fruit!'

Pattie rolls her eyes.

I march her out of the house. If only she does what I tell her until she turns eighteen, we'll have a lovely time. We walk to the park in stony silence, but after a while I realise Pattie's running to keep up with me, so I slow down. I tell her some sanitised stories about The Tube days to keep her entertained.

'You're not cool, Dot,' Pattie replies.

I stop walking and my eyes water a little. This is the most hurtful thing anyone's ever said to me. Then I remember that I'm talking to a small child, so I poke my tongue out at her and we continue walking.

At the park Pattie tugs her hand out of mine, running off to play. I'm the only person standing alone. As usual, there are more adults than children at the park and they cover the equipment like helicopters on a battleship, tailing their kids. When Jack and I played, Mum must have been there somewhere, but I don't remember her. It was just us kids. If children can't play unsupervised, how can they create their own magical worlds? I check work emails to give Pattie some privacy as she plays.

When we get home, Jordan is cooking a stir-fry while talking to Peter From Work on speaker. Pattie hugs him around the legs then runs off.

'What did she get up to at the park?' Jordan asks, when his phone call ends.

'Oh, I don't know. I had emails to answer. Ask her.'

By the time we eat, it's nearly eight and Pattie quickly finishes her meal.

'Thanks, Daddy! I was hungry!'

'Dot, don't you think it's a little late for her to eat?' Jordan asks. 'We should ask Helena to cook her dinner at five.'

'Nonsense, Jordan! I'm not having my child eating dinner in the afternoon like some sort of bogan. Besides, there's a bowl full of perfectly good fruit she knows she can eat.'

I feel an argument coming on, so I say to Pattie, 'Go and put your *Operation Ouch!* DVD on. You can watch one episode before bed.'

As she trots off, Jordan mutters, 'Jesus, Dot, she's a little kid.'

I grumble, 'Well, I just don't like the idea of her eating dinner in the afternoon. It's tacky.'

'Tacky? On which planet does anyone think what a little kid does is tacky? Don't confuse her meals with your fancy bloody dinner parties.'

I'm not thinking of fancy dinner parties. I'm thinking of the dinners my family ate at Graceland: a kitchen full of pots and pans and kids, the floor vibrating with Dad's foot tapping as he played the accordion. Dinner was served any time between seven and ten, and we all sat down together, yelling to be heard over everyone else.

I don't know how to recreate this joyful scene with Jordan and Pattie, so in the end I say, 'I just wanted us to eat as a family…but maybe she is a little young. We'll tell Helena to give her dinner at six.'

'Or we could eat earlier with her?'

'How do you propose I get from the city to this far-flung place any earlier?'

Instead of answering, Jordan clears the dinner things.

I go into the lounge room and ask Pattie, 'Do you want to help me water the plants?'

'I don't care.'

I want to make these little activities fun things we do together, but she's turned away from me back to *Operation Ouch!* so I snap, 'Well, you *can* help.'

I've decorated the house with succulents in all sorts of containers – tea-cups, cut-open plastic toys and glass bottles. I let Pattie squirt water on to the plants and she does so without spilling a drop, but holding the water bottle stiffly and moving around with heavy limbs, the same way I used to move when Mum made me unload the dishwasher.

I admire our collection of plants, but there's something sterile about them, even when they sit in their ridiculous containers. 'Maybe we need some flowers too,' I say.

'Daddy's allergic. Did you forget that?' Pattie asks.

'Oh yeah… Well, that was fun anyway, wasn't it?' I ask in a voice that dares her to say it wasn't. She doesn't answer, so I say, 'OK, teeth, toilet, bed!'

'No! Wanna watch *Operation Ouch!*'

'Oh boy, if you're like this now, god help us when you're a teenager. Teeth, toilet, bed! Now!'

'You love clean teeth so much you should marry them!' Pattie shouts, but she stomps off to the bathroom and I hear the tap come on.

When she returns I sniff her breath to make sure it smells of toothpaste, and ask Jordan to read her a story.

'Yay, Daddy! Let's have *The Muddle-Headed Wombat!*'

While Jordan's reading to Pattie, I answer some emails before going in to give her a good night kiss. She air-kisses me and I head to my room, grabbing my bathers to go for a swim.

The pool is where I go to think, relax and stretch my back muscles that cramp up from spending so much time in front of a laptop.

I don't like it that Pattie is so awkward and oppositional with me, and I don't like it that I'm so awkward and oppositional with her. Even when we're doing something fun, like going to the park or watering the plants, we don't connect. When she was a baby, I would hold her face to get her to make eye contact with me, searching for something that wasn't there in those black olive eyes. And what's with the air-kissing as though she's a haughty fashion designer instead of a five-year-old?

The people in my lane are swimming far too slow, so I switch to the fast lane and continue thinking.

It's not Pattie, it's me. But I can't work it out, because I think I have pretty good parenting skills. I don't mollycoddle her, or neglect her, or fight with Jordan in front of her. Maybe I should spend more time with her, maybe I shouldn't have gone back to work early, maybe I shouldn't have insisted on controlled crying, maybe I should post pictures of her on Facebook, maybe I should talk about her nonstop with my friends; but I'm scared of losing myself.

Pattie's eyes are as dark as the view from my capsule window when I have that dream about being stuck in space, the dream that won't stop no matter what I do. Pattie should be in Major Tom's capsule with me, but she's in her own one and it's a universe away. I don't know how to find her.

My brain is too tired to think any further, so I shut down my thoughts and finish the last few laps as fast as I can. When I get home, both Jordan and Pattie are asleep in our bed. I'm too worn out from the swim to do anything about it, so I take a shower and go sleep in Pattie's room.

I wait for bits of her soul to enter mine, but nothing happens.

TRACK 41 – LUST FOR LIFE

There's not much difference between the gym and The Tube – fast, loud music, sweaty bodies jumping about in skimpy clothes and more than one person who looks like they've consumed illicit substances.

Cat and I change into neon shorts and singlets, step out of the changing room, pausing a little to make sure everyone's aware we have arrived, then commence our workout. We point men out to each other, using the same sign language we've been using for over twenty years. Afterwards, we share a smoothie in the café downstairs.

'So the girls have banned me from using teenage expressions,' Cat tells me, as she sips our watermelon and kale beverage.

'How basic of them!'

Cat laughs. 'They say every expression I use is three years out of date.'

'Ooh, just like when Mum started saying 'pash'!' I try the drink. It's disgusting, so clearly must be doing us good. I take another sip.

Cat says, 'So…dinner tonight?'

'Yep,' I say. 'There's this new place in one of the laneways off Little Bourke Street that's supposed to be dope, as the youf would say. No reservations, but if we put our name down at about five, they'll call us when a table comes up. Usually takes about two hours.'

'Sounds great. Can't get there at five though, can you?'

'No. Some fool thought it would be a good idea to hold a meeting at four thirty on a Friday afternoon. Laure can get there earlier though.'

'Sweet! Well, I've gotta launch,' Cat says. 'Later.'

'Ha! If your girls could hear us, they'd die of embarrassment.'

'Care factor zero!'

We head off in opposite directions, laughing to ourselves. I wonder how Cat and I are going to sound when we're living together in an old folks' home, using seventy years' worth of teenage buzzwords. No one will be able to understand us; they'll assume we have dementia!

Kai is waiting for me in the office. 'Morning, Dot!'

He makes us both an espresso and we bustle into one of the meeting rooms. I open my laptop, but it's just for show.

'Tell us about The Tube again,' Kai breathes.

I can hear Pulp in my head as I start talking, 'Oh Kai, I wish you'd been there with us! The drink cards, the ultraviolet lights, the boys we'd pick up!'

Kai's eyes are shining and I'm sure mine are too.

'We would literally dance all night. And you could wear whatever you wanted – a fairy outfit, a school uniform or a three-piece suit just like you're wearing now!'

'Wow, Dot,' Kai sips his espresso. 'I wish I could've experienced the original scene rather than the retro one.'

'Oh, everyone's scene is someone else's retro,' I reply, feeling wise.

'You're my oldest but coolest friend.'

We sing a verse of 'Common People' together, before dissolving into laughter. I'm never allowed to be nostalgic for long though. Irene comes tapping on the door, keen to fill my day with work, no doubt. I sigh, and head to my desk. I wish she still gave me writing assignments, but now it's all just reporting and presentations. I'm already counting the hours before I can leave for the day.

When I finish work, I go to the bathroom to touch up my makeup and spray on a little perfume. I wonder when it was that I forgot to be punk. I let out a long breath and tell myself I'm good looking. Once I start to believe it, I leave.

I strut down the street to meet Cat and Laure in a bar, where we wait for the call for dinner. It's the same bar Cat and I went to when we first started working. In those days it was dingy and stunk of cigarettes and the odd joint.

Now it's decorated with white furniture, is tiled top to toe and has succulent plants growing from a vertical garden.

'So ladies, are you ready for the retreat?' Laure asks.

'Certainly am!' I reply.

Our annual Mornington Peninsular weekend is coming up, with its regime of yoga, massages, mineral springs and facials during the day, and escaping to Mangiare at night for a seasonal degustation meal accompanied by matched wines. Raj, Jordan and Laure's boyfriend think we're going to one of those strict detox places, and we let them think this.

Throughout dinner I'm buzzing with anticipation for the weekend away, but as I say goodbye to Cat and Laure, and head off down the freeway, it wears off.

Like Sarah Jessica Parker in a rom-com, I've managed to retain my social life, my career, family life, health and exercise. On paper things are excellent, and my life is probably enviable, but despite all I've cultivated, I still have those dreams.

With Jordan lying there beside me, I wake from the emptiness of space calling out 'Ba!' and shivering from the cold of Major Tom's capsule. When David Bowie died, I wondered if he'd stop my dreams about Major Tom's capsule, but that wasn't the case.

When we were first married, Jordan would show concern, but after a lifetime of the same dream I'm now adept at calming myself within seconds of being jolted awake, so I downplay it. Now he doesn't even wake up, even when I shuffle about, turn my lamp on and comfort-read for a bit. It's no big deal, everyone has recurring dreams, and they're more or less forgotten by the morning.

I know why I still have the dreams, though. It's because the man with the music isn't here. There's been no music for years. I'm so busy with other stuff, there's no time for the jangly guitars and the synth keyboards. Sometimes in the past I thought I could see him, sometimes I felt like he was near; but now it feels like he's not anywhere at all. Maybe he's dead; maybe he never existed. If I let myself think about it I start to panic, but I'm good at not thinking about it.

The next day I go for a walk during my lunch break and a big-nosed man carrying a stack of drawings limps up to me.

'Hi. Remember me,' he says.

'Zack!' I say. 'How are you?'

'OK. My mum died last year, so now I live alone in South Yarra.'

I feel the way I should when Pattie falls over and cries. 'Do you want to have lunch with me, Zack? I'd love to see your drawings.'

His face lights up and I wonder if this is the first time I've ever made someone truly happy.

After we've eaten, Zack gathers up his pictures and says, 'Do you want to keep in contact?'

And this time I say, 'Yeah, Zack. I do.'

TRACK 42 – SHOULD I STAY OR SHOULD I GO?

Ever since I've known him, Jordan's worked hard. He's a good man, but I wonder if he needs something more. He says that of work, family and personal interests, you can only pick two. I need to believe you can pick all three, and I want Jordan to believe that too.

It's a rainy Sunday afternoon, and Jordan and Pattie are playing a *Peppa Pig* game on the iPad. I'm pacing the house, bored. I pass the spare room, which we never enter except to vacuum, but today I step inside. The carpet is white, the walls are white and the linen on the bed is white – a canvas of potential. I wonder if Jordan became passionate about something, whether I'd become passionate about him.

Back in the kitchen, as I make myself a herbal tea, I feel a whisper of an idea. I jiggle the tea bag, trying to think what it is, and then I realise. It's music; for the first time in ages I'm thinking about music. Then I realise that there's no music in this house.

I feel almost shy as I call out to Jordan, who's sitting on the corner couch, 'Hey, why don't we convert the spare room into a music studio? You could do some mixing in there.'

'Nah…we need it as a guest room.'

We never have guests. I take a sip of tea, but it has a horrid, bitter flavour, matching my disappointment with Jordan's answer. I pour it down the sink.

Maybe spending time together outside this house is more the answer then. It's been such a long time since we've had a night out. Memories of romantic dinners with Jordan are beyond foggy. As I rinse my cup, I remember something Cat mentioned a few days ago.

'Jordan, DJ Shadow is playing at the Forum Thursday week. Why don't we go see him?'

'On a school night? I don't think so.'

'Just as a one-off. Wouldn't it be nice to have a night out together? It'll be just like the old days.'

'Some other time, maybe. Work's been hectic and I'm wrecked.'

How does he know he'll be tired in two weeks' time? I don't want to beg him though, and so instead I go to the concert with Cat and Laure. We have a great time, and I get home after one am. I'm tired, but good tired, like how I feel after a workout. I'm surprised to see that Jordan's still awake, sitting at the kitchen table, surrounded by documents. A trickle of irritation runs down my spine; if he's going to be awake, he should have been awake with me!

'I don't understand why you didn't come with me to see DJ Shadow,' I say. 'He was really good! Seeing you're awake anyway, it would have been something fun for us to do together.'

'It's just not my thing, Dot,' Jordan says.

Not his thing? I know back in the day Jordan only worked as a DJ to support himself through university, but he was playing music at The Tube every week. Surely some of that rubbed off on him, etched itself into his soul, formed neural pathways in his brain.

'I'm a family man now,' he continues, trying to explain away the disappointed expression that must be on my face.

His explanation doesn't help. Everyone loves their family, but if that's the start and end of a person's identity, how can they fly?

♫ ♫ ♫

I finally get an opportunity for a night out with Jordan. To celebrate how much money it's made, the bank puts on a function for employees and their partners.

We've given up knowing what each other does for a job – I'm not sure I even know what I do. We both work long hours, get paid decently and go to work events, but really it's just a blank in the day, like the time between falling asleep and waking up.

I can tell that Jordan is important in his world of work though, because the colleagues at this function speak to him with deference. I leave him with them to track down a waiter carrying a tray of drinks. I help myself to a glass of wine at the same time that this youngish guy grabs a beer.

'You're Jordan's wife, right?' he says. 'I'm sorry, I forgot your name.'

'Dot.'

He shakes my hand. 'I'm Peter. And how is Pattie? Does she still like *Operation Ouch!?*'

Peter From Work introduces me to his wife, who also asks after Pattie. The three of us head back to Jordan. Mrs Peter and I stand at the edge of the group and talk, but at the same time, I'm watching Jordan. Tonight I'm presented with a different Jordan who I haven't met before. This Jordan enjoys holding court and regaling his minions with wondrous tales of his exploits as a DJ, when the world was his very own *Choose Your Own Adventure* book. I suspect by their overly civil expressions that they think he's an old fart, and I wonder if they think the same about me.

Peter From Work's wife is one of those people who talks at you and doesn't expect a reply, so I can appear to be in conversation with her, but really I'm listening to what Jordan's saying.

'When I was a DJ, I'd start work at eleven pm and play for six hours straight...'

We'll be home by ten tonight.

'Back in my clubbing days, I saw some pret-ty wild sights, let me tell you...'

Now he won't even take the train in case one of the passengers is odd.

'Pattie and I were watching *Peppa Pig* together last night...'

Yes, it's true. He is a grown man who watches Peppa Pig.

Jordan's stories are all about events where I featured, but I don't get a mention. Mrs Peter excuses herself to go to the bathroom, and I go for a wander.

I take my wine and stand by the window, gazing at the city lights. As I stand there, sipping my drink, I glimpse myself in the reflection of the window. I'm glamorous, I'm cool, I'm Jocelyn, but no one comes up to talk to me.

It's not long and we're back in the SUV, driving down the freeway, back to Wintergate Gardens. At home we sit on opposite ends of the corner couch drinking water.

'Did you enjoy yourself?' I ask Jordan.

'Sure.' He reaches for the iPad.

'I didn't know you were so popular at work.'

'It's just because I'm senior to them.' He switches on the iPad.

I want to reach out and pat his hand or something, but when his face lights up from the glow of the iPad screen, I change my mind.

Jordan and I settled, and what does settling produce? It produces a child, a nice home, affluence, stability and a plus-one. What it doesn't produce is music, passion, all the things they write books about and it doesn't stop my dreams about being stuck in space.

'Jordan, what do you like?'

'Um, why do you ask? Hmm, I like Pattie, my parents…and you. I like our house and I like my job. What do you like?'

It's the first non-Pattie related question he's asked me in forever, so I dive in. 'I like olives, and the smell of spring in the air at the end of winter, and post-punk music, and the way my lungs feel after a long swim, and Pattie's laugh when you play with her, and Jack's jokes, and Cat's slang, and Laure's French accent, and hearing Dad's accordion, and red wine, and cheese, and conversations about nothing that last all night, and feeling a connection with someone new, and never forgetting my childhood, and the inner city, and little old workmen's cottages, and the colour green, and judging bogans, and Dr Ivanskiy's funny sayings, and Mod-style dresses, and black mascara, and tapas, and walking through the streets without a destination, and the yellow colour in the air before the sun starts to set, and little bars and sailing even though I've never been sailing, but I know what it feels like and I like it.'

Jordan's staring at me, looking like a confused Harold Bishop, but he's put the iPad down.

I can't take myself out of rant mode. I continue, 'We need to do something about this house, Jordan. It isn't a home. A home smells of woollen jumpers, tea leaves and ash. Not cleaning products and plastic.'

Jordan looks at me like I'm a lunatic. 'Those are just details, Dot,' he says.

Without the details, what do you have? I hold Jordan's gaze, willing him to understand, but we've never really been in the same spaceship, headed in the same direction. How can he possibly understand?

'Never mind,' I say. 'I'm tired. I'm going to bed.'

I pile up the pillows in bed and pull out my own iPad. I grip it for a moment, thinking about what to do, and then I type 'post-punk' into Google. The blog of some Melbourne guy is one of the top results. I read the first post and I'm shocked. It's almost the same as my failed blog, but his posts have hundreds of comments, whereas mine had none. I search back through the years his site's been running, looking for an explanation. His blog is like a song, it started with a weak drum beat, then after several months, guitars joined in, followed by voices a year or so later. The site grew louder and louder, and right now it's at its penultimate chorus, the loudest and best part of any good song. That was where I went wrong with my blog – I started with the chorus, and from there I had nowhere to go.

The blogger talks about a future that's bright, and there's something familiar and comforting about his words. I read for most of the night.

♫ ♫ ♫

On the weekend, we go to Glen Huntly for a visit. While Jordan and Pattie are playing in the garden, I take a look in my old green room. One of the wardrobe doors is unaligned and won't close. I see an old shoe box sitting on the top shelf.

It's full of my concert tickets from London. I hold them in my hands, and all the music comes back to me. At the bottom of the box are some band stickers. The Clash, The Specials, Blondie and other old favourites are all here.

'What're those?' Pattie's standing in the doorway.

'Stickers of old bands.' I show them to her.

Pattie steps closer. 'I like the stencil writing,' she says.

When we're out the front saying goodbye to Mum and Dad, I walk around to the back of the giant car. The My Family sticker is glaring at me; the mother sticker is holding groceries. With a sudden compulsion, I cover the three figures with a Clash sticker.

'Ooh, Dot. Don't bugger up this lovely car like you did with your Barina,' Mum says as she hugs me goodbye.

Jordan and Dad exchange looks, implying that I'm a looney. Only Pattie smiles at me.

TRACK 43 – BELA LUGOSI'S DEAD

I read in the newspaper about a man charged with aggravated assault and burglary. When I look at his photo, I don't see a dangerously hardened man. I see little, rock-throwing Milo from primary school, prematurely hirsute and screaming out for his parents to take notice. According to the article, he was in and out of juvenile detention centres and prison his whole life, just like Mum predicted. If I didn't laugh at him and tried to make friends, would his life have turned out differently? Or would he have just seen a little girl, silly in her stable capsule, and pushed me to the ground?

If I'd stayed in contact with Martin Jones, whether or not he wanted me, would he have heard me knocking on the window of his capsule and realised he wasn't alone and that his life didn't need to end in a bath? Or would he have laughed bitterly at my easy and pain-free existence?

I leave these people alone and float onwards. I don't notice the passing of time until I look at old photos. To me, Cat, Jack, Julie Ann, Dobbler and Jade are still children, laughing so hard at life their backs spasm. My parents, aunts and uncles are still fresh-faced young adults who kick up their heels and get a twinkle in their eyes at the very whiff of a party. Grandma is still here, praising my pale skin. Dr Ivanskiy still sings and dances, calling out 'ay yi yi!' with more lust for life than Iggy Pop could ever have sung about.

I don't see the lines, the grey hair and the floppy bodies, and I don't hear the breathlessness in the ay yi yi-ing. Life continues and the Kellys huddle together, asserting our unity every time Dad plays the accordion, or Julie Ann has a concert, or Dr Ivanskiy drinks too much 'wodka' and stumbles about making inappropriate comments.

♫ ♫ ♫

It's Christmas, and this year Aunty Mary-Margaret Rose is hosting. The family is bloated with in-laws and new children, so she reasserts her old request not to bring presents, and all but Dr Ivanskiy obey. Jack and Dobbler help him carry piles of brightly-wrapped boxes from his taxi.

I open my gift, and it's a beautiful ornament of a Japanese lady, identical to the one he gave me long ago.

For some reason, I water up and can't speak, but Jack says, 'I won't smash this one, Dot, I promise.'

I give my brother and Dr Ivanskiy a tight bear hug, and I don't feel like letting go. I'm interrupted by a tapping on my shoulder.

'Dot, do you know what the wifi password is?' Jordan asks. 'I need to send something to Peter From Work.'

I untangle and say, 'No. Go ask Mary-Margaret Rose.'

Once he's wandered off, Dr Ivanskiy says, 'Why you marry a boring fella like Jordan I'll never know, Dot. But tell you what, that Pattie is a lovely little girl.'

I glance over at Pattie, who's standing next to Mum, eyeing off the other kids. 'Yeah. She is,' I say.

'Coco, stop talking about *Star Wars* and play with your cousin!' Jack barks.

'Ay yi yi!' Dr Ivanskiy chuckles.

'Sometimes your truths are hard, Dr Ivanskiy,' I tell him.

He takes a sip of his vodka before replying, 'When you live through war, you're grateful for truth.'

I don't really know what he means, so I look over at Pattie playing with her cousins.

♫ ♫ ♫

I thought Dr Ivanskiy was a forever-dentist, but he retired years ago, and even then he was well into his seventies. To fill the place of teeth, he took up Bridge and these days enjoys more female attention than he ever received. He still takes annual trips to Ukraine to visit his nephew Kolia.

Shortly after Christmas, Mum calls me.

'Kolia and his family have been in a car accident.'

'What? Are they OK?'

'They've been killed.'

'All of them?'

'Yes.'

They were Dr Ivanskiy's only surviving family.

The Kellys assemble at Dr Ivanskiy's flat in St Kilda Road. It's too small for so many of us, but we squeeze in, gathering around Dr Ivanskiy who's sitting in his armchair, gripping and ungripping his walking stick. I never thought of Dr Ivanskiy as alone in his space capsule until now.

Over the next few months, we unite to revive him as best as we can. He still attends every family function, although he's wobbly on his feet even without vodka. He still tells us whose partner he thinks is 'crafty, like KGB', whose child is 'right daft, like peasant from neighbouring village' and who has become a 'really unusual character', but if we reach out to comfort the man, he shrugs us off and tells us to go and dance.

♫ ♫ ♫

The Mornington Peninsular retreat weekend rolls around again. I turn off my phone so I'm free to enjoy the hot springs, soupy warm sea and vanilla slices without being disturbed by work or home. I'm needled by guilt, but resolve to make it up to Jordan and Pattie when I return. When I get back to Melbourne, there are two voicemails on my phone from Mum.

'Dot, it's your mother. Call me back.'

That's unusual; Mum normally leaves long-winded voicemails.

'Dot, it's Mum again. Call me back as soon as you can. It's important.'

Cold liquid flows through my veins at the mention of the word 'important', and I call her back even though it's late at night. She answers the phone straight away.

'Dot?'

'Yeah. What's happening?'

'It's Dr Ivanskiy. He's passed away.'

Passed away? Passed on, departed, off to a better place, gone the way of all flesh, shuffled off his mortal coil, deceased, demised, at rest, died, dead, dead, dead, he's dead, I'm dead. Yesterday he was here and today he's not; yesterday he was breathing and 'ay yi yi-ing' and today he's floated away to join his Ukrainian family, his friend Grandpa Kelly, Grandma and Martin Jones. People are going away, like Zack's mind went away and Milo's innocence went away, and they're taking with them the links to my childhood, leaving me all alone in Wintergate Gardens.

'Dot?'

Mum is still on the phone and the sound of her voice hushes the waterfalls in my ears. I remember that I've never really been alone and probably never will be, no matter how many dreams I have about that space capsule. I pinch myself into adulthood and turn my thoughts to others.

'Oh! What happened?'

'He went peacefully in his sleep. One of the neighbours found him.'

'Oh… When's the funeral?'

'We aren't sure yet. I'll let you know.'

When Mum hangs up, I go into the spare room, closing the door so Jordan and Pattie can't find me, and I cry. It's half an hour later when I realise that this is the first time I've cried about someone other than myself.

Dr Ivanskiy was – thinking of him in the past tense makes me start crying again – an atheist who really did regard the Church as the crow from *Animal Farm*; but the Kellys arrange for his funeral to be held in a gold-domed Ukrainian Orthodox church, so that they can take comfort in rituals that are as close to Catholicism as they can get away with.

Before we enter the church, I kneel down to Pattie's level and say to her, 'OK Pattie, I want you to sit very, very quietly when we go inside. It might be a bit boring for you, but if you stay really still during the service, when it finishes we'll go back to Dr Ivanskiy's flat, and there might be some cake and some other kids to play with.'

Pattie scowls like a teenager when they're told something obvious.

'Give it a rest, Dot,' Jordan says in the patronisingly earnest voice he uses whenever something serious is happening.

I follow the two of them into the church.

The place is full of Kellys, dotted with a few people Dr Ivanskiy knew from the dental industry and his Bridge ladies. There are no Eastern Europeans here, and we all stare blankly at the bearded priest as he recites the service in Ukrainian. I can hear the whirring of Jordan's phone coming from his pants pocket, and sigh. Pattie sits up straight, her eyes on the priest, but I glance around at the ornately decorated church. Jack, who's sitting next to me, pokes me in the ribs.

'Right showy, this place. Got more dollars than sense, the greedy crows,' he whispers to me in a mock Dr Ivanskiy accent.

I stifle a laugh, but Julie Ann and her daughters, who are sitting in the pew in front, turn around to give us a good glaring. Jack and I bite the insides of our cheeks to suppress further laughter. We'll always be children, but Dr Ivanskiy wouldn't mind.

We squeeze back into his flat for the wake. I'm not sure if Ukrainians have wakes, but the Kellys do, and we've claimed him as our own for nearly seventy years. I can feel Dr Ivanskiy in the apartment. The carpet is worn flat from his vodka-enhanced stumblings, the cabinet is full of bottles of clear liquid in varying stages of fullness, the coffee table is strewn with packs of cards and nowhere in the house is there a single item that could entertain a child. But if you let yourself laugh along with Dr Ivanskiy, your heart will sing.

'What was Dr Ivanskiy's first name?' I ask Mum, who's making tea for everyone. 'I never knew.'

'Ivan.'

'Ivan Ivanskiy? Ha!'

The tea won't do, so we drink the bottles in the liquor cabinet and we sing. We don't know any Ukrainian songs, so we sing Irish folk songs. Dad's accordion is produced from nowhere, and Julie Ann and her daughters strike up in voices so pure they could be fairies from the glen. This is Dr Ivanskiy's day though, and he won't let us stand around prettily, with a tear in our eyes. He demands something more robust. As Julie Ann and her girls start on the second verse, Jack joins in with a voice that's rough, choppy and very out of tune. Dad's foot is counting the beats, and he stomps so loud the liquor cabinet rattles. Bit by bit, people join in. We finish the first song and start 'Danny Boy' without a moment's hesitation. Even Pattie is mouthing the words; only Jordan stands there awkwardly, shoving his hand in and out of the pocket where he keeps his phone. I grab Pattie and hug her against myself.

♬ ♬ ♬

My family has revived me and for several weeks I'm calm and content. Unfortunately it's not enough. Normality returns, and with it, dreams of space capsules. I start giving Pattie a hug and a kiss when I get home from work, but the spontaneity has gone and we're both stiff. Whenever I look at Jordan, the same feeling overcomes me as when I'm suppressing a giant yawn during a meeting.

I take a few days off work and spend them pacing our white suburban home. I call Mum, and we talk for an hour about nothing in particular.

'It's good to hear your voice, Dot,' she says. 'Your father wants to say hello too. I'll put him on.'

After the phone call, I resume my pacing. Our house is so large that my Fitbit clocks up the requisite amount of steps in no time. When I realise my endless humming of 'The Ballad of Lucy Jordan' is about to drive me to climb onto the rooftop, I go back to the office. I fill my days with the gym and work, and I alternate between feelings of panic and the giant yawn.

♫ ♫ ♫

Dad calls me at work one day. 'Well Dot, he's left the lot to you kids.'

'What? Who?'

Irene appears in front of my desk, but I turn away from her.

'Dr Ivanskiy,' Dad says. 'He's left everything to you, your brother and cousins.'

'But I wasn't expecting anything…'

'Expect the unexpected, Dot.'

From the moment he pushed Grandpa Kelly out of the path of the oncoming tram, Dr Ivanskiy has been saving my family. Now it's my turn to be saved by him.

'Ay yi yi!' is all I can say. Irene looks at me blankly.

TRACK 44 – THE TIDE IS HIGH

The house is silent. Clutching my laptop, I pace from generously-sized room to generously-sized room, and even with the tiles and other echo-enhancing surfaces, I don't make a sound. Pattie is in bed and Jordan stretches out on the corner couch, working with the television on in the background.

I stand in the doorway of the spare room, contemplating its sparseness, and then I enter. I sit on the soft, unused carpet, open my laptop and read my old blog files. I'm taken aback by the explosion of musical joy. I took my blog offline in a rage at the lack of appreciation, but I never kept it live long enough for the world to react. It doesn't take me long to create a new website and upload the old posts. I write a couple of new ones too. My language is tentative, but I know I'm just warming up.

I bring my shoe box of London concert tickets into the spare room and shuffle through them. I remember every concert, the songs, the audience, the magic. I'll take photos of each ticket and add them to my old posts. Maybe everyone will read what I've written, maybe no one will. This time it doesn't matter. I'm writing for me.

I dig out my old hard-drive of MP3s from the storage closet and plug it into the laptop. The music starts to return. Like my writing, it's hesitant and tinny at first, but I turn up the volume and snakes of noise slither out and fill up the room. I don't yawn; I breathe.

Jordan taps prissily on the door. 'Don't you think the music's a little loud? Pattie's asleep.'

When I was Pattie's age, I was lulled to sleep by the sound of people talking in loud voices, accordion playing and the tapping of Dad's foot. It was only when I woke to silence, after dreaming about being stuck in space, that I couldn't sleep. My god, how can Pattie sleep in this silent space station lost in Wintergate Gardens?

'A little noise will do her good, Jordan. Life is noise and she needs to get used to it.'

I've spoken in a tone of voice he won't challenge, and he pads away in his woolly socks.

The spare room transforms into a music shrine. I buy a retro-style turntable that comes in a small bright-orange case. I also buy a couple of preposterously-priced vinyls. The sound of music is growing more and more confident in this little room.

Songs are constantly playing and I plug in lamps that give off a yellow subdued light, instead of the blinding white of the rest of the house. I take my books from the bookshelf and stack them in piles on the floor. I cut out pictures from magazines and stick them on the wall – pictures of the ocean, of little houses, of spaceships, of punks, of smiling faces, of accordions and one of the sky and sun Ukrainian flag. Jordan stays away from the spare room, but Pattie comes in to sit silently on the bed. She looks at the pictures, and it's with curiosity rather than her usual disdain.

♫ ♫ ♫

On a Sunday visit to Mum and Dad's, I search my old room for treasures I missed on my last visit. Mum must have given away my old clutter years ago though, as the cupboards are empty, aside from spare sheets and towels. I open my old chest of drawers, but they're empty too. I slide the bottom drawer closed and notice it doesn't shut all the way. Something that looks like a square of cardboard is blocking it, but my fingers are too big to get a proper grip.

'Pattie!'

She materialises in the doorway; she must have been hovering close by.

'Can you get this cardboard thing out with your little fingers?' I ask her.

She rummages around in the drawer, then hands me an object. It's my old 'London Calling' single. I take the vinyl disc out of its cover, and it's all scratched. The cover's faded too, but I can still make out the picture of a girl and boy sitting with a pile of records.

'They look happy,' Pattie says. 'What is it?'

I put the single in her hands. 'Someone gave it to me a long time ago. So long ago I can't remember. It's yours now, Pattie. Look after it because it's the future.'

We sit together on the bed, looking at the happy teenagers listening to records.

♬ ♬ ♬

At night I work late on my blog and stream post-punk from One Eleven FM. I close my eyes and imagine I'm in the original *Dogs in Space* house in Richmond. Those days must have been heady and chaotic, yet the thought of them makes me feel calm. The announcer comes on, and an echo of an echo lights up like a match in my brain. I abandon my blog and listen to the rest of the program, sitting motionless on the floor.

Instead of going to sleep in the room I share with Jordan, I hop into the bed here. I sleep soundly without dreaming of space capsules. Jordan doesn't say anything, so I continue sleeping in the spare room. The rest of the house is an abandoned space station, but this room is my yacht and it's taking me across the bay.

♬ ♬ ♬

I'm still working long hours, though. When I think about it, so much of my adult life has been filled with work. And for what? I had a couple years of joyful writing, but was soon moved on to what were supposed to be more prestigious tasks.

One night on the way home from work, I stop off at Prahran to look at the little run-down houses of my childhood, only they're not here. The whole area has been gentrified beyond recognition, and the only real things left are the council flats. I wonder about Dobbler's soccer-playing kids. I assume they grew up and flew away from the flats, but I hope they still play soccer, maybe with their own kids now.

The next morning my alarm goes off at four am. I roll out of bed and lie face down on the carpet, waiting to feel awake, which doesn't happen. Like an internee of a concentration camp lining up for the daily parade, I force myself off the floor, into the shower, into clothes and out of the house. I'm on the road at four thirty for a business trip to Sydney and I won't be back until late tonight.

I stare out of the Uber car window and even though it's still dark, there are other people up and about, beginning their days.

'But this isn't living!' I want to yell at them.

Even though it's freezing, I wind down my window and take big gulps of air as the streets of Wintergate Gardens glide past. This isn't the life I chose; the man with the music isn't here. Stop, stop, I got on the wrong ride and I want to get off! My capsule is zooming through space at warp speed and my compass has stopped working. It hurtles me down Melbourne's tollways, to the airport, on to the plane and across the sky all the way to Sydney.

As I approach the Sydney office, I switch to autopilot, enter the building and attend meetings. It's only towards the end of the day when a few of my colleagues suggest a quick drink before my flight that my autopilot switches off.

'OK, give me a minute,' I tell them.

Something like panic is rising in my chest, so I go to the toilets to wash my face. I exhale three times and stare at my frightened-looking eyes, willing them to become calm again.

'You have options,' I tell the woman in the mirror. 'You've always had them and you always will.'

Still in the toilets, I call Irene and tell her I'm resigning. She's surprised, but says she understands and hopes I'll keep in contact, maybe catch up for lunch every now and then. Most people are pretty awesome, once you give them a chance and let them in.

A few hours later, I'm sitting on the plane back to Melbourne. I've switched off the motor and opened the sails. I have no idea where the yacht will take me, but like the certainty that people who play songs out loud on public transport have shit taste in music, I know it'll take me to the right place.

The next thing to be done is to tell Jordan, but I want to do it properly and respectfully rather than freezing him out with my usual disconnectedness. I try to think of his safe haven, where he'll feel most protected when I tell him, and come up with the corner couch.

The following morning I ask Mum to mind Pattie.

When Jordan comes home, talking on his phone, I'm waiting for him on the couch. The television is on low, murmuring and giving off bright, comforting colours.

I wait for him to finish the call and pour himself a Coke before I say, 'Jordan, come sit with me for a bit.'

We sit side by side, which is good, better than face to face and ready for conflict.

As Jordan reaches for the remote to turn up the television volume, I say, 'We need to talk.'

Sometimes only a cliché can convey your message and with those four words, Jordan knows. He blinks, taken aback, but when he speaks his voice is steady.

'You're leaving?'

He always did look handsome when he was surprised, and I reach out for his hand.

'I'm sorry I never was very nice to you,' I say. 'We should free each other up for people who can love us properly.'

'Pattie?'

'She'll be happier because we're happier.'

'Uh-huh…'

Jordan turns the television off and plays some songs from his iPad. They're the old chill-out tunes he used to play at The Tube; I didn't know he still listened to them. We listen to the music in silence for a while.

When we've heard our fill, I ask him, 'How do you feel?'

'Um…' Jordan pauses and thinks. 'Disappointed, I guess.' His phone rings, but he shuts it down and continues, 'My heart's in this house, but yours is not.'

That's his honest answer; he's not blindsided or heart-broken. Disappointment will be easier for him to deal with. We spend the rest of the night in conversation. I hope Jordan gets what he deserves.

The next morning, I pick Pattie up from Mum's and take her to a café on the beachfront of Elwood. It's a crisp, blue-sky day and we sit outside, rugged up, watching the sailing ships. Pattie pokes at the marshmallow in her hot chocolate, as I explain to her that changes are coming.

'What about me?' she asks.

'You will live some of the time with Dad and some of the time with me, but wherever you are, you're going to have lots of fun because everyone will be happy.'

I watch Pattie's little face digest the news. There'll be less tension and stony silence in her life, but am I seriously fucking up my child? Am I going to turn her forever black-eyed, a product of a broken home? Pattie stirs her hot chocolate vigorously, creating a small whirlpool in the glass.

'Pattie?'

She shifts her attention from the drink back to me. 'Can I stick pictures in my new room, like you've got in your room?'

She falls into my arms. 'Of course you can, sweetie. Whatever pictures you want,' I speak into her hair.

♫ ♫ ♫

I rent a ramshackle workman's cottage in a neighbourhood close to the city that's still gritty for now. There's a saggy old couch on the front porch and a banana tree in the garden. I'm home.

'Slumming it, are ya?' Cat jokes. 'Just kidding, this place is great!'

'When's the housewarming?' Jack asks.

'Right unusual hovel you found, Dot,' Dr Ivanskiy's ghost says. 'But tell you what, it could be a nice little home for you and Pattie.'

I fill the rooms with candles, old furniture and plants, and I park my new twenty-year-old car out the front. Pattie decorates her room with pictures of butterflies and fairies surrounding the 'London Calling' single, which she's Blu-Tacked to the wall.

I take a part-time job and fill my life with details, but this time I involve Pattie. Our little house is full of visitors and the barbeque is always on.

♫ ♫ ♫

The housewarming is a blast of Kellys and music that'll keep us warm forever. Now and Then squeeze together in the tiny lounge room, playing all the old favourites. They take a break to drink a cup of tea, but Pattie marches up to them.

She stomps her foot three times, counts herself in 'two-three-four!' and starts singing.

And I shall hear, though soft you tread above me
And all my grave will warmer, sweeter be
For you will bend and tell me that you love me
And I shall sleep in peace until you come to me.

Dad plays along with the accordion, his foot tapping so loudly I can hear the dishes in the cupboard rattling. Everyone sways and sings along with Pattie. Her voice is sweet, clear and perfectly in tune, as good as Julie Ann's ever was. It's a detail I hadn't noticed before. We clap wildly when she's finished, and I feel a tear in my eye.

'Thank goodness she didn't inherit your voice,' Jack says, patting me on the back, and everyone laughs.

'I'm in your band now,' Pattie tells Dad.

He beams at the thought of one of the kids finally wanting to join Now and Then.

The next morning, the house smells like stale beer and there's mess everywhere. I'm washing dishes when I hear three perfectly timed knocks at the door. It's Zack.

'Zack!' I move to hug him, but he steps back. 'You missed the party last night.'

'Yes. I do not like parties because they are too noisy. So I am visiting you now.'

I take him to the kitchen where Pattie's eating cereal.

'Who're you?' she asks him.

'I'm Zack. From primary school.'

'I was probably your age when I first met Zack,' I tell Pattie. 'He's a really good drawer.'

'Uh-huh.' Pattie gets up from the table and leaves the room. Before I can wonder what she's up to, she's back, carrying paper, textas and the 'London Calling' single.

'Can you draw this?' she asks Zack.

'Yes, I can.'

Zack replicates the single cover perfectly, but instead of a yellow background, it's pink, as requested by Pattie. The three of us go into her room and stick the drawing and the single side by side on her wall.

Pattie smiles at Zack. 'Next time you visit, can you draw me a green one? It's Mum's favourite colour.'

'Yes. I will do that.'

Zack leaves and I finish washing the dishes. It's too quiet though.

'I've got an idea,' I tell Pattie.

I bring my laptop into the kitchen and find The Tube playlist I recently created.

'These are some of my favourite songs. Let's have a listen and see if they help us clean,' I say.

The first song is 'Connection' by Elastica. As soon as the music starts, Pattie stomps her feet up and down. She shuts her eyes tight and jumps and jumps and howls like a wolf.

'I love this song, Mum!' she cries.

Pattie skips about the house, gathering bottles and dishes and bringing them to me at the sink. I wash up and nod my head to the music.

BONUS TRACK

I walk past little old houses, bluestone laneways, street art, warehouse studios and pop-up restaurants. Post-punk music is in the air, so I follow it to a café where I order a coffee. I don't bury my head in a smartphone or a newspaper; instead, I sit up straight and observe. I make eye contact with people who enter the café and smile at them; they smile back and I know we're all passengers on the same ship. The sky is blue, and the wind blows in just the right direction. Music continues playing; guitars and drums march me along, and Joe Strummer starts to sing. Under the table, my feet tap out the beat to the song that became part of my memories before my memories even started.

♫ ♫ ♫

I finish my show at One Eleven FM and walk down the road towards the tram stop. I need to get to the city to interview Discombobulation. This is massively exciting because tonight will be their first gig since 1979.

I walk past a café and hear 'London Calling'; my mouth waters at the thought of coffee. I'm in a rush, but the idea of sitting a while, soaking up the music, is enticing. The boys won't mind waiting forty minutes, seeing they've keep me waiting almost forty years.

♫ ♫ ♫

I'm sitting facing the doorway, listening to 'London Calling'. A man walks in. He's older than me, with closely-cropped grey hair. He's thin and lined, but I like how he looks. I look at him and smile. He stands in the doorway, smiling back at me.

Then he says, 'Hello. Great music they're playing here. Sounds like the future.'

He has a kind voice, and he talks a little slowly, like he's considering things.

ACKNOWLEDGEMENTS

To my wonderful editor, Lu Sexton, your enthusiasm blew a breath of fresh air into this first novel.

To Fiona Byrne for your kick-arse design skills and for being my nineties clubbing buddy extraordinaire.

To Jessica Hoadley for being a fantastic proofreader.

To the following people (in alphabetical order because that seems fair): Steve Abrahall, Alby Blazo, Darcy Conroy, Nicola Cordel, Ruby Ewens, Cleo Fleming, Penelope Gollop, Lee-Ann Hawe, Lauren McDermaid, Nikki McWatters, Gail Pascoe, Danica Ralston, Louie Richmond, Sonia Rosa, Melita Rowston, ST Smith, Chloe Trindall and Kav Vignarajah. Thank you times infinity plus one for taking the time to read my drafts (at various stages of quality) and sharing your wisdom about the literary world. Your feedback and support has been invaluable and I can't say in words how much I appreciate it.

To Jane Coghlan for coming up with the name of Dot's school.

To all the amazing people I've met through school, university, work, share houses, travel and friends of friends I've commandeered along the way. I'm so lucky to have met you all. Thanks for all the fun times and thanks for keeping in contact.

Finally, to my family, immediate and extended, for giving me the best childhood ever, for always being there and for raising me not to expect three Tim Tams for lunch.

ABOUT THE AUTHOR

Nichola Scurry is a proud and cynical member of Generation X who was born in England and grew up in Australia. She majored in English Literature at Monash University and has been writing stories since childhood.

Nichola has lived in London and Barcelona, but Melbourne is her current home. *With the Music* is Nichola's first novel. You can visit her at www.scurry.com.au